Who was the other Judith?

When Judy entered the old house in the Highlands, she knew she had lived there before. She
knew that love was waiting for her—and she
was possessed by joy.

But before she and Ian could acknowledge their
love, they must understand the past that had
brought them together . . . the past that was
shaping their lives to its own strange design.

Then—as a storm swept over the ancient house
—Judy slipped into the other Judith's lovely
dress. The door to the past was open and Judy
knew what she had to do. . . .

> **"THE MIDDLE WINDOW has charm and
> humor and romantic beauty"**
> **—Books**

THE
MIDDLE WINDOW

•

Elizabeth Goudge

PYRAMID BOOKS • **NEW YORK**

Dedicated to
EILEEN THORNDIKE
*who asked that this story,
written originally as a play,
be made into a novel.*

THE MIDDLE WINDOW

A PYRAMID BOOK

Copyright, 1939, by Elizabeth Goudge

Renewed © 1967 by Elizabeth Goudge

All rights reserved. This book, or parts thereof, must not be reproduced in any form without permission. Published by arrangement with Coward, McCann & Geoghegan, Inc. Printed in the United States of America.

Pyramid edition published October 1973
ISBN 0-515-03177-1
Pyramid Books are published by Pyramid Communications, Inc. Its trademarks, consisting of the word "Pyramid" and the portrayal of a pyramid, are registered in the United States Patent Office.

Pyramid Communications, Inc., 919 Third Avenue, New York, New York 10022

THE

MIDDLE WINDOW

PROLOGUE

The Search

To those who cry out against romance I would say—
You yourself are romance. You are the lost prince herd-
ing obscurely among the swine. The romance of your
spirit is the most wonderful of stories.

—Æ, THE CANDLE OF VISION

PROLOGUE

I

THE queer change began to creep over Judy as soon as they reached the Highlands. They had come by easy stages, with Judy at the wheel of her Morris car, right up from London to the north, across the border into Scotland, through the Lowlands to the mountains of the west. They could see them coming, great giants standing with their heads in the sky as though yearning toward it with a still impatience, cloaks of torn rain clouds streaming from their shoulders and the cold breath of them sweeping down into the valley like a wind of warning, "Don't come too near," they seemed to be saying. "Those who come to us we hold forever. Be careful." But Judy was not careful. She put her foot on the accelerator, and she went to those mountains like a bird to its nest.

And suddenly they were among them, so suddenly that it seemed a gate had opened and shut behind them, locking them into a new country. The giants leaned from the sky, brooding over them, their lower slopes seeming to gather them in like the folds of a purple cloak. There was the sound of rushing water quite close to them, and red rowan berries glimmered in the muted sunshine. They could hear sheep bleating and whaups crying and see the mist swirling beneath the arc of a rainbow. Then wet gray rocks closed in around them, and the light paled as a rainstorm swept down from the heights. . . . They had arrived. They were captured.

Not only by a new country, thought Judy, but by a new life as well. With the shutting of that gate behind her not only were her surroundings changed but she herself was surely changed too. She had known it would be very wonderful, this first visit to Scotland of a girl to whose forebears this country had been home; but she had not known it would be quite like this, she had not known that the mere fact of coming home could enfold one in such joy and peace that one felt a different and a finer person, as though a hidden personality were unfolding within one minute by minute. All the way up from London she had been happy, but now she was more than happy, she was possessed by joy. She thought suddenly of the lotus flower, of the patient growth of the long stalk upward through the darkness of the water, of the bud resting at last upon the surface of the pool, tasting the freedom and lightness of the air, and then of the joyous unfolding of the petals in the sun. That was how she felt. All her life until now had been a reaching upward through darkness to some unknown, unimagined lovely destiny. It was not, surely, far off now. She was so glad about it that she began to sing softly under her breath.

Charles, the quite excellent young man to whom she was engaged, sat beside her wrappped in the gloom which seemed to him inseparable from life in the wet high north. He hated the north. Only love of Judy, who had insisted on this Scotch holiday, could have dragged him to it. Sarah, Judy's little dog, seemed to feel the same; for she had crept inside Charles's coat for warmth, and her wet black nose and bright black eyes, gleaming inquiringly in the mat of black wool that was her face, quivered and blinked with distinct apprehension. Judy's father and mother, too, swathed in rugs in the back of the car and meditating on the old house in the western Highlands that they had at Judy's command rented for ten weeks without having the least idea what it was like, seemed also a little apprehensive, for they spoke little and sneezed much. . . . Charles sighed and stirred restlessly. . . . The frowning heights of the mountains, now revealed and now hidden by the drifting clouds, pressed upon him like an actual physical oppression; the sound of falling water was to him as the sound of weeping and sent a chill into his very bones.

It was because he felt so cut off from Judy. This strange joy of hers that had fallen about her as soon as they slid into the mountains, was something that he did not understand. It was almost like a cloak of darkness that hid her from him. She was, he felt, moving away from him to where he could not follow her.

He looked with apprehension at this girl whom he loved, and the sight of her familiar dearness cloaked in that unfamiliar and illusive joy, a joy that had nothing to do with him or his love, gave him a twist of almost intolerable pain. He had to take a firm grip of himself to force himself to look at her calmly, noting about her all the things that he loved that were just the same. Judy Cameron was arrestingly attractive. In spite of the delicacy of her pale pointed little face, strength and courage were apparent in her. There were sparks in her dark eyes, she carried her head proudly, and when she walked the swing of her small slender body was the least bit arrogant. Above all she had that vitality that is like a flame burning; and never before, thought Charles, had he seen it burning with so intense a brightness. She was ablaze with happiness. Looking at her, he was reminded of all warm and glowing things—orange flames and golden crocuses and red berries and clove carnations. Her golden-brown tweed coat was open at the neck, showing the orange scarf twisted round her throat, and there was a yellow feather in her little brown cap. Her face was flushed, and the dark curls that escaped from under her cap had unexpected glints of gold in them.

"Are you happy, Judy?" he asked softly.

"Yes," she said, and sighed out of her joy. "Yes, I'm happy."

11

II

To Charles that journey seemed endless, but to Judy it passed with the swiftness of a dream. She drove unerringly, with no doubt as to the way she should take, and she was only conscious of the passing of time as a deepening of her joy, a slow and steady deepening that became at last a sort of pain. On and on they went, up steep twisting roads between dripping gray rocks, up and up into the clouds, and then down again between walls of gray mist, accompanied always by the sound of wind and falling water and the crying of the whaups.

"Judy," said Charles suddenly. "Judy, are you all right?"

She turned toward him, and he saw that her face was white and set and her eyes quite black, like mountain tarns, with no light in them.

"Judy," he said sharply.

She did not answer, and he did not think that she had heard him. It was queer: He didn't like it.

"What's the time?" asked Lady Cameron. "Surely we ought to be nearly there. We must have come the wrong way. What's the time, Charles?"

"My watch has stopped," said Charles.

"I'm quite sure we've come the wrong way," complained poor Lady Cameron, "and James has gone to sleep again, and Judy isn't even looking at that route the R.A.C. gave us. She hasn't looked at it for hours. . . . Judy!"

Judy did not answer, and Lady Cameron prodded her in the back. "Look at that route, dear; I'm sure we're all wrong."

Judy stirred and sighed. "No," she said, "we shall be there in twenty minutes." Her voice seemed to come from very far away. "We're just climbing up Ben

12

Caorach. In ten minutes we shall be at the top. Then we shall drop down into Glen Suilag."

"Judy!" exclaimed Charles. "How on earth do you know?"

She did not answer. Her ungloved hands were gripping the wheel so tightly that the knuckles were white, and her face was shining in a queer way, as though there was a lamp alight in her. She felt as though something were stirring inside her, something imprisoned, with wings, like a bird. Something that wanted to get free, and was longing to speed on ahead of her slow body and be in its nest. Its impatience was a pain at her heart, and she cried out voicelessly to it, "Be quiet a little. . . . We shall be there soon. . . . Soon. . . . Soon. . . ." But the Morris was so slow. Grunting and squeaking, it toiled up the long, steep mountain road. The mist shut them in like a wall, and there was nothing to be seen but the wet pebbles of the road and the tussocks of heather and turf that edged it. . . . So slow. . . . So slow. . . . "It was quicker on horseback," said Judy to herself.

And now they were at the top. Driven by an impulse so strong that she could not resist it, she jumped out of the car, banged the door shut on her outraged family, and ran off over the grass and the heather to the right, until she was hidden from them by the driving mist. Here she was alone. The muffling mist was like a cloak that shut her away from all sound and sight of her normal world, and she was alone with that winged thing within her that was struggling for life. As she stood there she felt as though it were growing, penetrating her whole being with its life, pouring new thoughts into her mind and new loves into her heart, even subtly changing her body. "What is it?" she whispered to herself. "Is it me myself coming alive? Or is it something else possessing me?" She felt a thrill of fear and pushed out her hands against the mist, as though to ease the pressure

13

that shut her in so closely and so secretly with that winged and struggling thing. The mist swirled about her just as closely, but mentally she was eased and her horizons widened.

She stood and gazed in front of her. She could see nothing, but she knew quite well what she would have seen if the mist had lifted and the sun had come out. She would have seen mountains, peak beyond peak and ridge behind ridge, azure and amethyst and topaz, scarred with gray rocks and pierced with silver spears of falling water. She would have looked out and away through miles of limpid air, north, south, east, and west, with no barrier to check the outward flight of her mind. Space would have been hers, with the full glory of the sky over her head and the glory of the earth a carpet beneath her feet. And to the west she knew there would be a straight, blue line drawn between earth and heaven, the sea. She knew just how it would look, so cold and far away and lovely, like the slab of sapphire pavement that paved the door to paradise. Though she could not see it she knew that the wind was blowing straight from it, for she could taste salt on her lips. Then, closing her eyes, she stood and listened. There was no sound at all. The tinkle of falling water was far away below her, so muffled by the mist that its faint murmur was only the silence talking. The humming of the wind in her ears was not sound, it was the harp music that her heart gave out as fingers plucked at it, a faint plaintive sound that told how the fingers hurt her. . . . Why was she in such pain and yet so happy? . . . She realized suddenly that she was lonely, that something vital to her life was missing, that she was hungry for something with a hunger so desperate that she could hardly bear it. . . . Someone should have been here with her, listening with her to the silence talking, someone who was as much a part of herself as her own body; but that someone was no one whom she knew. There was no one to satisfy this terri-

14

ble ache. She was sobbing a little, and her hair and her face were wet with the mist. The heather and grass had drenched her to the knees, but she did not feel wet or cold, she felt nothing but the pain at her heart. . . . A hand seized her arm, and she looked round eagerly. . . . It was Charles. . . . The reaction was so great that she almost hated him. . . . Charles! . . . It was not Charles whom she wanted.

"Judy, Judy!" he said. "Darling Judy, what is it?"

But Judy could not tell him. Something was happening to her that concerned herself only. With every moment that passed she was being carried further and further away from all that she knew and loved, away into a beautiful and dreadful loneliness.

Charles led her back to the car and tenderly mopped up her face with his handkerchief.

"It's this mountain," he explained to her astonished parents. "Mountains make one feel dashed queer. It's the height, you know. Makes one lightheaded. . . . I'll drive now, Judy."

"Yes," said Judy, and climbed meekly in beside him.

They slid down the steepest hill ever seen, dropping cautiously foot by foot from the heights to the valley, slipping round corkscrew bends and bumping perilously over stones in the road.

"What a road! What a road!" moaned Lady Cameron. "Once we've got to this horrid place, goodness knows how we're ever going to get out of it again."

"Perhaps there's another road out, dear," comforted Sir James.

"No," said Judy.

Charles, clinging wildly to the wheel, was incapable of speech.

As they came lower the mist thinned a little. Judy leaned eagerly forward, and suddenly she gave a little cry.

"Look!" she said. "There!"

They were nearly on level ground now, and in front of them they could see the loch. It was iron-gray, wild and stormy looking, with litle rippling waves. It was edged with weed of an indescribable golden color that was not quite gold and not quite orange, and over it sea gulls were wheeling and crying. They were approaching it from the south. Through the mist they could see that on the north and west mountains descended sheer into it, and that the lower slopes of the mountains were dotted with crofts. On the east its shore was edged by a larch wood.

"I can't see any house," said Lady Cameron. "I said all along we'd come to the wrong place."

"The house is hidden by the larch wood," said Judy softly. "It curves round the house and garden on two sides, the south and the west. The road turns to the right, Charles, before you reach the loch."

Charles swung to the right. In front of them in the glen was a village that seemed to consist only of an inn, a church, a post office, and a school. Those chief necessities of life and death, the grocery and the graveyard, were standing in stern isolation up the hill to their right. On their left the larch trees, vividly green, were rustling and whispering in expectation.

"Now to your left," whispered Judy gently.

An old broken gate in the wall was propped open by a stone. Charles turned through it, and they were in the green gloom of the larch wood.

"Straight on," said Judy, "and you'll come to the front door. It's at the south end of the house."

"How in the world do you know?" asked Charles.

Judy was a little puzzled. "I don't know how I know. But I do know."

The larch trees thinned, and the grass-grown lumpy road, which could be called a drive only by courtesy, brought them into a graveled sweep completely covered with green moss. In front of them was an old gray house so battered and stained by time and weather that it looked perhaps older than it was, so grown over by creepers that it seemed more like a natural growth than a thing built by man. They stopped and looked at it. It dominated them all, even Lady Cameron, for it had character and charm. It looked solid and strong, built to withstand wild weather; yet it had beauty and dignity, and gave one that sense of depth and space that is so lovely in old houses. There would, Judy knew, be no overcrowding inside it. The rooms would be spacious and the stairs wide and sloping very gently. There would be roomy cupboards and quiet, unexpected corners, and everywhere a sense of peace and leisure. It had an air of dreaming, humble withdrawal, as when an old and lovely woman with a gracious gesture of apology draws aside from the hubbub of life to think in peace.

"A monastery," said Charles, and was surprised at himself.

"A refuge from the pleasure of life," said Sir James, and screwed in his eyeglass more firmly.

"It's beautiful, but it'll be damp," Lady Cameron warned them.

Judy said nothing. She jumped out of the car, banging the door behind her so that the others were shut in, and ran alone across the moss-grown gravel to the front door. Again there had come upon her the overmastering impulse to get away from her family, to be alone with this place and this country. She must be alone with it. It was hers.

A curved half-moon of shallow steps led up to the front door, protected by a porch supported on slender columns. The door itself had once been painted green by man, but was now painted all colors by the weather, like a lichened stone. It was an eighteenth-century door, tall and wide, with a fanlight over it. It had a brass knocker in the form of a stag's head with branched antlers.

For a moment Judy stood in front of it, her arms uplifted, her palms laid lovingly against the old wood; then she lifted the knocker and knocked once, loudly and imperatively. Then she listened. She could hear footsteps shuffling across a stone-flagged hall, the footsteps of someone who was very old. A bolt was pulled back, a key was turned, and the door swung slowly open.

In front of her stood the queerest old man she had ever seen. His garments, green with age and ornamented with tarnished brass buttons, had perhaps once been a butler's livery and hung loosely on his shrunken figure. His face and bald head were the color of old leather, crisscrossed with thousands of fine wrinkles. His nose was very red and protruded bleakly into the world out of a wild thicket of gray beard and whisker. His eyes were a vivid and startling blue, like the eyes of a very young child.

For a full moment they stared at each other, the old man and the young girl, and then the old man smiled. It was a very slow smile, that crept over his dour old face with difficulty, as though it had not been used for years; it almost seemed that his features creaked with the effort.

Then he bowed to her, and spoke:

"Mistress Judith, ye've coom back."

BOOK I

Individuality

The high goal of our great endeavour
is spiritual attainment, individual worth,
at all cost to be sought and at all cost pursued,
to be won at all cost and at all cost assured.

—ROBERT BRIDGES, *The Testament of Beauty*

CHAPTER I

I

IT had been as they passed into the Highlands that Charles had noticed the change in Judy; but Judy herself knew that it had begun much earlier than that. It had begun months ago in London, on the first day of spring. For a moment, as she stood with her hands against the closed door, that day had been back with her, living again in her memory as though it were the present moment.

Spring came with utter suddenness that year, in the night. The excitement of its arrival awakened Judy earlier than usual that morning, and running barefoot to the window she looked out at this lovely new world that seemed as light and airy as a rounded bubble, sun-warmed and rainbow-tinted, bouncing and bounding along before a westerly wind and held and protected by a curving, mothering sky.

As the morning went by she pictured to herself this miracle of spring rippling over London. Eight o'clock in Soho, and the silver lamps hung by the rain on the area railings twinkling and swinging in the sun. Nine o'clock in Harley Street, and the brass door plates winking at the blue sky and the front door steps, freshly scrubbed by singing charladies, snowy as apple blossoms. Ten o'clock in Hyde Park, and the crocuses topaz and amethyst set in jade. Eleven o'clock in Kensington Gardens, and the sparrows mad with ecstasy. Twelve o'clock, and she herself was in Regent Street, one of a laughing, gaily dressed crowd that jostled joyously upon the pavement while the hoot of the taxis, the rumble of the busses, the laughter and chatter and cries,

21

blended together, made an anthem in praise of spring as triumphant as the song of robins and wrens in far-away coppices.

As triumphant but not as varied, she thought, strolling along through the shifting kaleidoscope of color. There was an appalling sameness about the rumble and jungle and rattle. In the budding coppices the clear bird notes would be rising and falling, pausing, trembling, cascading, as varied as the shifting pattern of leaf and bud and slender twig etched against the windswept April sky . . . . An April sky in the country. Great clouds racing their shadows over the tawny downs. . . . Quite suddenly Judy wanted to cry. Ridiculous. She blinked furiously, for what in the world, she asked herself savagely, had she to cry about?

She was young and healthy and good to look at, she had a large dress allowance and nothing to do all day but enjoy herself, she had a couple of doting parents whom she kept firmly under her right thumb, and a doting fiance whom she kept firmly under her left thumb, she had a cairn called Sarah and a Persian kitten and a Morris car, and yet she wasn't happy.

She was fed up. She was more utterly fed up than she could ever remember being before, and that on a day when the world was a rainbow-tinted bubble bouncing before a west wind. . . . The case was serious.

This particular attack of fed-up-ness was taking the curious form of lost identity. It seemed to Judy that there was no such person as Judy Cameron. She was just one of a crowd, one of the peas in society's pod, so tediously identical with all the other peas that her loss would simply not be noticed by that blaring merry-go-round, the life of London.

Her mind traveled back to the dance she had been at last night. She saw again herself and all those other girls, exactly alike with their reddened lips and plucked eyebrows and waved hair. Identical. And the men. Each wearing the same black coats and white shirt fronts, with the same fatigued carnation popping up out of their buttonholes, all drawling the same silly talk and eying the girls with the same slightly insulting look of patronage. The beautiful familiar scene had suddenly turned Judy sick. Was it a gathering of individual spirits pausing in their individual adventures to greet each other, or was it an auction of painted dolls waiting to be knocked down to the highest bidder? Judy, under the influence of post-influenza depression and an unbecoming frock, had decided that it was an auction. She and the other dolls were not real people at all, they were just the peas on the other side of society's pod. What would happen to them? She supposed they would just dance and dance until they were married to the peas on the other side of the pod, and after that both sets of peas, the male and the female, would spend years in performing what was known as social duty, which consisted, as far as Judy could see, in standing about in crushes eating and drinking and longing to sit down. . . . And then they would die. . . . Well, anyway, death would at least permit one to sit down. Kind, merciful death, that plucked the marionettes out of the merry-go-round and let them sit down.

"Good heavens," thought Judy, "I'll have to get a tonic"; and she quickened her pace.

But not for long, for a flower shop rose up out of the pavement, and she adored flowers. With a great breath of delight she stood and stared.

Daffodils golden as the sun-kissed limbs of the boy Spring himself, bluebells blue as his eyes, narcissi white as the clouds that raced over far-away downs, fat pink and white and blue hyacinths, like stout little girls in gingham pinafores, wet purple violets, tulips, jonquils, and primroses.

Their lovely familiar scents drifted through the open door and assailed Judy's nose. She sniffed. The scents were all different, all individual, and the flowers that were throwing them to her were as different each from the other as the woods and the clouds and the birds. Each had looked for and found a different perfection. Judy, sniffing, decided suddenly that nature, not man, knew how to live. Man, left to himself, did nothing but glue his nose to his neighbor's back and play follow-my-leader round and round in circles till he died of exhaustion. But natural things, flowers, grasses, trees—these unfolded each after its own individual pattern, spread their perfection under the sun, and, rooted in quietness and peace, lived out their lives in union with the earth that bore them.

Through individuality to union—was that the way of life? Was unity the final good and individuality the road to it? Must one discover and know one's individual self before one was fit for union with something else?

A sudden resolve flamed up in Judy. She turned away from the shop window with her lips set in the obstinate line dreaded by her family. . . . She would get out of this. . . . She would break free from this machine-made life that stifled her and somewhere, somehow, she would discover her real self, that Judy who was surely alive deep down within the doll she despised.

Somewhere. . . . But where? . . . Where could one find oneself? . . . Surely where the flowers grew, who were so gloriously themselves, and where the earth was old and still and very wise and unpolluted by the foolishness of men. . . . Yes, but where?

And then a curious thing happened to Judy. Walking along the pavement, she stopped mechanically in front of a picture shop and stared at a picture there, the picture of a mountain, and the whole of her life was changed.

She had not realized that she was staring at it, but quite suddenly Regent Street was gone, the hum of the traffic was gone, everything was gone, nothing was left in the whole world but a great purple-black mountain, its jagged outlines savagely defined against a cold, stormy sky and its summit hidden in clouds. In the foregound of the picture was a larch wood, and seen through its vivid green branches were the silver waters of a loch. Down the side of the mountain, falling from the smoky gray clouds to the silver loch, tumbled a burn, showing against the rocks and heather like a rent torn in a purple cloak. The scene had a cold and stormy beauty that was a little frightening, but at the same time utterly satisfying, in its sheer perfection. There was something ultimate and final about it. It did not seem like a picture, it seemed like a vision from another world. Judy, staring at it, felt that she was looking through a window. It was as though the comfortable Regent Street world that she had seen a moment ago was nothing but a painted curtain, having the appearance of reality only, and that now hands had torn it aside and she looked beyond it to a reality that was terrifyingly real. And not only her eyes but her whole body was made aware of it. Through the window a cold mountain wind blew upon her. She could feel its icy fingers creeping over her body, touching her, stinging her awake, making her shiver with a fear that was half ecstasy. In her ears was the sound of water falling and the crying of mountain birds. She could smell wet earth and green things growing, and under her feet was the feel of springing turf.

And then, as she stared, the whole of her being gathered up into concentration; she became gradually aware that she herself, that individual spirit that she had thought did not exist, was confronted with a choice the most momentous to her that she would ever have to make. On either side of the picture of the mountain were two other pictures: the one on the right the picture of a glittering London ballroom, the one on the left the picture of an interior, a comfortable country cottage in the shires. Slowly these two pictures came forward from their background and forced themselves on Judy's attention, changing as they did so from pictures to windows. She found herself looking through three different windows at three different worlds. And she knew what the worlds were; and she knew, too, that within the next two minutes she would have to decide which one was to be her home. On the right was the world of brilliance and wealth, into which she had been born and for which she had thought herself destined; and on the left was the world of compromise that united pleasure with a love of nature and of homely things and achieved a placid comfort; and in the middle—what was she looking at through the middle window? A world of stark and terrible beauty, of sorrow and failure, shorn of wealth and comfort but yet ablaze with joy, the world of the heights of the human spirit. It seemed to Judy that her little shivering self was flitting from side to side, unwilling to choose either of the worlds to left or right, yet cowering back in fear from that terrible middle window. And yet—she had to choose it. It was where she belonged. The courage and strength that were the essence of her drove her on. She took a step forward on the pavement and fixed her eyes on that purple mountain against the stormy sky, and as she moved forward her spirit moved too and was caught and held. She felt the grip as of fire that seized her, and the whole world reeled.

II

"Hullo, Judy." A hand gripped her arm and, turning, she saw Charles. She clung to him, thankful for his support while the pavement heaved beneath her and Regent Street swayed as in an earthquake.

"That picture!" she gasped. "The one like a window —the middle one. Look!"

Charles looked and saw the usual conventional picture of a crude purple Scotch mountain, with larch trees of a sickly green sprouting in the foreground. It was framed in a particularly loathsome gold frame with knobs on it.

"Good lord," said Charles, "what a frightful object."

"Frightful?" said Judy, and looked again. Yes, it *was* frightful. It was cheap and tawdry and quite small, though a moment before it had been terrifyingly lovely and had filled the whole horizon. What in the world had she been thinking of? What in the world had been happening to her?

"Charles," she said, "I feel funny."

Charles surveyed her. She was very white under her makeup, and there were little beads of perspiration on her forehead.

"That blasted flu," said Charles, and putting one arm round her he signaled for a taxi with the other.

"A cocktail and a spot of lunch is what will meet the situation," he told her as he heaved her in. "It was that dance last night. I told you not to go. Obstinate young donkey."

In the taxi she sat with her head against his shoulder and listened while he scolded. Charles, good-tempered as a rabbit and placid as an owl, had a particularly gentle way of scolding that was as soothing as a lullaby. He was really very nice. So nice was he that it is difficult to do him justice. He was fair and rosy and easy-going and kind. He had money and a commission in a crack regiment. He hadn't many brains, but his moustache was perfect and his clothes a dream. He was perhaps a little inclined to *embonpoint*. He had a roundness of outline and a solidity of substance that hinted at the extremely substantial major he would eventually become. He had never in all his life done an unkind thing or said a sharp

27

word. His thoughts, when he had any, were like a child's for simplicity. He was an eminently desirable husband. Judy had seen that when she met him first at the age of eight and had immediately appropriated him for that purpose, training him carefully through the intervening years in obedience to her every wish and veneration for her whims.

"Charles," she said, "when you get your leave we'll take mother and father and the car and go to Scotland."

"But we were going to Bornemouth," objected Charles.

"I've changed my mind," said Judy. "We are going to Scotland. We ought to go to Scotland. I've Scotch blood in me, and I've never been there. It's disgraceful."

Charles sighed. He liked Bournemouth. The food was good and the sun was hot and one could ride in the New Forest. Scotland he did not care for. It was cold and draughty and one felt perpetually clammy, and he had never acquired the meditative habit of a fisherman.

"Must we?" he asked.

"Yes," said Judy, and stuck out her chin.

"I suppose the Mater and the Old Man will gambol in leading-strings as usual? They're partial to Bournemouth, you know."

"We are going to Scotland," said Judy slowly and distinctly. When Judy was slow and distinct there was never any more argument, and Charles capitulated.

III

Everyone capitulated. Charles easily obtained the promise of immense quantities of leave. His regiment expended so much strength on being crack that it had very little left for work, and lengthy periods of recuperation from crackness were considered necessary by authority. He was to come and go throughout the summer, and it would be mostly come.

Sir James and Lady Cameron complained bitterly at the loss of Bournemouth, but with firm handling were in time brought to heel.

Judy, who appeared to have gone—temporarily, one hoped—quite mad, sent an advertisement to the papers demanding that some human being unknown should let to them, for the space of ten weeks, a house in the Highlands of Scotland which looked out upon a mountain, a loch, and a larch wood.

"It's an insane advertisement," sighed Lady Cameron, "and no one would dream of answering it except a madman as crazy as you and it."

"If that mountain and that larch wood and that loch exist upon this earth," said Judy, "that advertisement will be answered."

"What mountain and wood and loch?" asked Lady Cameron, irritably counting linen—they were to let the London flat.

"I saw them in a picture," said Judy, "and I'm going to find them or perish in the attempt."

"It's me that'll perish," moaned her mother. "All this fuss with the agent, and my best pillowcase missing. . . . Go and ask your father if he feels equal to canned strawberries for lunch or if he'd rather be on the safe side and stick to rhubarb."

Judy obediently departed, and on the way down the passage heard the thud of the second post arriving in the letter box. She pounced on it. . . . The electric light bill. . . . A catalogue from Woollands. . . . A gentleman offering to lend them money simply, he assured them, for reasons of benevolence only. . . . And a large blue envelope bearing a Scotch postmark and addressed to Sir James in a queer, neat, angular handwriting.

Judy stood in the middle of the hall, her heart thumping, the letter in her hands. She looked at the handwrit-

29

ing. It had character. Fierceness in the downstrokes, delicacy in the curves. Something queer and contradictory in it. Individual. It seemed like a voice speaking to her, and she ripped open the envelope. It was addressed to her father, but it was, she felt, her letter. Inside was a short business note on a halfsheet of paper, headed Glen Suilag and signed I. C. Macdonald. Glen Suilag, it said, was an old house in a lonely part of the Highlands. It looked out on a mountain, a loch, and a larch wood; but then, it added with a touch of humor, most Highland houses did. It was to let at a moderate rent. The fishing was good. I. C. Macdonald did not say whether he was a man or a woman, but the entire absence of all necessary information in the letter made it quite clear that he was a man. . . . Besides, the voice that Judy had heard speaking was a man's voice. . . . She rushed with the letter to her father and never so much as mentioned the rhubarb.

IV

Then followed a period of endless delays that drove Judy nearly frantic. Sir James, who before his retirement had been a barrister of distinction, insisted tiresomely and monotonously upon references. Lady Cameron wrote passionate outpourings to Mr. Macdonald on the subject of household supplies and received terse replies commenting on the excellence of the fishing and the beauty of the view and answering none of her questions. Charles wasted days messing about at the stores with fishing rods and then went and had jaundice To crown all, when everything was ready for departure, Sarah, Judy's black cairn, eloped with the butcher's boy and was not retrieved for four days.

It was the end of June before they got under way and

slid out of London in Judy's Morris, on a day of rain and wind and cold as intense as that of March.

Everyone but Judy was perfectly miserable. Charles, seated beside her at the wheel, with his coat collar turned up and the corners of his mouth turned down and his complexion the color of a rather *passé* lemon, wondered if perhaps before the matrimonial knot was tied it wouldn't be as well to take a firm stand with Judy, to indicate gently but firmly that a husband's position was an authoritative one, and that occasional submission in a woman was desirable. But by the time they reached the suburbs he had decided that he felt unequal to the effort of indicating anything, and as for a firm stand, a soft sit was a lot more in his line at the moment.

As for Sarah, wedged between Judy and Charles, she felt bad. During her sojourn with the butcher's boy she had eaten lots of things, and it had been nice at the moment, but not afterwards; and the afterwards was lasting longer than the moment had, and she hoped she wasn't going to be sick in the car because she quite well remembered from past experience that that was never a popular move. . . . She lowered her silky black lids over her lovely, lustrious brown eyes and lolled against Charles, hoping for the best.

Sir James and Lady Cameron, wrapped in rugs in the back seat, were cold and resigned. Sir James was always resigned. He was a kindly, gray-haired man, with an eyeglass and a deprecating manner. In the courts he had been renowned for his decision and his swift, vigorous handling of cases; but at home he had always found it best to be meek and quiescent. Lady Cameron was the kind of wife who made a husband find that best. She loved him dearly, but she believed very firmly in the molding properties of love and the strong guiding of a woman's hand. . . . Sometimes when Charles woke up at two in the morning with indigestion, he wondered if

31

Judy would become as strong-minded as her mother, and devoutly hoped not. Somehow, though he was quite used to the spectacle of Judy managing her vigorous mother, it never occurred to him that she was already the stronger character of the two. . . . Judy in her sweet youth was so soft to the touch, soft as velvet; only the discerning felt the full strenth of the iron in her.

"Liking it, Judy?" he asked.

But she did not answer, for she had not heard him. It was not like her not to hear what was said to her. He suddenly felt cold with foreboding and tugged at the collar of his coat.

"Rotten day," he muttered.

"Deplorable," said Lady Cameron's voice behind him. "It's probably quite sunny at Bournemouth."

Judy was oblivious of them all. As the day wore on and they left London further and further behind them, she felt that the Morris was a boat launching out into unknown seas. Where it was taking her she did not know. To the Fortunate Isles, to Utopia, to a Hidden Country, to adventure, to romance—whatever it was she welcomed it. Looking around her at the storm, she reveled in the wild beauty of the day. It was in tune with her mood. Warm sunshine and drowsy fields would not have kept pace with the singing in her heart and the pulsing of her blood, but this tossing storm was a rapture and thrumming of savage music, elemental and grand, like the music of the sea.

The world was just like a sea today. The sheeted rain, blown by the wind, was rushing to meet them like waves, and the branches of the trees, with their little green leaves clinging desperately to life, were streaming in the wind and the rain like mermaids' hair floating out on the water. The clouds, driving low over the green earth, were stretched out like racing horses, and every little pond and stream held long lines of wind-blown ripples. . . . Silver and green. . . . A magic sea of romance. . . . The birch trees passed by with a gleam of silver trunks swaying in silver rain. The blackness of brooding pinewoods protected as in a cave the fragile, heart-piercing green of the young bracken. Each hawthorn hedge, cascading with green leaves, sent showers of green foam spurting up into the sky at every gust of wind. Beneath them, nestling as though in the curve of the wave, were the round moon faces of the yellow celandines; and now and then, spilled along the ditches and wandering streamlike through meadow grass, were pools and threads of pure gold, the buttercups. . . . Gold. . . . Now the world seemed to Judy made of silver and gold, the precious metals. Not tinsel and gilt, but silver and gold. Real things.

V

And that sense of reality deepened in her as the strange journey wore on and they reached Scotland and the Highlands—Glen Suilag. Upon nothing in her life hitherto had she been able to lay hold as she was now laying hold of this country and this place. All that she saw was instantly hers, and so real to her. When she stood with her lifted hands laid against the wood of the old front door her fingers were thrillingly conscious of the texture of the wood, holding it, possessing it. When the door opened and that queer old man stood before her they looked at each other with an instant love that made her feel that he, too, was hers. How blue his eyes were, and how young. How strange that so old a man should have the eyes of a young boy. He did not speak again, but he stood aside from the door and held it open for her.

Judy hesitated a moment, thrilling with that excitement that seizes every human being standing on the threshold of a strange house. . . . A new world opening its gate to take one in for good or for evil, changing perhaps the whole tenor of life. . . . Yet to Judy this new world did not seem unknown. She had the feeling that she was not stepping forward but back. . . . The old man stretched out a bony hand, seized her arm, and pulled her very gently over the threshold. As he did so she was gripped by an extraordinary feeling of finality. The old life was ended and a new life had begun.

She was standing in a dark, cold paneled hall, uncarpeted and smelling of damp and rotting wood. The stairs, wide and shallow, sloped gently away into the shadows. Stags' heads were round the walls, and she could see the branching antlers, like the leafless trees of a forest, spearing the gloom high up over her head. On a table near her stood a bowl of pale pink cabbage roses. Their sweet smell brought a note of tenderness into the cold, grim darkness of the hall, and Judy buried her nose in them for a moment and felt reassured.

"Coom this way," said the old man sourly, and turned his back on her. The sudden affection and delight that had lit up his face at the sight of her had vanished, and he now looked the crossest old thing possible.

She followed his bent, shambling figure through a door on the left into a large dim room. It was sparsely furnished, and yet Judy, as she came in, had the feeling that it was crowded. But not with furniture. It was thronging with memories. They gathered round her, pressing in on her; and she stood bewildered, uncertain, her conscious mind too confused to gather any impression of tangible things or to lay hold upon any one of the intangible things that overwhelmed her.

There was a commotion in the hall, heralding the arrival of the family, and instantly that mounting wave of intangible things receded. Judy's mind, untroubled by it, was able to grasp the outward aspect of the room. Facing her were three long, low windows, looking west over

34

a lovely tangled garden to the larch wood. Through the trees she could see the gleam of the loch and beyond that again a great purple mountain, its sides gashed with a corrie and a tumbling burn and its summit hidden in clouds. To the right of the windows was another door. The room was dim, for the middle window of the three was blocked up. . . . How strange. . . . Why should they have blocked it up? . . . In front of it, as though shielding it from a too great inquisitiveness, stood an old oak chest. The room was paneled in wood painted a pale and lovely green. At the windows hung very shabby but very beautiful brocade curtains patterned with roses and carnations. To Judy's right as she faced the windows was a great open fireplace with a chintz-covered sofa beside it. There were a few Sheraton chairs and a little spindly-legged writing table. To the left was a harpsichord, the old ivory keys yellow as buttercups and the wood of it, that must once have been so bright and shining, dulled and cracked by time. A few framed miniatures hung on the walls. The carpet on the floor was faded and threadbare. The room was like a piece of music, a sad little minuet played very softly. Tears pricked behind Judy's eyelids, and the eruption of Sarah and her parents into the room seemed to her like the sudden blaring of a horrid trumpet tearing the lilting tune to pieces.

"Charles is putting the car away," said Lady Cameron. "What an appalling place!" She seated herself despairingly on the sofa and sneezed. "There! My throat is going up into my head. The damp's enough to give a mermaid cold."

Sir James, the Scotchman in him thrilling to the sight and sound of mountain country, was for once oblivious of her sufferings. He strode to the left-hand window.

"Judy, come and look." Judy came to him and looked again.

"Yes," she said. "I feel I've come home."

Unseen by any of them, the old man standing in the shadows by the door crept forward a few paces, his eyes fixed on her.

"That's the Scotch blood in you," said Sir James. "There'll be fish in that loch. . . . By Jove, Judy, we're going to enjoy this holiday!"

"I'm not," snapped his wife. "James, ring the bell. I must have a hot bath and go to bed."

Sir James, once more the dutiful husband, turned from the window with a little sigh.

"There does not appear to *be* a bell, dear."

"What, no bell?" Lady Cameron glanced despairingly round the room, and her eye fell upon the strange figure of the old man. She erected her lorgnette. She had had the handling of all sorts and conditions of domestics in her day, but never anything like this. She remembered that the Macdonald man had said Angus the butler would be left in charge of the house.

"Are you the butler?" she demanded incredulously.

The old man, standing close behind Judy, turned on her with something like fury. It was as though any interruption to his intense preoccupation with Judy was more than he could stand.

"Hae ye no een i' yer head?" He indicated his livery with scorn. "Would a mon dress his puir body up i' ridiculous garments the like o' these for a joke? Do I look like a mon to waste the wits given him by God Almighty makin' jokes wi' 'em?"

Sir James held out a friendly hand. "You are Angus? Mr. Macdonald told us about you. It's very good of him to let his house to us."

Angus reluctantly put his horny hand in Sir James's. "The Laird was aye a fule," he growled.

"I dare say, but go and see about my bath," Lady Cameron urged him. "Go and tell the housemaid to get it ready."

"There's no' a bathroom i' the hoose."

36

"What? . . . Not even water laid on?"

Angus rubbed his hands together, and the pleasure consequent upon annoying someone he disliked was apparent in him.

"Na. The young Laird has bin here but twa three year, an' the old Laird, that's his uncle, no cared for modern contraptions."

"One forgets how modern washing is," murmured Sir James.

"The old Laird was of opeenion that those who like to be kep' awake o' nights wi' cisterns gurglin' ower their heeds could be kep' awake wi' cisterns gurglin' ower their heeds, an' be damned to 'em; but as for himself he prefairred to sleep sound."

"How did he bathe then?" demanded Lady Cameron.

"He no bathed."

"How does the young Laird bathe?"

"I' the burn."

There was a moment's frightful pause.

"I expect you can have a tin tub in your room, dear," countered Sir James gently.

"What's the good of a tin tub to a woman of my size?" demanded Lady Cameron passionately. "The moment you get into those prehistoric things, if you're large, all the water slops over onto the floor. What's the use of that?" Sir James and Angus, eying her contours, could not tell her, and a chill fell on the room.

Judy had not heard a word. She was still standing in the window, leaning forward and looking out. To her left she could see the upper part of the road down which they had come, a white ribbon winding up into the mist. It was, she knew, the only entrance to this little world shut away in the mountains. She realized what that white ribbon must have meant always to the people who lived in this house. It would have been their one connecting link with the world outside. Tidings of joy or pain, of peace or war, would have come to them down

37

it. When they left their valley to join in the tumult of the world beyond they would go up it. When they came home again they would come down it. The people who loved them and waited for them would watch that white ribbon day after day, eagerly, perhaps torn with anxiety because an expected traveler did not come. She almost felt as though she herself were expecting someone. She put up her hand and pushed one of the brocade curtains further back, that she might see better, and as she did so she saw a tiny kilted figure, dwarfed by distance, coming down the road. She looked at him. Even from so far away she could appraise the swinging kilt, the free stride, and the tall, lithe figure. . . . A shepherd perhaps. . . . She took her hand from the curtain, and it fell back into place, hiding the figure from her. She saw that where her hand had been there was a worn patch on the curtain, and a little thrill went through her. . . . So someone else had stood at that window and watched so often that the roses and carnations of the curtain were all worn away. . . . She drew back a little, awed, and found herself standing in the middle window. She looked up at it, a hand on each of its curtains, deeply resenting the barrier of wood and stone that shut out the air and the light. She heard Angus's voice crying out warningly to her, "Hae a care, Mistress Judith, hae a care!" and even as he spoke that tide of memory, that had risen a little and then ebbed when she first came in, rushed over her like a terrible, choking flood. It seemed as though it came to her from the middle window, and it was a tide of grief and despair. She started back, crying out, and in a moment Angus was by her side, holding her arm, almost as though he had expected this moment and had been watching for it.

"Mistress Judith! Mistress Judith!" he said, comforting her. She clung to him with one hand and to her father, who had come to her, with the other. She felt as though the two of them were lifting her up out of a terrible salt sea of misery that was drowning her. Her mother's voice, sharp with the irritation of anxiety, seemed to come to her from very far away.

"What in the world is the matter, Judy?"

Judy clung to her father. "That middle window! It made me feel awful!" She looked up into his face, urgently demanding an answer to her question. "Why did they block it up?"

The astounded Sir James patted her shoulder gently. "How in the world should I know? . . . Judy! Judy!"

She turned to Angus. At that moment the answer to her question seemed to concern her more vitally than anything else in the world. "Why did they block up that window?"

His eyes met hers. She thought that he knew, but he would not answer. Muttering and shaking his head, he turned from her and ambled out of the room.

Judy, seated between her parents on the sofa, was patted and soothed. That terrible tide withdrew and she was her normal self again. "How silly of me. . . . I felt funny suddenly. . . . That middle window made me feel funny."

Lady Cameron, as always was instantly ready with a normal explanation for abnormal phenomena. "It was the lunch you ate at the hotel. If you will have an ice on top of lobster and then hot coffee on the top of that, what can you expect? . . . Do you think that man means to get us any tea? Where's Charles all this time? It can't take him half an hour to put the car away."

"Charles?" said Judy. "What Charles?"

Her parents stared at her. "Judy!"

"Oh, yes. . . . Charles." Judy laughed a little nervously, twisting her hands together. Somehow Charles, who in London had meant so much to her, seemed in this place to mean almost nothing at all. . . . She had completely forgotten him.

Steps sounded on an uncarpeted floor, and the second door, the one behind the sofa on which they sat, opened.

"Tea at last," said Lady Cameron, and pulled a little table close to her. "Put it here, Angus."

"It's not tea," said Judy, without turning her head, "it's Ian Macdonald."

She spoke very quietly. All feeling of tumult and confusion had left her, and she felt at peace. She slipped off the sofa and went to him, and their hands met.

"How do you do," he said, "I'm so——"

He stopped abruptly and looked at her, smiling. She, her hand still in his, smiled back at him. There was in their greeting the quiet delight of two friends who meet after a long separation, two friends whose affection is of such longstanding growth that it does not call for comment or emotional expression. With one glance at him Judy knew exactly what he looked like, and her glance was not the appraising one of a stranger but the swift, rather anxious look of one who reassures herself that the beloved has not changed.

He was a tall man, strongly and finely built, cleanshaven, naturally fair but tanned by sun and wind. His gray eyes, shy and gentle, were the eyes of a dreamer, but there was strength and almost a touch of hardness in his lips and jaw. His manner was queerly contradictory, decisive sometimes with the resolution that was a part of his character, then suddenly awkward and hesitating, the shrinking of a recluse from human contact. A man lonely and emotional, imaginative and strong; a man who for good or for ill would leave his mark on his world. His kilt and tweed coat were appallingly shabby and wet with the mist. His boots were muddy and his hair ruffled. . . . Lady Cameron didn't think much of him.

"Might one ask who you are?" she demanded.

Her voice broke the queer spell that held the two together. He dropped Judy's hand and came round the sofa.

"Forgive me, Lady Cameron. I'm Ian Macdonald, whose house you've taken. I just came in to see if I could do anything for you." He turned to Sir James. "How do you do, sir."

Sir James liked him. Odd, but very much in harmony with his background. Sir James liked people to be in harmony with their backgrounds. This, to Lady Cameron, was no recommendation—she had taken such a dislike to the background.

"Oh, haven't you gone away?" she asked with ill-concealed annoyance.

Ian smiled. "I know it's awful to sit down at one's tenants' gates, but I can't afford to go away. I've taken rooms at the inn in the village. But I shan't keep my eye on you, you needn't worry. I'm sure you're the perfect tenants."

"This is the perfect house," delcared Judy.

He turned back to her, pleased but puzzled. "I'm glad you like it. . . . How did you know my name before I told you who I was? Have we met before?"

"I don't think so," said Judy, and then stopped abruptly, for that queer winged thing inside her seemed to be laughing. . . .

Lady Cameron made a violent effort to be hospitable. "Well, do sit down, Mr. Macdonald, and have tea with us. So kind of you to come. We hope your man Angus has gone for tea."

Ian flushed shyly. "Thank you very much, but I think I oughtn't—after all—I've just cleared out."

Sir James pulled forward a chair. His liking for the man grew with every moment. "Please. We'd like to talk to you. Have a cigarette?"

They sat down and cigarettes did their blessed work of destroying constraint. "We've taken a great fancy to Glen Suilag—especially Judy."

"This room," said Judy, "talks to you."

Ian looked at her again, startled. "Yes. That's what I feel about it."

"I could wish, Mr. Macdonald," said Lady Cameron, "that there was a bathroom in the house. I think you should have told me that there wasn't."

Sir James waved his right hand in the soothing way which in his days as a practicing barrister had always poured oil over troubled courts, and was now frequently successful in quelling the tactlessness of his wife and daughter. "My dear, surely an unimportant point."

"I don't think so. How is one to bathe?"

Ian was distressed. "I'm so sorry. I didn't know you wanted—I didn't know you expected—you see, lots of these old Highland houses haven't modern conveniences."

"So I see," said Lady Cameron, and sneezed.

"You're catching cold," he said. "Let me light the fire."

In a moment he had the peats in the grate blazing. The warm glow crept over the dim old room, giving it a rich and lovely life. Ian's face, as he knelt by the hearth, was lit up by the flames. Judy leaned forward, looking at him. "Just the same," sang the spirit within her, "just the same."

Angus came ambling in with a tray containing a plate of bread and butter an inch thick and an extraordinary assortment of cups and saucers. Lady Cameron eyed it with horror.

"What a frightful tea set! Is that the only china there is?"

Ian flushed again with mingled confusion and annoyance. . . . He had taken an instant dislike to Lady Cameron. . . . Angus snorted.

"Losh! Do ye want to drink yer tay out o' gold an' siller? Na, na, tay's tay whatever ye drink it oot of. 'Tis the tay itsel', an' the stomach into which ye pour it as must be in guid condeetion. The crockery's of no importance to a body wi' a grain o' sense."

"Angus!" said Ian warningly.

"Hoots!" said Angus, and departed, growling.

"I like that man," said Judy, and again the spirit inside her laughed. Like? What a word to use to describe what she felt for Angus!

Ian turned to her gratefully. "Yes. He's rare. We don't know where he came from originally, and he doesn't seem to know himself, but he's been at Glen Suilag ever since I've known it."

"And you've been here two years?" said Sir James.

"Yes. I inherited from my uncle. I've been here off and on since I was a boy, of course. I love the place." He paused, and a note of despair came into his voice. "But I've hardly a bean. That's why I've let the house. . . . There's such an awful lot needs doing."

Lady Cameron glanced from the threadbare carpet to the smoke-grimed ceiling. "Yes," she said pointedly, "a lot needs doing."

Again Sir James waved a soothing right hand. "Estate in a bad way?" he asked sympathetically.

Ian spoke jerkily, with deep feeling and a note of challenge in his voice. "Yes. . . . Crofters beastly poor. . . . An awful lot of illness. . . . I'm a doctor, though I've never practiced, and can do a bit for them in that line, but it's going to be a tough job to get things right here."

"If you've never practiced you're only half-fledged," said Judy. "Why didn't you sprout the final feathers?"

"I came up here instead."

Lady Cameron banged down her teacup in its saucer and spoke with force. "Do you mean to tell me, Mr. Macdonald, that you abandoned a promising profession to bury yourself alive in this damp, draughty back of beyond?"

"Yes." He leaned forward, looking at the fire, speaking queerly. "At first I didn't really want to. . . . I didn't mean to. . . . I had to."

"How very silly of you. . . . Very silly. . . . How silly young men are."

Ian smiled. "That's what my sister and uncle say. You must meet my sister. I think you'd get on."

"I'm sure I'm thankful to hear you've sensible relations to keep an eye on you."

"They're here now, as a matter of fact, staying with me at the inn. They come for the fishing and to keep my loose tile from blowing off."

"Oh, have you a tile loose?" said Judy. "I thought so."

"Judy!" expostulated her father, and half raised his right hand.

"I'm paying you a compliment," said Judy to Ian. "Odd people are the salt of the earth. I'm odd myself."

"Thank you," said Ian, his eyes on her.

Suddenly she leaned forward. He, she felt, would perhaps be able to answer that question that so vitally concerned her. As they talked it seemed to them both that they were quite alone in the room.

"When was that middle window blocked up?" she asked him.

"After the 'Forty-five."

"Why?"

"I don't know."

"Who lived here then?"

"Ranald Macdonald, the Laird of Glen Suilag, and his wife Judith."

"What happened to them?"

"I don't really know. . . . History has it that he was killed in the 'Forty-five and that after his death she blocked up the window."

"But why?"

"I don't know." He smiled at her urgency. "It's nice to find a stranger so interested in my family history."

44

"A stranger?" said Judy, and gave her head a tiny shake. "And you don't remember any more than that?"

"No."

The queer little dialogue ended abruptly, and Lady Cameron's suppressed annoyance burst forth. "My dear Judy, how can you expect the poor unfortunate man to remember what happened here two hundred years ago?" She turned to Ian with sympathy. "Have another cup of tea, Mr. Macdonald. . . . James, I think you'd better go and look for Charles. The poor boy's tea will be cold."

"Is Charles your son?" asked Ian.

"Not yet. At the moment we've only one child to bully us. But Charles is engaged to Judy. He's outside putting the car away."

"Father, go and see about him," said Judy. "I believe Glen Suilag has taken a dislike to him and done him an injury, as it has mother."

Lady Cameron stared. "You mean my cold? Judy, don't be absurd!"

Sir James went off to look for Charles, and Lady Cameron, her tea finished, went off to look for larger handkerchiefs. As the sound of her footsteps died away a still, intimate silence settled down on the room, and it seemed satisfied, as though it had waited for this moment. The two who were left sat without speaking. A shaft of sunlight slanted into the room and touched Judy's cheek, and she glanced round.

"Look!" she cried, and ran to a window, opening it and leaning out. The sun was just piercing through the mist, gathering it up from the earth with long, golden fingers and rolling it away up the mountains. Far up it still lay like cotton wool in the folds of the hills, but below color was creeping back to the earth, the yellow of lichened rocks, the green of the bracken and larch trees, the blue of the distance, the jeweled mosaic of the flowers in the garden. The steamy air held a thousand scents.

"What a heavenly smell!" exclaimed Judy, sniffing. "What is it exactly?"

Ian was standing just behind her, holding back the curtain. "Wet bracken and bog myrtle, the roses in the garden and the peaty smell of the hills just touched with a tang of the sea. . . . I'm glad the sun's come out for you. . . . Doesn't it bring out the color?"

"Yes," said Judy, "the sun and the earth have met, and all that color is born." She turned to him. "Some meetings are very exciting in their results, aren't they?"

"That meeting certainly is."

"It's like when two people meet and the whole of their world is made new."

"What?" he said, and looked at her strangely. They stood very close to each other, expectant, their hearts beating fast. . . . Charles erupted from the hall.

For the second time that day Judy could cheerfully have murdered him. In this new world there were only two people whose presence did not jar on her: Angus and Ian Macdonald. The others seemed alien to its life.

Charles was limping, and his manner was slightly aggrieved. He sat down suddenly on the nearest chair and extended a leg.

"I'm sorry to disturb you, Judy, but I've sprained my ankle."

Judy struggled desperately and unsuccessfully to get the better of her irritation. "Have you?" she said crossly. "The place evidently doesn't like you. It doesn't like mother either. She's got a cold. How did you do it? I hope you weren't tinkering with the car because we shall want to use it tomorrow."

Charles felt his ankle peevishly. "Heartless jade! I twisted the damn thing trying to shove some of the rubbish in the garage out of the way so that I could get the car in." He cocked his eye at Ian. "Look here, if you're the gardener, or the angel in the house, or whatever you are, why the dickens didn't you clear out the garage?"

Emotion and annoyance and mirth combined to make Judy feel quite hysterical. She waved her hand. "May I introduce Mr. Macdonald, the Laird of Glen Suilag, and Captain Anderson, my intended."

Charles flushed to the roots of his hair. "Good lord, awfully sorry an' all that. No idea, of course. Dashed silly ass."

"Clothes maketh man," said Ian humorously.

"Will you have some stewed tea, Charles," asked Judy, "or shall I massage your ankle first?"

"You don't massage a sprain, you silly goat, you bandage it. I'll get the mater to see to it later. You're no earthly at this sort of thing. . . . Yes, tea, please."

Ian Macdonald moved shyly toward the door. "I think—perhaps——"

Judy flung out a detaining hand. "No, no, don't go!"

Her urgency startled her as much as it startled Charles. She turned away and sat down behind the tea tray, pouring out tea to hide her confusion. "Charles and I don't want to be left alone together," she said hurriedly, "we're long past that stage. We've been engaged since we were in long clothes, and we're going to be married as soon as this holiday is over."

Charles, utterly bewildered by this queer new Judy and this odd, untidy, silent Highlander who never, blast him, took his eyes from Judy's face, tried loyally to back her up in the stupid conversation she had chosen.

"Keen on each other an' all that, no end keen, but sentimental backchat ran dry long ago. Quite like a married couple now." He drank some tea and smiled at her. "What filthy tea you do make!"

To his surprise she flamed out at him furiously. "I didn't make it. Angus, the butler did."

"I bet it was you who forgot to put in more water."

"That was mother."

"Well, have it your own way," he said good-humoredly, "it's filthy tea anyhow." He turned from her to the Highlander standing there stiff as a ramrod, waiting. Blast the fellow, what on earth was he waiting for? Was he waiting for him, Charles Anderson, the affianced husband of Judy Cameron, to take himself off? Confound it, if any taking of oneself off was to be done, surely it should be undertaken by the Highland fellow who, when all was said and done, had let his dashed house and had no business to be there at all.

"Good shooting and fishing?" he asked amiably.

"For those who like it, yes. I'm a rotten shot myself and not much good with a rod either."

Charles was astonished. "Then why live in Scotland? If you don't go in for shooting and fishing I'm dashed if I know what you can go in for, except economy and getting wet."

"Mr. Macdonald," said Judy, "came to live at Glen Suilag because he was forced by an inner compulsion."

"Inner what?" said Charles. He gulped down the dregs of his tea, tea leaves and all, and rose. He might not be very quick in the uptake, but he knew when he was not wanted. . . . Compulsion, she said. . . . These two and, he felt, the room itself, were forcing him out of it. He felt bitterly, miserably hurt. "If you'll excuse me I'll just go and have a bath."

"There isn't one, " said Judy.

"What?"

Judy spoke slowly and distinctly and with annoyance. "I repeat, there *is* no bath. There is no water laid on."

For the moment Charles's irritation got the better of his wounded feelings. "Look here, Judy, it's too bad. Dragging your poor parents and your long-suffering intended to this beastly hole without ever asking if there was a bath. I told you not to be in such a damn hurry. Silly little donkey, you are, always hurrying an' scurrying your panting family after this and that without giv-

48

ing 'em time to think. . . . Your mother'll have something to say about there being no bath."

"She's said it," snapped Judy, "and I think you forget
that Mr. Macdonald is here."

"Good lord, yes. . . . Sorry. . . . I've been standing on
my head in the garage, you know. Confusing." He
bowed stiffly to Ian and withdrew with, for him, considerable dignity.

Judy was seized with compunction. "Poor Charles!
How cross I've been, " she murmured.

"Yes," said Ian.

She looked at him and saw that his eyes were bright
with amusement. She had the queer feeling that he
knew all her faults; that he knew quite well just how
cross she could be, and how wilful and how set on her
own way; but that he knew, too, lovely things about her
that she did not know herself. . . . How strange it was.
. . . She went back to the window and he followed her.
The quiet, expectant moment that Charles had shattered came back to them again.

"Please forgive Charles and mother," said Judy.
"They've really been very rude about this perfect house.
You see, it's not the sort of place they're used to. They
don't feel at home here as I do."

"I'm glad you feel at home here," he said softly.

"Yes. I seem to remember it all." She paused, a little
scared. "I don't understand."

He turned to her hastily, reassuring her. "Don't
worry. Perhaps you are what they call a sensitive. The
atmosphere of a place affects you. Old houses are always full of memories that one seems to remember. A
place like this, so hidden away that it never changes, is
like an underground cavern with a stream running
through it. It holds the echoes of the running water that
is coming and the running water that has gone and
keeps them both alive."

49

"Yes," said Judy, very low, "but how is it that I remember *you?*"

He was silent a moment, as puzzled as she was but trying to find a reason that would satisfy her. "There have been Macdonalds at Glen Suilag for centuries. Perhaps you met one in the hall as you came in, and I reminded you of him."

"You mean a ghost?" said Judy.

"Let's call him an echo that the cavern keeps alive."

Judy looked at him again, at his dreaming eyes and the purposeful set of his jaw. Surely a man of dreams who, unlike so many dreamers, had the power to translate his dreams into action. . . . What were his dreams? She felt she knew, but yet the knowledge eluded her.

"May I ask you something?" she said.

"But of course."

"You said that when you first came here you didn't mean to stay, but you had to."

"Yes."

"What made you stay?"

"Love of the place. . . . And then it felt as though hands out of the past were forcing me to do a particular thing here."

"What particular thing?"

"To build Utopia in this glen."

Judy had a slight feeling of shock. It was an odd confession for a man to make. Then she remembered how, as she drove through the fields of England, she had wondered where she was going to—to the Fortunate Isles—to a Hidden Country—to Utopia. Was this a fairy story or was it real? "Building Utopia?" she said. "But how? What *are* you doing here?"

He turned a little away from her, embarrassed and muttering. "It sounds so silly when I tell it. . . . Rebuilding the cottages. . . . I work like a laborer to do it. . . . Doctoring the crofters. . . . Patching up their quarrels and so on. . . . The neighborhood think me mad." He

50

turned back, his embarrassment gone, blazing with sudden passion. "I'm trying to make this place absolutely perfect, and I will before I die."

"But isn't Glen Suilag rather an isolated place to build Utopia in?"

"Utopias are built best in isolation. In the filthy modern world you can't make a thing that's not at once smirched; but here in these glens loveliness can be ringed round and protected by the mountains."

"That's the monastic ideal," said Judy, "and I've always thought it rather selfish—a creeping away from life."

"Then you have misunderstood it. The monastic ideal is a core of sanity in a loathsome world, a core of sanity that spreads. Again and again men have gone into solitude to create beauty, and the beauty, created, has revolutionized a whole country."

Judy was still unconvinced. "But if nothing can get through the mountains to contaminate your Utopia, how can the beauty you create get out into the world?"

"If you light a bonfire in a sheltered valley the protection makes such a huge blaze of it that those outside see the whole sky lit up." "I see," said Judy, smiling. "Forgive me for being so slow in the uptake, but I'm used to Charles, and Charles does not talk like this."

Ian's shyness came back and he flushed a little. "No sane man does. Living alone, all sorts of crazy ideas come into one's head. . . . And there's something about the place."

"Yes," said Judy, "as you say—there's something about the place." Then she began to laugh. "What a conversation for a first meeting!"

"But I don't feel as though it were a first meeting," said Ian.

"No more do I," said Judy lightly, and then, slowly and wonderingly, "no more do I."

They looked at each other.

51

"Judith! Judith!" he said, and flung his arms round her. They clung to each other exultantly for a brief minute, and then he took his arms away so suddenly that she nearly fell. She heard him give a choking exclamation, half horror at himself, half pain and bewilderment, heard his footsteps cross the room, cross the hall, and go up the drive, running as though afraid. She listened as they died away.

Oddly enough she was not frightened now nor bewildered, only exultant and gloriously happy. She did not in the least understand what had happened, but somehow she was content not to. That day in Regent Street, looking through the middle window, she had deliberately chosen a strange, unfamiliar world. She had stepped into it and hands had seized her. They were the hands, she felt now, of Eternity, that great angel who stands with arms outstretched, one hand in the future and one in the past, linking the two togehter. She had given herself into his hands, choosing to belong to him rather than to Time, courageously willing to be broken by time that she might live in eternity. Now she would be tranquil and quiet in the hands that guided her, unafraid even though a bandage were over her eyes.

Very tired and very happy, she wandered quietly round the room, loving it and caressing it. She ran her fingers along the edge of the spindly-legged writing table, she struck a few tinkling notes on the harpsichord, she smiled at the Sheraton chairs and the miniatures, she talked a little to the whispering flames on the hearth and nodded to the roses and carnations on the curtains. Then her tour of love brought her to the middle window, and instantly her happiness was gone from her and misery drowned her. She crumpled up on the oak chest, sobbing.

CHAPTER II

I

NEXT morning Judy woke up before dawn, while the world was still dark.

She was lying in the four-poster bed in the big bedroom over the drawing room. Beside her on the bed, curled up in a round black ball, was Sarah, who was dreaming of rabbits and whose queer internal barks had awakened Judy.

It was too dark yet to see her room, so she lay and thought about it instead. There had been a great argument over it last night, for though there were plenty of rooms they were inadequately furnished, and the fitting of themselves in was a problem. This one was the best bedroom, and Lady Cameron had therefore quite reasonably cast her eye upon it. But Angus thought otherwise, and had declared, monotonously and disagreeably, that it was Mistress Judith's room and that Mistress Judith must therefore lie in it. Entirely disregarding orders to the contrary, he had placed Judy's luggage in the big room and Lady Cameron's in a smaller and inferior room over the dining room, where the bed was hard and the wardrobe inadequate. Before dinner Charles changed round the luggage, and during dinner Angus changed it round again. Everyone got rather cross, and Judy made matters worse by behaving with the utmost selfishness and saying that she wanted the big room for herself and she didn't see why she shouldn't have it. After all, she said, there was plenty of room for mother in the single bed in the other room provided she didn't try and get father into it too, and father could quite well have the north room with no wash-stand.

"And what about Charles?" said Lady Cameron. "He was to have had the north room with no washstand."

"Anything will do for me," murmured Charles sweetly. "There's the room over the porch with no bed, for instance."

Sir James, as always in moments of domestic crisis, went away to have a quiet pipe somewhere.

It was Elspeth, the rosy-cheeked Highland maid, who finally solved the difficulty. "The wind is rising, and her ladyship will find the big room draughty," she said. "Ye ken, it has three windows, and the wind from the sea blows over the mountains. 'Tis the Laird's room, and he always has to peg the windows with his razors to stop the rattlin'. And then, ye ken, there are more mice in the big room than in the other. Three mousetraps does the Laird keep in his room and sets them all before he takes to his bed."

At this Lady Cameron began to regard the smaller room with a more favorable eye. It had thicker curtains, she noted, and though the bed was undeniably hard, yet it would not give her the shivers as would that ghostly four-poster. "I never did like a four-poster," she said. "It's so easy for spiders and what not to swarm up the posts and drop down on your face in the night." That nice little north room, she told Sir James, would do beautifully for him, and a basin and tooth-mug could easily be provided. As for Charles, dear boy, another bed could surely be procured from somewhere, and anyhow he was so placid that he never minded much what he did have or didn't have.

So Judy had the big room and, what she deserved, a restless night. The wind, as Elspeth had predicted, rose and blew over the mountains from the sea, and in the absence of razors Judy's comb and toothbrush were quite inadequate to keep the three long windows from

54

rattling. She lay awake listening to the wind soughing in the trees and sighing and tapping at the windows. The house was full of mutterings and plaintive whispers, boards creaking and curtains rustling in the draught. Now and then a mouse ran across the floor pursued by Sarah. All night long the wretched Sarah jumped on and off the bed, alternately indulging in the pleasures of the chase and sleeping off its effects. Sleep for Judy was impossible, and she lay awake on her back in the great four-poster, her arms opened wide but yet, so big was the bed, not reaching its edges. Clouds were flying across the moon, and the room was now dark, now dimly lit by waves of silver light that showed her the softly swaying curtains of her bed and her own slim form under the ghostly white blanket.

She began to be a little afraid. She was terribly tired, and her fatigue robbed her of the ecstatic happiness of the afternoon. She began to wonder about the bed in which she lay. It must have been there for years and years. Generations of Macdonalds must have been born in it and perhaps died in it. Death? What was death? People talked a lot about the death of the body and the life of the spirit, but what did they know about it? What did anyone know? Men laughed and talked and ate and drank inside a little lighted house of life, and outside was a great windy darkness that stretched they knew not where and held they knew not what. Those dead Macdonalds who had died in this bed—was it their voices she heard in the wind and their footsteps that went up and down the stairs and backwards and forwards along the passage outside her door, making the old boards creak so strangely?

She thought of them all. The men in their tartans who had ridden their horses up and down the glen road and marched to the wars with their clan. The women who had borne their children and cared for their homes and wept at their death. Their little children who had laughed and played up and down the passages. The old servants like Angus who had served them from childhood to old age. The dogs and the horses who had loved them and been a part of their life. Judy dozed a little, and they seemed to pass by her bed in procession, their faces gray in death and their eyes sightless. Then she woke up, trembling with fear, the horrible immobility of nightmare holding her in its grip; and it seemed to her that one out of all those passing figures had remained behind and was still there. She thought she saw the gleam of a woman's white dress in the moonlight, and the room seemed full of a voiceless crying. . . . Judith Macdonald. . . . Judith, who had blocked up the middle window, no one knew why. . . . Judy was aware of her, grief-stricken and lonely and frustrated. . . . "Judith! Judith!" she whispered. . . . Then the last of her dream slipped away, and she knew there was nothing in the room but the draught whispering over the floor.

But still she felt afraid. Her mind, hot and tired, went back over all that had happened the day before. She remembered how, as the car climbed to the top of Ben Caorach, she had first become aware of something stirring inside her, something imprisoned, something with wings, like a bird. It had been with her all the day, and it had made her feel familiar with people and things that she had never seen before. It had made her feel joy and pain more deeply than she had ever felt them before. What was it? Was it Judith? Had the spirit of the dead Judith come to her at the top of Ben Caorach and taken possession of her? Possession by the dead. She had heard of such a thing. But could it happen? Had it happened to her? And if so, why? Why had Judith come to her? What did she want her to do?

She turned over, terrified, and hugged Sarah's warm protesting body close to her. The feel of the warm little furry creature comforted her, gave her a sense of companionship. Then she began to think of Ian Macdonald.

56

Did he, she wondered, when he had pegged his windows and set his mousetraps, lie awake as she was doing and listen to the feet of the dead on the stairs and their voices in the wind? She remembered how they had clung together in the room below, his horrified, astonished exclamation and then his precipitate flight. He was as puzzled as she was. It seemed that some adventure had caught them both and that neither of them understood it. Well, whatever it was, they were in it together. At that she felt warm and comforted and fell asleep.

II

When she woke up she knew that dawn was not far away. From the garden there came one lovely, clear call, like a faraway fairy trumpet. It was a robin. Then there was silence again. Then a pearly light crept through the drawn curtains, slowly filtering into the room like phosphorescent water into a dark cavern. As its radiance grew, little bursts and trills of music came from every corner of the garden, answering other little trills that woke and died and woke again in the depth of the larch wood. The music rose and thrilled and mounted higher and higher, voice answering voice, until the whole world was echoing with a glorious symphony of praise that was almost unendurable in its beauty. Judy sat up in bed and listened, pushing the heavy hair back from her face. All night she had been thinking of death; but who could think of death, or even believe in it, when the whole world echoed with that song? Judy suddenly thought, she did not know why, of the slaves of old entombed in the Roman mines and of how they had scratched on the walls of their prison the word Life! Life! Life! Even in death they had believed in it. . . . Perhaps there was no death. . . . Perhaps it was only an illusion.

She jumped out of bed and ran to a window. There was nothing to be seen yet. The garden and the mountains were all veiled in gray. She pulled back the curtains and went back to bed. It had been so dark last night, the room lit only by a couple of guttering candles, that she had hardly taken in the details of it. Now, as the light grew, she looked at it intently, almost reading it, as one would read a page of print read long ago and then forgotten. It looked very bare and empty, the floor uncarpeted except for one shabby rug. The bed, a big old dressing table and washstand and wardrobe, a couple of chairs and a bookcase full of books seemed lost in the huge room. The windows and bed were curtained with an old shiny flowered chintz, so thick and stiff that it looked like china. The paneled walls were painted white, and there was only one picture. The room had a look of austerity that was almost monastic. Judy, loving it, yet wondered exactly how cold it would be on a January night. She shuddered at the thought. Ian Macdonald, who looked as hardy as his own mountains, would probably hardly notice it; but anyone else, surely, would be driven to a fire.

There was a lovely old fireplace opposite the bed, with fluted wooden pillars on each side of it and surmounted by a carved wooden frame which was of a piece with the paneling. Inside the frame hung the picture, the growing light shining on it.

Judy suddenly shot out of bed and pattered across the floor on her bare feet to look at it. It was a glorious picture. It might have been a Reynolds. Why in the world had she not noticed it last night? She supposed she had been too tired and overwrought. It was the picture of an eighteenth-century Highland gentleman in tartans and a bottle-green coat, with lace ruffles at throat and wrist and powdered hair tied back in the nape of the neck. Behind him was a background of blue sky and mountain and glen. The scene had the glorious clarity of all Reynolds' pictures—the brilliance of a world just washed by a shower of rain and now illumined by sunshine.

But it was the man himself who excited Judy, for he was Ian and yet not Ian. The dreamy eyes and the purposeful mouth were the same, but the Ian she had met yesterday was shabby and diffident, marked by poverty and struggle, nervously conscious that everyone thought him a fool, while this man was a person of importance, proud, confident, prosperous, happy. Judy suddenly set her jaw and tilted her chin. This was what Ian ought to look like. This, she said to herself, was what he *should* look like. How he was to be made to look like it she was sure she didn't know, but she hopped back into bed and sat glaring at the man in the picture, as though angry with him for daring to compare too favorably with his descendant. . . . How *dared* he. . . . And yet she couldn't be angry with him, for he was so splendid, so gay and colorful. Was he the Macdonald who had died in the 'Forty-five? What a pity that anything so vital should be dead. . . . Life! Life! Life! sang the bird. . . . There was no death.

The now almost wild ecstasy in the garden brought her back to consciousness of the outside world. The dawn had arrived in good earnest. She bounded from bed again, put on her scarlet dressing gown over her red-and-blue striped pajamas—in the worst of taste, Lady Cameron said they were—and went to the window. She flung it wide open and knelt down, her arms on the sill.

The cold air was like fingers of snow creeping over her body and stinging her awake to vivid consciousness of the loveliness in front of her. The shadow of night still lay over the garden and the larch wood and the loch and the lower slopes of the mountains, but up on the summits day had come. There were no clouds now to hide the top of Judy's mountain; it was outlined in indigo and violet against a golden sky that melted through

59

apricot and primrose yellow to deep blue overhead. Far up the sun's fingers just touched the bog myrtle and bracken to green flame. The wind had dropped now, and beyond the song of the birds and the sound of falling water Judy was conscious of a deep and heavenly silence. She felt she must get into it, sink down into it. After the roar of London, the aimless noisy bustle of life there, silence was what she wanted more than anything. Here in the house there would soon be the sounds of awakening life, people talking and cans clattering; but up there on the mountain there would be no sound at all. . . . She would go there.

She turned away from the window, poured cold water into her basin, stripped off her pajamas and washed herself. Heavens, how cold the water was! Her warm flesh shrank from the touch of the sponge, but she set her teeth and went on sponging. She was determined to teach her pampered body discipline and endurance even in little things. It seemed to her very necessary that the whole of her, body as well as soul, should be brought into harmony with the austerity of this place. She laughed a little as she thought of her London uprisings. At this hour, had she been in London, she would be still wrapped in piglike slumber, from which she would be awakened at eight o'clock or later by a starched maid with a can of hot water and a cup of tea, who, if the morning was the least bit chilly, would switch on her electric fire. She would drink her tea and then, if she felt like it, get up. If she didn't feel like it she would have her breakfast in bed. . . . Well, this was better, she thought, even though cleaning one's teeth in ice-cold water gave one toothache in every one.

She put on her brown tweed coat and her orange scarf and her little brown cap with the yellow feather, then, carrying her brogues in her hand and followed by an ecstatic Sarah, she crept downstairs to the hall. . . . Creak, creak, creak, went the stairs, just as they had creaked last night. . . . She opened the front door and let herself out. It was not necessary, she knew, to go round by the road; she could reach her mountain by going through the garden and the larch wood. She turned to the right and came round to the west side of the house. Here its long, low gray front was almost entirely covered with creepers, honeysuckle, roses, and jasmine. They covered the outside of the middle window so closely that one could scarcely see that it had been blocked up at all. A terrace was under the windows of the drawing room, dropping to a strip of lawn. Judy crossed it, leaving the prints of her feet in the wet grass and noting the handsome crop of dandelions and plantains that ornamented it. . . . Either Ian Macdonald's gardener was worse than useless, or else he couldn't afford one at all.

Beyond the lawn was the flower garden. Judy had never seen such a place. Lavender and rosemary and roses and hollyhocks and snapdragons and weeds grew together in wild confusion, and every now and then immense unbrellas of rhubarb sprouted up like palms in the desert. The whole amazing collection of fauna melted off into the larch wood. . . . One bit of rhubarb even grew inside the wood, and a climbing rose was scrambling up a larch trunk and rubbing its crimson cheek against the green spikes.

Judy pushed her way through the gloom of the wood and found herself on a path that skirted the loch at its southern end. She crossed a narrow strip of turf and heather and stood beside it. It was very still and very cold, for the sun was not yet high enough to reach the valley. The surface of the loch reflected the sky and the great purple mountain so clearly that it seemed like a painted picture.

Judy turned and, following the path round the loch to its western side, found herself right underneath her mountain. She made for the burn. It came tumbling down the corrie, foaming and cascading over boulders, spreading out now and then into quiet pools under the branches of rowan trees, then leaping down mossy precipices and finally falling headlong into the loch. Its rippling, noisy little waves spread fanwise over the still water and then were lost in the quiet, calm depths.

Judy gazed up the mountain. It was all very well to talk about climbing to the silence, but it didn't look particularly easy. She decided to stick to the burn, for where it came down she could perhaps go up. She climbed and climbed, slipping and sliding on the slippery stones, clinging to the trunks of the rowan trees. Sarah, unused to mountaineering and puffing like a traction engine, sprawled behind her. She was soon panting and straining and aching in every limb, but she had seen above her a lovely hollow in the mountain, covered with green bracken, and there she would get or die.

When she did get there, after what seemed an hour of climbing, what with an empty interior and the fatigue of a bad night, she felt very like dying. She lay flat on her back in the wet bracken and wondered if she wasn't rather silly. Sarah, with her tongue hung out to its furthest limit and her eyes narrowed, hadn't any doubt about it. It was quite impossible to appreciate any silence with the blood humming in her ears and her heart beating like a kettledrum. But gradually she revived, sat up and looked about her.

She had left the burn now and was in a lovely amphitheater hollowed out of the mountain. On three sides of it heather and rocks rose steeply from a still black mountain tarn, and the fourth side, where Judy sat, was a flat ledge of heather and bracken. Looking down she could see the whole of Glen Suilag laid out like a map at her feet. There was the loch and the garden and the wood and the house with the village behind it, all dwarfed by distance to the size of toys and all ringed round by the protecting mountains. How lovely the glen was, with its crofts and whitewashed cottages, like an enchanted country, so hidden away that only its lovers could find it. She understood what Ian had meant when he talked about the creation of loveliness in solitude. Surely beauty would be safe in such a hidden country; the mountain rampart would protect Utopia from Vanity Fair.

Sitting with her hands clasped round her knees, she shut her eyes. High up and facing east, the sun was gloriously warm on her face. There was no breath of wind, no sound at all but the sound of the burn and the delicious, heavenly tinkle of some sheep-bells. But the silence was charged with life. Sitting there she felt it all round her, running through the visible world like an invisible flame and rising up inside her like a bubbling spring, different in each of its manifestations yet the same in its essence. Out of the silence and the loneliness there came to her a vivid sense of her own individuality. The sense of unity with created things made her feel not a pea in a pod but a separate unity, and she wondered why. Perhaps, she thought, if you come, by yourself, very close to the fount of life in nature, you are washed clean of the follies that seem to lie like a coat of dust over men when they move about the world in herds, kicking it up and covering themselves with it, so that they all look exactly alike. She did not feel dusty now, she felt washed, with her true colors showing; and she could have shouted for joy. She was becoming herself.

Then, for a moment, her thoughts slipped back to the fears of the night before. Possession? No. That winged thing in her was no alien spirit but herself, the real Judy. And all those queer memories and emotions? She would not think of them. She would forget them. She would accept Ian's explanation of them. What mattered now, she felt, was she herself. She must grow. In these lovely spaces her cramped self would have room to expand and stretch itself, and on these mountains her wings would mount high. She would be a stern surgeon, she promised herself, lopping off all that hindered and clogged her, that her wings might go free.

A sharp bark beside her made her open her eyes. Sarah, planted belligerently on her four feet, with her tongue withdrawn, her teeth showing, and every hair erected, was glaring at a huge tawny wolfhound standing in front of them in the bracken. Judy leaped to her feet, clasping a growling, kicking Sarah in her arms. For Sarah believed in taking the offensive instantly, no matter what the size of her antagonist. She believed in moral strength rather than physical, and in fastening instantly on the hind leg of the enemy before he had time to think. The wolfhound, a very great gentleman indeed, considered the pair of them beneath his notice; he blinked contemptuously, turned his back, and scratched himself.

"Lochiel!" shouted a voice, and Ian Macdonald came slipping and scrambling down from the heights.

"He's not doing anything except despising us," Judy reassured him. "It's Sarah who's so bellicose. . . . Shut up, Sarah!" and she smacked Sarah's nose.

"Don't smack her," said Ian. "Put her down, and I'll hook her onto my stick till she calms down."

Judy did so.

"Are you going up or down or staying put?" asked Ian.

"I'm staying put," said Judy, and sat down again.

"So am I," and he sat down beside her. The wolfhound, his back still turned, lay down and went to sleep. Sarah, straining on the end of the stick, choked as one in the final throes of asthma.

"It's incredibly early for you to be out," said Ian, astonished.

"Well, *you're* out," said Judy, a little nettled.

"Yes. I come up here nearly every day."

"Before a hard day's work?"

"Yes."

Judy looked down at the glen spread out at their feet. "I suppose you came to look at your Utopia?" she said lightly.

Ian flushed. "I wish," he muttered, "that you'd forget all the nonsense of yesterday."

Judy turned to him eagerly, earnestly. "I wasn't teasing you," she said. "I liked what you said about Utopia." She paused, flushing in her turn. "And I liked *you* for it—and telling me." She turned back to the valley. "Most of us never say what we really think and really feel. It's so silly. I suppose we're afraid of sounding prigs. . . . And so we are never ourselves with each other and not often ourselves with ourselves."

"I think it's easy to be yourself in this country," said Ian. "It's a very stark world. No illusion about it."

"That's what I want," said Judy. "I want to get rid of illusion, and of the things that clutter one up."

"What things?" asked Ian.

"Too many possessions," said Judy, "and silly conventions, and duties that are not really duty and amusements that are not really funny. You see, we are well off, and the richer you are the more you get cluttered. . . . It makes one feel very bloated."

Ian considered her slim figure and smiled. "You don't look it. You look as though you could get through the eye of a needle."

"Oh, the poor camel! I have tried very hard not to grow the rich man's camelious hump, but it wasn't easy. Dieting isn't. . . . I wish one hadn't got to diet to get into the kingdom of heaven."

Ian laughed.

"I didn't mean to be funny," said Judy in a small voice.

He was instantly grave again. "Forgive me, I didn't mean to laugh. . . . You'll find your dieting easier here."

"Why?"

"Because Utopias are built best in isolation."

"You've said that before, and *I'm* not building Utopia."

"Then what's all this struggle to get through the eye of a needle? What's all this effort to be humpless?"

"You mean I am building it in myself? . . . I see." She paused and laughed. "There! Now I've unburdened myself to you as much as you did to me. . . . We're quits."

"No," said Ian, and began digging holes in the ground with his stick.

Judy sighed. She knew what was coming, and she wished he'd let it alone. It was one of the unexplainable things that she did not mean to think about.

"Yesterday," he said, "I went quite mad. Please forgive me, and don't think of it again. . . . It was as though another man possessed me."

Possession again. Judy thrust the idea away from her. "No," she said, "it was just old memories alive in the room that got hold of us both. That was all. . . . Don't let's think about it."

"No," said Ian, and they sat silent for five minutes, thinking about it.

"Do you think," said Judy suddenly, "that people live on in their homes after death?"

"Perhaps," said Ian guardedly. "That is, those of them who have spirits that *can* live on."

"Haven't we all?"

"No, I don't think so. Spirits are made by life."

"But we all live," objected Judy.

"It depends," he said, "which world you live in."

Judy stared at him, round-eyed, remembering the three worlds that had confronted her in Regent Street. "You mean," she said, "that you can't expect, so to speak, to sprout a spirit unless you choose to live in the world of the spirit."

"Yes," he said, "there's a germ in us, a spark, that only flowers in the right soil."

"And when it flowers?"

"It flowers forever."

"That's rather frightening."

"Yes. If you choose that particular world you let yourself in for it."

"I think" said Judy suddenly, "that I'd like to go home to breakfast."

"Just have a look at this place before we go," said Ian, and he took her round the little tarn, lying in its semicircle of rocks. Its waters were of an impenetrable blackness.

"How deep is it?" asked Judy.

"No one knows, and no one knows what is at the bottom of it. I dare say some of my savage ancestors disposed of their enemies there."

"Ugh!" said Judy ,"how nasty of your ancestors."

"And perhaps," added Ian, "when times were bad they disposed of themselves here."

He led her round a great boulder and there, hidden behind it, was a cave. They went inside. It was very small but perfect as a little shrine. A tiny spring bubbled up at the back and seeped over the pebbles that formed the floor, losing itself so secretly in the tarn that the black polished surface was hardly distrubed by more than the faintest ripple. The domed roof of the cave was purple and dark green and glistening with diamond drops of moisture, as though a myriad candles were lit there. There was just room for the two of them to stand upright.

"It is beautiful," said Judy.

"This mountain is called Ben Fhalaich, and this is the cave of Ben Fhalaich, though my crofters call it Macdonald's cave."

"I wonder why?" said Judy.

"I expect because a Macdonald fugitive hid in it."

"What a perfect place to hide in," said Judy, "with that spring water to drink and the tarn to bathe in."

"And nothing to eat," said Ian. "No. On the whole I'm glad it's my fate to be Laird of Glen Suilag in the twentieth century and not the eighteenth."

"Your head touches the roof," said Judy. "If *you'd* had to hide here you'd have been a tight fit."

They stood side by side in the tiny cave laughing like two children. Ian stood with his back to the cave's opening, the clear, rain-washed morning behind him. Through some trick of the shadowed light his face was the face of the man in the portrait in Judy's room, and the laughter died out of her face. "Let's go back," she said, and pushed past him out into the wholesome sunshine.

They scrambled down the mountain, the now reconciled dogs at their heels. As they went they talked of everyday things, the view and the weather and the car and the habits of Sarah and Lochiel; but Judy all the time was marveling. She had talked to this stranger as she had never talked to anyone before. . . . If Charles had heard her he would have died of shock. . . . She was usually reticent about her private thoughts and so, she thought, was he. And yet she was not ashamed. It was as though she had been talking to herself.

They parted at the larch wood, and Judy was very late for breakfast.

CHAPTER III

I

THE weeks went by, and the strangers from the outside world, "they foreigners" as Angus contemptuously called them, began to find their places in the Glen Suilag world. Sir James, Lady Cameron, and Charles sought for and found the amusements and consolations

68

that should while away time; but Judy, it was noticed, began to dig herself in and to form settled habits as though she meant to stay here forever. The boundaries of their common life, that had contained just the four of them and Sarah, widened to take in Angus, Elspeth the maid, Macgregor the utterly incompetent odd man, Ian, Lochiel, his dog, and, lastly, his uncle, Major Murray, and his sister Jean. These were the inhabitants of the Glen Suilag world; yet to Judy it seemed that there was a world within a world and that in the inner, secret one were only herself and Ian and Angus. They three, she felt, lived in the sanctuary of Glen Suilag while the others knew only its outer courts.

Yet they seemed moderately contented there. Sir James had been reluctant to come to Scotland at all in the first place, having reached that age when one feels reluctant ever to go anywhere for anything, but now that he was there he was happy. He was an ardent fisherman, and every morning he took himself off to the middle of the loch, where he sat in a boat all day in the grip of that awful paralysis of mind and body that afflicts fishermen all the world over. Yet he appeared happy and, on the rare occasions when he caught anything, more than happy.

Lady Cameron did embroidery and complained of her lot, but as she enjoyed both these activities it is possible that she was happier than she thought she was.

Charles was definitely unhappy. Judy was living some queer, aloof life of her own and was hardly ever with him, and on the rare occasions when she was with him she treated him as though he was a religious duty, an insult which no self-respecting man could be expected to put up with for an instant. Yet, outwardly, Charles put up with it. He was not given to making fusses, and he was aware that some change was taking place in Judy that made her want, very urgently, to be let alone. He knew nothing about psychology, but he loved Judy enough to realize that at this particular moment of her life she must have her way if things were to be well with her, and he let her alone. But he was not enjoying himself. Sometimes he fished with Sir James and sometimes he held embroidery skeins for Lady Cameron, but both these activities palled. His only consolation was the society of Major Murray and Jean and expeditions in their car.

The Major was an elderly garroulous man who had been in India and trumpeted in his talk. He could shoot straight and talk politics—Conservative and Winston Churchill politics—and appreciate the charms of Lady Cameron. He shot with Charles, talked with Sir James, and appreciated with Lady Cameron. They all three liked him, especially Lady Cameron.

They also liked Jean. She was what they called a nice sensible girl, and not in the least like her brother, thank heaven. She was pretty and well dressed and modern and had no queer ideas. Judy in the old days would have got on well with her, but now she hardly seemed to notice her. Jean, when she was not shooting with Charles and Major Murray, sat and poured out her worries to Lady Cameron, with whom, as Ian had predicted, she got on. The chief of her woes was Ian himself.

"He never used to be like this," she mourned. "It's the place that's turned him queer. He was perfectly normal in London. We had a jolly little flat in town together when he was at Barts, and he was quite jolly and sensible then, a bit dreamy and inclined to be socialistic, but nothing out of the ordinary."

"You mean he didn't wear a red tie with handkerchief to match, or look handsome in a black shirt or anything dreadful of that kind?" asked Lady Cameron.

"Perhaps it would have been better if he had," sighed Jean. "They do say that if the 'isms' break out in haberdashery they're got out of the system quicker. It's like the rash in measles. One's better after."

Lady Cameron made sympathetic noises.

"Since Ian came here," went on Jean despairingly, "he's become simply silly. He ought to sell the place, but he won't. . . . And he's thrown up everything to live here. . . . There's no money, mind you; there's nothing at all but sea gulls and a tumbledown house and poverty-stricken crofters. How can he do anything with it without money? He's taken on too big a job. It's breaking him, and he's killing himself with overwork. He never goes anywhere or sees people. He's getting odd. And you should hear his ideas."

"I don't want to, dear," said Lady Cameron hurriedly. "The ideas of the overworked and underpaid are usually very nasty and uncomfortable. . . . Revolution and supertax and that sort of thing. . . . I'm sure Sir James and I are nearly crushed out of existence with the supertax."

"Ian's ideas are not that sort," said Jean. "I only wish they were. For the poor to want to murder the rich is at least normal and natural and has been thought of before, but he mixes up medieval ideas about Utopia with Franciscan ideas about poverty and Benedictine ideas about the monastic life, and dishes it all up with a lot of Jacobite sentimentality and spiritualistic rubbish until— well—I don't like it."

"No more do I, dear," said Lady Cameron fervently, "and I only hope he doesn't hand it all on to Judy. She's very impressionable to nonsense."

"He doesn't see much of Judy," comforted Jean. "He works too hard to see much of anybody."

"No," said Lady Cameron.

There she stopped, apparently absorbed in threading a needle, and silence fell.

"Poor Charles!" said Jean suddenly. "I like that man."

"So do I," said Lady Cameron, almost with passion. "Such a good family and so well off. One of the Worcestershire Andersons."

Silence fell again. It was true that Ian and Judy saw little of each other, yet the whole of the Glen Suilag world saw, without knowing how it saw, that each day that passed strengthened the link between them. They felt, all of them, as though they were living in the hush before a thunderstorm. A moment was creeping closer to them, they knew, when the hush would be shattered.

II

Judy knew it subconsciously. Consciously she was as absorbed in herself as a little child just learning to walk. A great change had taken place in her, that greatest change of all, a change of outlook. In London she had been conscious chiefly of her bodily life and of the physical world that was in harmony with it. Sometimes, when she heard Beethoven played or saw the sticky green buds opening in the parks in the spring, she wondered if she had a soul, but she didn't wonder often. Her physical life was so gay and carefree and satisfactory that it absorbed her whole attention, and her body weighted the scales very heavily. And then had come that queer, unexplainable moment in Regent Street. The scales had trembled, and very slowly the balance had begun to change. It had been changing all these weeks, and now it was beginning to drop down on the other side. But it had not fallen yet. Judy, struggling with herself and thinking hard as she had never struggled or thought before, was more conscious of conflict going on in her than of the predominance of one world over the other. Yet she knew that in time, after she had struggled, the new world would seem much more real than the old. She would, perhaps, achieve a sort of divine carelessness about the things of the body. Sickness and health, poverty and wealth, even life and death, would not matter very much. They would seem light as air, trivial; the weight of importance would be all on the other side. But she was not there yet; she was still in a sort of no-man's land between one world and the other, fighting to achieve personality; and she felt that at this stage she must fight alone. "Spirits are made by life," Ian had said; and she knew that presently she must go back to the world and let human relationships and human activities do their work in her, but just now she must be alone. She had discovered a tiny spark in herself and she must bend over it, sheltering it with her two hands while it steadied into a flame. When it was burning strongly the winds of the world would fan it into a blaze, but if they blew upon it now, while it was still so weak, they would only put it out. . . . That was what Ian had said about the creation of loveliness in solitude. . . . It must be sheltered in the valley until the protection made such a huge blaze of it that those outside saw the whole sky lit up.

So Judy lived by herself. She thought a great deal and she went for long walks with Sarah, and very occasionally with Ian, and she sat alone up on Ben Fhalaich, by the black tarn, thinking of nothing at all but letting the silence and the beauty of Glen Suilag become a part of her. And she practiced very vigorously, and with courage, little austerities of thought and action that in themselves were trivial, but which took some doing and were, she knew, valuable to her.

And she also read a great deal. Ian had left his books behind him in the west room, poetry and history and philosophy, and, with frightful effort, she read them nearly all. She had never used her mind much, and now it positively ached with the strain. Yet, when the aching died down a little, it exulted. It had entered into a new kingdom. She realized that to the questing mind and spirit there are worlds beyond worlds, never ending. To enter into possession of one was to stand on the threshold of another, and it seemed to her that on each threshold there took place a death and a birth. Any laziness or weakness of mind or spirit, conquered and killed, seemed always to be followed instantly by an inrush of new energy, and the harder the death the more joyful the corresponding life. Judy began to think of death and birth as different aspects of the same act of advance, like a being with two faces who, when you had faced the gorgon's mask of terror, swung round to you the fair face of an angel.

Then, turning her attention from the alternation of death and birth in the life of the mind and spirit, she considered the heart. That unaccountable and tiresome organ was, on and off, occupying her attention a good deal; for soon, she knew, when she emerged from her retreat, its development was going to be very upsetting to herself and everyone else. . . . For the old love was dying, and a new love was being born.

In the old life she had loved Charles. She had lived then in certain expectation of a certain program. . . . One left school. One was presented. One had one's first season. One fell in love. One was married at St. Margaret's, Westminster, with all the usual ornaments. One settled down to a life of social duty. One died. . . . Charles had seemed to fit into place very naturally in items four, five, and six of the program. It had all seemed very nice and very right. But now everything was different, and she felt that she was behaving very badly to Charles, and sometimes she was very miserable. But she couldn't help it. The old life was receding further and further away from her and taking Charles with it. He didn't belong any more. And the new life was coming nearer and nearer, and at the heart of it was Ian. She could not quite understand what she felt for Ian, for it was quite different from anything she had ever felt for Charles. There was nothing at all emotional about it, except for that crazy moment on the first afternoon, but that had passed and gone. It had been more like a foretaste of something that was coming or a memory of something that had gone than an actual existing fact. In the old days, when she had danced with Charles, the feel of his arm round her waist had given her delicious prickles in the small of the back and when he kissed her or touched her hand little ripples of physical pleasure had seemed to go all over her body. But there was nothing of this in her feeling for Ian. It might come, for after all the body had its place in love; but when it did it would not be important, it would not be what mattered in their relationship, and its passing would be equally unimportant. But in every other department of her life Ian seemed a central fact. Into whatever new world her mind penetrated it seemed to find him there with her, and in the new life of her spirit she found him too. He was there before her. He belonged.

But what was she to do? Must she turn out her dear Charles, who was so good to her? She was so fond of him and she did not want to hurt him and then, too, she would be so safe and comfortable with him, while with Ian there was no knowing. She didn't think she would be very comfortable with Ian. He was an idealist and a reformer, and neither idealists nor reformers are comfortable people. He would not, perhaps, always give her a very easy time. . . . But then she had not chosen an easy time. That day in Regent Street she had deliberately chosen a hard time. . . . And then her relationship with Ian was a fine thing, she did not yet understand how fine, and therefore it must be deliberately accepted. It was feathered with fine love, and it would bear them up and forward. So, at whatever cost, it must be Ian. Wherever she turned he seemed to be there, a part of

75

her. Some words that she had read in his tattered Shakespeare came into her mind.

As easy might I from myself depart
As from my soul, which in thy breast doth lie;
That is my home of love: if I have ranged,
Like him that travels, I return again.

Meanwhile she waited for time to show her how to pass from one love to the other, and while she waited she wondered—what of this combined life of mind and heart and spirit that was herself? Would her death, too, be followed by a new birth?

III

But Judy was not by temperament a hermit, and one Sunday morning in August she issued forth from retreat with startling suddenness.

"I'm going to church," she said.

Her family looked at her with astonishment, for, as usual in a Scotch August, the rain was descending in a solid sheet and the wind in the chimney sounded like a storm at sea.

"Church?" asked her father. "What for?"

"Curiosity," said Judy.

"I shouldn't dear," said her mother. 'It's very wet, and they stand while they pray, and I believe it's all most exhausting. If you go take your father's shooting stick."

"The English service at ten," said Angus helpfully, dumping the coffee pot on the tray, "an' the Gaelic service at twelve."

"Go to the Gaelic, Judy," said Sir James. "You won't understand a word and you will be mostly deeply impressed." He helped himself to porridge and added

76

gloomily, "Nothing's impressive when you understand it."

"Which shall I go to, Angus?" asked Judy.

Angus snorted. "Ye should pray to Almighty God in a tongue ye can understand," he told her severely, "or ye micht be sayin' Amen to somethin' undesirable. Wi' our meenister ye hae tae keep yer wits aboot ye."

"But why?"

"It's a dangerous man he is. Last Sabbath he prayed that we micht all ken the blessings o' poverty. . . . Now, a nice thing 'twould hae been if he'd prayed the bit prayer i' the Gaelic an' ye, unknown', had said Amen i' a loud voice an' woke up the morn to find yersel' a starvin' woman."

"Thank you for the warning, Angus," said Judy. "I'll go to church at ten."

"And keep yer wits aboot ye an' tak' a peppermint drop to keep the damp oot."

"That will do, Angus," said Lady Cameron. Angus's habit of breaking into the conversation at meal times drove her perfectly distracted. Ian Macdonald, it seemed, did not understand the first thing about training a servant.

Judy put on her mackintosh and her little brown cap, and Angus gave her boots a final polish with his dirty yellow duster and presented her with one of his own peppermint drops to suck during the sermon.

"Will the Laird be there?" she asked him.

"He should be so," said Angus severely. "If he's no' there ye micht be tellin' me an' I'll gie him a piece o' my mind."

The rain poured down upon Judy as, armed with the shooting stick, she slopped along to church. The mountaintops were hidden in the driving rain, and the whole world was filled with the sound of rushing water. The last few days had been dry, and only the main streams had been alive and talking; but now, at the touch of the rain, hundreds of little cataracts had started into being and came dashing down the flanks of the mountains, streaking their angry purple with swords and scimitars of foaming white. The wind was whipping the smooth loch water into miniature waves and lashing angrily at the treetops. The few gulls who ventured to fly too high were caught by it and tossed contemptuously out of its path. The world, storm-buffeted, seemed shaken with tremors of fear, and Judy, too, felt in herself a little stirring of rather exciting alarm. On these stormy days some terrible power seemed taking the earth in its two hands and shaking it very gently. It was quite possible, one felt, that at any moment it might lose its temper altogether, pick up the earth, and throw it away.

Yet in Scotland Judy had come to love the wind and the rain. In London they were just inconvenient things that made a mess, but up here in the north they were great lifegiving forces whose strength was exhilarating. Nothing evil could live with them, Judy felt. If the power that let them loose was terrible, it was terrible only because of its purity. They and it were cleansing, scourging things.

A final buffet of wind brought her to the church. It was white-washed and gray-slated and plain to the point of ugliness. Judy wondered, not for the first time, why the Scotch seem incapable of erecting a beautiful building. Perhaps, she thought, the grandeur of nature depressed them. Setting to work to build a church, and happening to look up at the sculptured masses of the mountains, they felt unable to compete with it, and, despairingly slapping a roof on top of a few piled stones, they left it at that and went to have a drink.

In the porch she was met with enthusiasm by Mr. Campbell, the grocer and the minister's clerk. He helped her out of her mackintosh and galoshes and led her triumphantly into church. Here she had a little difficulty with him over where she was to sit, he wanting her

to sit in the front and she being firmly determined to sit
in the back row of all, because of the shooting stick.
However, Judy never had much trouble in getting her
way with the opposite sex, and Mr. Campbell was soon
routed. Sighing, yet mollified by the smile she bestowed
on him when he gave in, he presented her with a large
black book and left her.

She stowed the shooting stick under the seat for future use and had a good look round. The inside of the
church was worse than the outside. Rows of hideous
pitch-pine seats faced an equally hideous pitch-pine
platform for the minister. The severe windows were
filled with plain greenish glass, and the whitewashed
walls were bare except for the most depressing-looking
memorial tablets. Although it was nearly ten there were
very few people there, only the Campbell family in
white cotton gloves, Macgregor the incompetent odd
man, some school children and a few devout old ladies
in black bonnets. The glen was sparsely populated, and
most of the crofters, Judy thought, would be going to
the Gaelic service. It was very grim and rather depressing, for outside the windows the rain could be seen driving by in sheets and the draughts on the floor were
creeping about like live things. And yet she liked it. She
was surprised at her liking, for when on rare occasions
in London she had condescended to decorate a place of
worship with her person she had always chosen a
church where the upholstery, the lighting system, the
floral decorations, and the nice smells were all in keeping with her own charming appearance; and here there
was nothing to look at, nothing at all but the storm
beyond the windows and the memorial tablets on the
walls.

She looked again at these and caught her breath, for
they were all of them to Macdonalds. Macdonalds who
had died at the Crimea. Macdonalds who had died in
South Africa and India. Macdonalds, the sons of Ian's

queer old uncle, who had died in the Great War, Macdonalds who had stayed at home and died in their bed, Judy's bed probably, and most of them with wives and daughters, Margarets and Lavinias and Janets. Judy looked eagerly round to see if she could see any memorial to Judith Macdonald, but the church was too recent for that—there was nothing there earlier than the Crimea. Judith's memorial, Judy felt, was written in her own heart. It was because of it, perhaps, that she liked this place so much. This church, containing as in a casket the clear green windows with their view of rainwashed mountains and the rows of tablets inscribed with the names of the dead, brought the country and the race that Judith must have loved together into one place, holding them side by side in memory.

Memory, Judy thought, was a queer, odd thing, and a church was rather like it in the power that it had to destroy time and space. You entered into it, as you entered into your memory, shutting the door behind you; and instantly the destructiveness of the material world was shut out and inside the four walls were only the events and the existences that it could not touch. And suddenly Judy knew why she had come to this bare, bleak church; not for curiosity but because she had just discovered that there are some things that are indestructible, and she wanted, humanlike, to be with those who had made the same discovery.

She had not time to think it out any further, for a bang of the door, an appalling onset of fresh draughts, and the beaming face of Mr. Campbell as he hurried down the aisle told her that Ian had arrived. He stalked up the church without seeing her, taking off his dripping mackintosh as he went; but, turning round in his seat to put it behind him, he saw her and came stalking down again.

"Judy! Come up to the front and sit with me."

"I can't," whispered Judy, 'because of the shooting stick."

"Shooting stick?"

"I've got father's shooting stick to sit on in the prayers, and I don't want my back view seen."

Ian didn't seem to think it funny, and she thought that when they got outside again he would probably scold her, but he sat down beside her without further comment.

Then a door at the east end opened. The minister in his frock coat entered and mounted his pitch-pine platform, and they embarked upon the most somber service Judy had ever attended in all her days. . . . And yet she liked it. . . . It was like the storm outside the windows, grim and austere and yet shot through with sudden unexpected gleams of beauty. She supposed that the somber quality of the country had begotten a somber quality of mind in its people, and that in turn this grim religion. She thought of religion as she had seen it in Italy, of the bells ringing from the campaniles and the blue-gowned madonnas standing at the crossroads with their laughing babes, of the sweet singing of the monks and the smell of the incense and the bunches of flowers thrown down at the feet of the saints. There, in the hot sunshine, men and women worshiped their God with laughter and bells and beauty and color, but here in the bleak north with simplicity and austerity. . . . Strange how many doors there were leading into the very same country, and this particular door was the right one for herself and Ian. . . . Though tiring.

She did not use the shooting stick, for Ian, she felt, strongly disapproved. Her legs ached dreadfully as she stood through the minister's interminable prayers, but when she whispered to Ian, "May I sit down?" he only replied, "What for?" so she went on standing. There was no harmonium, but Mr. Campbell led them in a terrific voice a semitone flat, and they all followed his lead in the keys that seemed good to them individually.

Toward the end of the service the minister preached an overwhelming sermon on the rather curious subject of dew and persecution. Dew he saw as the symbol of renewal of life, and persecution as the highest good that life can know. But only the living can be persecuted, he told them with much shouting and gesticulation, only the living, not the dead; therefore must they pray that the dew of God's grace might fall on their spirits and quicken them to life again and again. Judy shivered a little as she listened, though it all fitted in with her recent discoveries. Life was to be renewed again and again only that one might suffer again and again. And to what purpose? Perfection, shouted the minister, waving his arms. The cycle of renewal and suffering must go on and on until perfection was an accomplished fact. Judy's thoughts wandered to the Covenanters with their savage joy in persecution and to Ian with his ideal of Utopia at whatever cost, and her heart fainted within her. She stole another glance at him. He was sitting very rigidly on the hard seat with his arms folded, and his figure looked dark and brooding. The roots of his being seemed to her to stretch back a very long way, and she felt, as she often felt, a little afraid of him. What a terrible people! And she, who might have chosen to walk softly all her days, had chosen instead to throw in her lot with them.

The sermon came to an end at last with a final burst of oratory. "Whoever you are," cried the minister, 'the dew can be yours if you choose it. It falls as willingly on a bit of dry bracken on the hillside as on the king's roses. . . . Enter into the land where the dew is falling."

Then, still obsessed by dew, they sang a paraphrase of the 110th Psalm, two lines of which stuck in Judy's mind for days.

In holy beauties from morn's womb,
Thy youth like dew shall be.

What did that mean exactly? Would her youth, that she so feared to lose, ever be renewed again?

And now they were outside and walking up the road together, and the storm had almost passed. The mountains were the color of grapes with patches of yellow-green where the sun touched them, and there was the hint of a rainbow across the slate-blue storm clouds.

"Tomorrow," announced Judy, "is one of your surgery days, and I shall come and help you."

"You'll do nothing of the sort," said Ian.

"Why not?" asked Judy, her eyes flashing.

"Because your mother wouldn't like it. You'd see sights, and you wouldn't understand how to help, and—well——" He waved his arms despairingly. 'Whatever should I do with you there?"

"*You* wouldn't have to do anything with me," said Judy grimly. "I never have to be done anything with, I always do all the doing myself."

"I dare say. . . . But no, Judy, it wouldn't do."

His tone was final, but so was Judy's.

"I'm coming, Ian."

They glared at each other, and Judy realized to her intense surprise that, for the moment only, she had met her match.

IV

But only for the moment. Next morning she got up earlier than usual and read history for an hour, going downstairs when the gong rang buoyed up by that extraordinary, and quite unwarranted, sense of virtue always produced by early rising. All through breakfast she was very sweet and sunny, perhaps a little too sunny; and her parents looked at her suspiciously. She wore a very workmanlike-looking frock, they noted, with the belt drawn tighter than usual; and her curls, usually so exuberant, were confined at the back of the neck in firm restraint. The decks were obviously cleared for action, and Lady Cameron sighed. Judy's recent saintly mood of meditation and withdrawal had been distinctly trying, leading her as it did to leave her galoshes about in awkward places and take not the slightest notice of anything said to her, but it had at least been harmless. The same thing, she felt, could not be said of this new phase. She knew quite well, from painful past experience, that when Judy drew her belt in tightly like that she was about to be tiresome.

"What are you going to do this morning, Judy?" she asked suspiciously.

"Go out, mother darling, and look at the world."

It sounded harmless, but Lady Cameron felt there was more in this than met the eye. Judy finished her breakfast very quickly, asked to be excused, kissed her mother with an astonishing display of affection, and disappeared.

"Now where has she gone?" demanded Lady Cameron. "She never kisses me like that unless she's going to do something she knows I'll disapprove of."

"I'll see what she's up to after breakfast," said Sir James, and waved a soothing hand.

But by the time he had got out into the garden Judy was halfway down the glen road. The house was at one end of the glen, and Ian's surgery at the other and more populated end, so that she had to walk the length of it to get there. It was a lovely morning, still and gray, with the clearness that comes before rain. The flanks of the mountains were indigo and the surface of the loch like polished steel. The mountaintops, usually so dominant, were hidden in low-hanging clouds, so that the crofts

84

below stood out very sharply and seemed in the clear light to take on an added importance.

They lay all round the loch, each small, low, whitewashed house standing in the center of its colored quilt of fields. Each crofter, she knew, must pay rent when he could for this tiny scrap of earth and must wrest a living out of it or starve. . . . Judging by the dilapidated appearance of both Ian Macdonald and his house, Judy gathered that their landlord did not press them very hard for those rents. . . . Those tiny domains struck her as both enchanted and pathetic, like fairy-tale farms that might at any moment vanish. The fields were so very small. Harvest fields and fields of yellow ragwort, dark green potato patches and shaven hayfields of emerald green with their stoops of hay protected each by its own private mackintosh, and all of them only the size of pocket handkerchiefs. Far up the sides of the mountain were more crofts, some visible and some hidden in folds of the moor or behind clumps of trees; and all of them sheltered Ian's people and formed his kingdom, her kingdom, that they would make perfect before they died.

Her kingdom? What was she thinking of? She stopped quite still, twisting her fingers together. The growing possessiveness of her thoughts startled her. She must remember that, whatever she was in her crazy thoughts, in sober reality she was only a stranger from London who had no lasting right to this place or to these people.

No right? That stabbed her so that she went hastily on again, talking to herself to change her thoughts. Ever since she had come to Glen Suilag she had fallen a victim to the habit of writing verse. In London she had never been afflicted in this way, and she could not understand it. But there it was. She could not help herself. The verse-making habit seemed to be a demon inhabiting her bedroom, for it was always when she was washing her ears that words began to string themselves together in her mind. The demon had been particularly active that morning and she said the words over as she walked:

> Born of winter's snow
> And April's rainbow showers,
> Cold as steel, and white
> As gleaming snowdrop flowers,
> Shining silver burns
> Slipping through the heath
> And golden bracken
> To the loch beneath.
>
> Splendid are the hills
> In golden glory growing,
> Lovely are the clouds
> Around their summits flowing,
> But I love to see,
> Sparkling through the ferns
> And sprigs of myrtle,
> The bright, falling burns.
>
> Through swaying larch trees
> The wind goes softly sighing,
> Up along the moors
> The lambs are gently crying,
> But there is no sound
> In the sweeping hills
> So clear as the song
> Of my silver rills.
>
> When I'm imprisoned
> In the roaring city street,
> The dusty pavement
> Hard to turf-accustomed feet,
> I can shut my eyes
> And dream of silver threads

Running through meadows
Where loch water spreads.

This brought her to the northern shore of the loch
and to the end of her journey; and she stood with a
beating heart in front of the disused crofter's house that
Ian had turned into his surgery. He had told her it was
thought to be more than a century old; no one could remember a time when it had not stood there. It was
haunted, they said, after dark. The walls were of unhewn, mortarless stone, and sloped a little inwards, and
it was thatched with rye thatch.

Judy walked softly to the open doorway and stood
looking in, and she saw a queer sight. She had just been
looking at the bright loch water lit by a passing gleam of
sun, and just at first she was so dazzled that the interior
of the house seemed to her black as night. The floor
seemed to be of trampled earth, and the black rafters
overhead were grimed with smoke. In the center of the
floor a peat fire was burning, the pungent smoke
wreathing up toward a hole in the roof. She heard no
sound at all, but the thick, smoky shadows were full of
huddled figures.

Then she blinked her eyes and found herself looking
at a bright, clean modern surgery. The floor was of
freshly scrubbed wooden planks, and the old rafters of
the roof had been whitewashed. Modern windows had
been thrown out to east and west so that the room was
filled with light and air. There were rows of white
shelves with bottles on them and a table of shining instruments. She could smell no peat smoke now, only the
sharp, clean smell of methylated spirit and iodine; and
there were no huddled figures in the shadows, only Ian
himself in a long white coat, standing at the table with
his back to her.

"Ian!" she gasped, and he swung round.

For a moment he flushed angrily, and she was afraid

he was going to turn her out; then his look changed and, seizing her arm, he pulled her inside and sat her down on a chair.

"Judy, what's the matter? You look as though you'd seen a ghost. Has anything happened?"

"No, but the room looked so odd."

"The room looked odd?"

"Yes. Pitch black and full of shadows."

"You must have been looking at the sun."

"Yes, I had been."

"Well, that's all right, then. You don't feel funny now, do you? Would you like a dose of anything nasty?"

Judy got up resolutely. "No, I wouldn't. I've come here to help you dose, not to be dosed myself."

Ian returned to the polishing of instruments with a perplexed frown. 'I don't know what I'm going to do with you. They'll be turning up soon, and I'm not used to coping with an assistant at the same time as I cope with the patients."

Judy cocked her chin indignantly. "Now I'm here I'm going to stay, and I'm not a bit like the usual kind of lady help."

"What's she like?"

"Neither a lady nor a help."

"Well, you're certainly a lady," Ian admitted meaningly.

Judy felt he ought to be punished. "It's a wonder to me," she said tartly, "that you're allowed to mess about like this. I should have thought all this free-lance chopping people up would have been resented by the medical profession."

"You see, I only treat little things," said Ian, "and the doctor is a friend of mine and trusts me. He lives a long way from here and is appallingly overworked. He doesn't want to come miles in all weathers to attend slight cases that he won't ever be paid for. . . . They're

88

usually too poor to pay their doctor's bills. . . . If there's anything serious, of course I send for him or pack the patient off to hospital, but often I'm able to take things in time and prevent them from becoming serious. You see, they come to me when they wouldn't go to him because they're not afraid of me."

He spoke so humbly that Judy was ashamed of herself. "I'm sorry I was such a pig," she said.

Ian laughed. "We're used to people on four feet in here. . . . Look at the first patient."

Judy looked round and saw a black and white sheep dog standing on three paws in the doorway. Ian whistled, and he came limping in, wagging his tail and holding up a beautifully bandaged fourth paw.

"He had it crushed in a trap," said Ian, fondling the silky ears. "It's been no end of a job."

"And do you mean to tell me," cried Judy, her eyes popping out of her head, "that he comes by himself to have it dressed?"

"Of course he does. His master brought him twice, and after that he understood all about it. He's a dog of sense." And Ian lifted the patient on to the table.

It was a strenuous morning, and Judy had never worked so hard in all her pampered life. Men and women and children and dogs and cats came in with poisoned fingers, boils and sprains and cuts, burns, sore eyes, swollen paws, and the toothache. They finished the morning with a boy who had chopped off two fingers and a cat whose son-in-law had taken a dislike to her and bitten a piece out of her ear.

Judy's respect for hospital nurses went up by leaps and bounds. At the end of half an hour she felt sick and faint, and it took every ounce of her considerable self-control to keep her on her legs. Yet, quick-witted and courageous as she was, she came through with credit. She managed somehow or other, more by instinct than by knowledge, to have the right instrument ready to hand to Ian at the right moment, and she rolled bandages and washed basins and held paws steady with fingers that trembled only a little.

And in spite of her absorption in what she had to do, she managed to notice Ian's amazing skill. His hands were like a musician's, strong and lean with sensitive finger tips, and his touch seemed in itself an anaesthetic. His voice, when he spoke to frightened children and shivering animals, was the most consoling thing on earth, and his patience was inexhaustible. What a crime, thought Judy, that this man should not be working in the London hospitals. What a crime that his skill should be wasted on cuts and bruises. . . . And yet, was it? . . . Serious injuries, like great tragedies, never lacked help; but the small woes of frightened children and furry beasts who could not say what ailed them sometimes went uncomforted.

At last even the bitten cat was disposed of, the last basin washed and the last bottle put back in its place. The doctor and his assistant straightened tired backs and looked at each other.

"Well done," said Ian. "I didn't know you had it in you."

Judy blushed crimson for perhaps the first time in her usually unembarrassed life. Never before had praise been so sweet.

After that Ian capitulated, and for more than a week they worked together. On surgery mornings Judy was as punctual in attendance as the sheep dog with the crushed paw, and each time she grew more skillful and more in love with the work she did.

On other days, when Ian had business at some faraway farm, they would spend the afternoon tramping together up one of the lonely mountain roads. These roads, hardly more than cart tracks, fascinated Judy. They seemed to wind on endlessly, piercing further and

90

further into the heart of the mountains, the solitude and silence seeming to grow deeper with every mile.

And then, at a turn of the road, they would suddenly find themselves at their journey's end. In a hollow of the bare, windswept moor, high up among the clouds, there would be a little kingdom, as beautiful as it was unexpected. There would be a peaceful tarn with a group of pine trees beside it sheltering whitewashed farm buildings, and on the mountain slopes all round would be sheep and cattle and goats. It would perhaps be sheep-dipping day, and the air would be filled with the clamor of barking dogs and bleating, outraged sheep. Ian would go to the sheep pen to talk to the farmer, and Judy would sit by the tarn with the sun warm on her face, listening to the tiny sound the water made as it whispered through the rushes and watching the slow lovely passing of the clouds. Then Ian would call to her, and they would go together to the farmhouse and be regaled by the farmer's wife with strong, scalding tea, freshly baked scones, and bramble jelly.

Judy always lost her heart to the hostess and her family. The dignity and naturalness of the Highland courtesy seemed to her perfect. There was no subservience in it and no self-consciousness. They welcomed her as one of themselves, and constrained by the sacred laws of hospitality gave her the best that they had with a genuine pleasure in giving that made of the meal a sacrament. . . . And Judy fancied, too, that in the short time she was with them they gave her affection because she came with the Laird. . . . Their admiration of him and gratitude to him delighted her. Usually those who slaved for the common weal as Ian did met with scant gratitude, but these people were so gifted with courtesy that they could take as gracefully as they gave.

As they walked home Ian would tell her all his hundred and one plans for Glen Suilag, some of them wise, some of them fantastic, and most of them hopeless for lack of money. The transport of the sick to hospital was a desperate problem. He wanted an ambulance specially built to get up these mountain roads to lonely farms and crofts. He wanted to give every child a stout pair of boots and an oilskin. "They tramp miles to school, Judy, in all weathers, and then sit all day in wet clothes. . . . Then they fall sick and die." Many of the crofters' houses were so old and damp that it was impossible for their owners to be either clean or healthy in them, and he wanted to rebuild them all. Then there was so much that he wanted to teach; modern methods of cultivation to increase the output of the crofts, the right care of animals, sobriety, bee-keeping, kindness, cleanliness, and not to beat their wives or stew their tea."

At the end of one of these outpourings Judy would sigh rather despairingly and say, "It will take you all your time, Ian," and immediately have an odd feeling that she had said exactly the same thing long ago.

"Time?" Ian would say contemptuously. "What's time? I have the whole of it." And that, too, or something like it, had surely been said before.

And each day as it slipped away, lessening by so much the span of their life on earth, made it up to them by adding its gold of sympathy and understanding to the growing wealth of their love. . . . And still they did not acknowledge it. . . . The pile of their wealth was mounting higher and higher with each day that passed, but it did not yet spill over and swamp them. Something more was needed to precipitate things, shock or parting or both.

And Lady Cameron, unintentionally obliging, provided the parting. She found out what they were doing and put her foot down. The walks into the mountains she did not object to so much: they were harmless and hygienic, though very hard on poor, dear Charles, mercifully absent at the time; but the discovery of the goings-on in the surgery sent her into what Judy, borrowing a phrase from the aeronautical world, called "one of mother's flat spins."

"Goodness knows," said Lady Cameron, summing up at the end of three-quarters of an hour, "what germs you haven't picked up and handed on to your poor father, and you know how tiresome he is when he's ill. I forbid you, Judy, ever to go near that dreadful place again."

Judy had been unusually sweet and docile throughout the "flat spin," which had begun some while before breakfast and continued through the repast without cessation. Now she kissed her mother very gently and quietly left the room. Five minutes later she was observed by Lady Cameron through the dining-room window crossing the garden surgery-wards, clothed in the workmanlike frock with the belt drawn very tight indeed.

"James," said Lady Cameron, "look at that!"

But Sir James, had, as always, evaporated; and there was no course left to her but the writing of a stiff note to Ian Macdonald, summoning him to an interview at two-thirty.

He came, and stood silently and politely upon the drawing-room hearthrug while Lady Cameron, seated on the sofa, expressed herself with the fluency that never deserted her. Yet in spite of her fluency she felt uncomfortable. This man always made her feel uncomfortable. Although she paid him rent for his appalling house his presence in it always made her feel an interloper. There were times, too, and this was one of them, when she almost felt that Judy was as much his as hers. . . . Ridiculous! . . . She gave herself a mental shake and brought her remarks to a close with an impressive peroration on the subject of germs.

"I am sorry," said Ian. 'I won't let Judy come again. . . .Where is she?"

"Sketching in the garden," said Lady Cameron.

"Where the rhubarb joins the larch wood. . . . I can't think, Mr. Macdonald, why you don't make Macgregor root up that rhubarb. Ridiculous, growing in the middle of the flowers like that. I must say that I find Macgregor the most incompetent——"

But Ian had bowed and left her. Through the window she could see him striding purposefully toward the rhubarb, and she smiled grimly. It was evident, from the set of his shoulders, that he thought he could manage Judy. . . . She almost had it in her heart to pity the poor young man.

Yet, to her intense astonishment, the door opened ten minutes later to admit an almost chastened Judy. She stood in front of her mother with her hands behind her back like a chidden child.

"I'm sorry, mother," she said, "I won't go to the surgery again."

"What in the world did he say to you?" asked Lady Cameron, when the power of speech was restored to her.

"He just said I wasn't to go again, and then——he said——"

"Well?"

Judy's lips curved in a smile, but she made no answer. What Ian had said was, "Be patient just a little longer, Judy."

CHAPTER IV

I

EARLY in September a spell of fine, hot weather settled down upon Glen Suilag. After the rain of August it was a gift of the gods, and Lady Cameron was heard to remark that it was really almost as sunny as Bournemouth. She and Charles, who had lately returned exhausted from upholding the bulwarks of Empire, with Jean and Major Murray, took to going for further excursions in Major Murray's car, leaving Sir James behind with the fish and Judy with her thoughts and her books.

This exactly suited her. She was alone with her darling house and her beloved Angus. Elspeth, shut in the kitchen, was an unseen presence whose soft singing of Highland songs and clattering of pans fitted into place as an accompaniment to the song of Glen Suilag, the bird songs and falling water and rustling of trees that murmured round the house all day.

One Wednesday, showery yet lovely, Judy never forgot. She cut sandwiches for the others with what seemed to Charles indecent haste, put rugs over their legs with enthusiasm, and waved joyously as they disappeared down the drive. Then she accelerated her father's departure from the loch and went upstairs to her room.

Here it was deliciously cool. The west wind, her favorite wind, was blowing from Ben Fhalaich, and the curtains of her bed were rustling and stirring. She stood still, listening to the sounds of the house, the tiny patter of a mouse, the creak of a board, the sighing of the wind along the passages, Elspeth's faraway singing, and the soft swish of Angus's broom as he swept the hall. She loved it when the house was empty like this. She was consicous then of its life, its quiet, wise life stretching so far through time. It had seen and heard so much, yet held its peace; it had endured so much, yet made no complaint. Yet she wished with all her heart that it would talk to her. If it would it could answer all her questions. Who was Judith and why did she block up the middle window? Who was the man in the picture over the fireplace? Why did she, Judy, love this place so much? Why was she so frightened of the middle window? Above all, why was her love for Ian growing so alarmingly?

For it was. The sudden ceasing of their almost daily companionship had seemed to shock and jar her into an overwhelming realization of love. From being the quiet background of her thoughts and her life it was becoming life itself, and it hurt her as life hurts. Standing there in the empty room, listening, it seemed suddenly that the house as well as she herself was crying out in loneliness. Its sighings and its murmurs were of sorrow. It seemed to her that she was aching with a double ache, her own and the house's too. They both of them felt empty and deserted.

She sat down suddenly on the floor and began pulling books resolutely out of the bookcase. . . . This wouldn't do. . . . She mustn't go back to the morbidity of her first night. It was silly. She wanted Ian badly; and union, she knew, with the increased strength that it brought, was the final goal in all departments of life; but individuality must come first, and she was still, she felt, a very poor affair, unfit to be any man's wife, let alone Ian's. She musn't think about union yet. She must go on reading and thinking, scourging her silly little mind into some sort of shape.

But everything today conspired against her. Whatever book she took up promptly fell open in her hands, as though of malicious purpose, at pertinent remarks about love that ran straight into her like sharp swords. She was reading *King John*, yet the moment she took up Shakespeare, though he had been opened firmly for the last two days at *King John*, he opened himself at the *Merchant*.

You see me, Lord Bassanio, where I stand,
Such as I am: though for myself alone
I would not be ambitious in my wish,
To wish myself much better; yet, for you

I would be trebled twenty time myself;
A thousand times more fair, ten thousand times——

She flung Shakespeare away disgustedly and took out a shabby brown book whose title was rubbed off. It looked dull. She opened it. It was, she hoped, on mathematics.

How do I love thee? Let me count the ways.
I love thee to the depth and breadth and height
My soul can reach, when feeling out of sight
For the ends of being and ideal grace.
I love thee to the level of every day's
Most quiet need, by sun and candlelight.

Good heavens! The "Sonnets from the Portuguese." Worse and worse. Mrs. Browning swished along the floor to join Shakespeare and Judy seized another book at random. It fell open.

For indeed he was a wonder to me then and always, not for his looks nor for anything that he did, but for the silent power of what he was, the power gathered up in him, as tremendous as a great mountain on the sky, that you couldn't measure nor name, but only feel. A man, it was. And if there be any meaning in what word as I hanna thought on, let them that read put it in. Let them put the strength and the power, the kindness and the patience, the sternness and the stately righteousness of all good men into that word, and let him wear it. For it was himself, the maister.

"A great mountain on the sky," Judy looked at Ben Fhalaich. Yes, he filled the whole world, as Ian did. . . . She jumped up with an angry exclamation and dropped *Precious Bane* on top of Shakespeare and Mrs. Browning. How dared Ian have novels in his bookcase! Mary Webb did churn one up so. And, what a sentimental passage! She would not read it again, she would *not*. . . . At least only once more. . . . Then she would read Trevelyan's *History of England*. It was on the bottom shelf and was, she felt, bracing reading for the lovesick.

Trevelyan was wedged in rather tightly. When she got him out, after much tugging, several other books fell out too, and there was a large gap. Standing up against the back of the shelf was a thin book with a worn cover patched with damp. It was so much the color of the wood behind it that it was only by a miracle that she noticed it. She took it out. It was filthy dirty. . . . Heaven alone knew when this room had last been spring-cleaned. . . . The edges of the pages were black with dirt, and the leather of the cover was peeling off. She opened it and gave a little exclamation, for it was very, very old. The pages were stained and yellow and torn, and in places the bookworm had bored his holes right through them, and it smelled very musty. Judy fetched a silk handkerchief from her drawer and very tenderly wiped the cobwebs off its face. Then she looked at it and found it was a manuscript book of songs. The notes of the music were delicately drawn in ink so faded that she could hardly read them, and the words of the songs were written out below the tunes in a lovely, spidery handwriting. She turned to the flyleaf of the book. Here there was an inscription written in a different handwriting, queer and neat, with delicacy in the curves and fierceness in the downstrokes. She read what was written. "Judith Macdonald, her book. Given to her on August 18th, 1745, by her husband, Ranald Macdonald. Dearest Judith, while I am away you are to write down all your pretty songs in this book so that not one of them is lost. When I come back you will sit at your harpsichord and sing them to me."

The room seemed to be turning round Judy. Judith's

book! Judith had written these songs. Her fingers were shaking as she turned the pages. Five minutes slipped by before she could pull herself together enough to try and decipher the words. When she did they absorbed her, and she sat perfectly still on the floor until she had read them all. There was nothing very arresting about them—they were just rhymes strung together to fit the tunes; but Judy, as she read them, seemed to feel the actual emotions that Judith must have felt when she wrote them, and by the time she had finished them all she felt worn out. At the beginning of the book were love songs and rhymes about the mountains and the sea and the birds, but at the end of the book were queer, wild laments that seemed to Judy to have in them the wailing of the bagpipes and the crying of the whaups. "Poor Judith!" whispered Judy, "poor, poor Judith!"

She got up and went downstairs to the drawing room, where she opened the harpsichord and sat down at it, the book propped open in front of her. Very softly, afraid that Elspeth might hear her, she picked out the tunes. Though she was something of a musician it took her a long time to decipher them, but when at last she had made them all out she found to her surprise that she seemed to know them by heart. There was one that she loved particularly and she sang it over and over again, forgetful of Elspeth, her voice echoing round the dim old room and flowing out into the garden.

Deep stillness of starlight nights and flooding of amber moonlight,
The strength of the dawn and the healing surge of the summer rain,
The sighing of winter woods and cry of the wind at midnight,
In the circling change of the seasons these shall return again.

Constant, changeless, eternal are mountain and rock
    and corrie,
Unmoved in their sculptured ranks amid thunder and
    storm and snow.
Youth and love will forsake me, and I shall grow sick
    and sorry;
Yet these my friends are faithful and these to the end I
    shall know.

When the burden of living is over and my life is a sor-
    row forgotten,
Only one love shall detain me when the door of death is
    wide,
Love of the earth shall hold me, love of the fields I have
    trodden,
Love of emblazoned midnight and love of the sea in its
    pride.

O you, my friends and my lovers, shall I come back
    from the darkness,
Shall I love again the sweetness, the color and glow of
    earth?
Shall I in a new-born body, fair and strengthened and
    spotless,
Worship again in the springtime the resurrection of
    birth?

So absorbed was she that she did not notice the door
open and shut. It was not until the last note died away
that she became aware of someone standing by her and
turned. It was Angus. How long he had been standing
there she didn't know. His eyes were blazing, and his
face wore the expression of joy that she had not seen
there since the day she came. "Angus!" she said,
"Angus!" and jumping up impulsively she took hold of
the lapels of his coat. "Angus, did you like my singing?"

"Na," said Angus. "Catawaulin'." But he was still

smiling and, taking her hands, he patted them. Judy could have dropped dead with shock, and it seemed that Angus shared her astonishment.

"Losh!" he ejaculated, and turning his back on her he ambled to the fireplace, muttering and growling. Still with his back to her he pulled his dirty old orange duster out of a pocket in the tails of his coat and flicked savagely at the mantelpiece.

"Don't you like music, Angus?" asked Judy.

"Na," muttered Angus, "I'm fond o' the pipes, forbye, but yon tin kettle——" he turned, his face now set in lines of the utmost disagreeableness, and pointed a scornful finger at the harpsichord, "gr-r-r-r."

Angus had a particular growl, used to express contempt, that was the most withering thing Judy had ever met. She got up meekly and shut the harpsichord, putting the book inside it.

"Gie me yon!" said Angus sharply. He came to her, opened the harpsichord and took out the book. Holding it close to his eyes he blinked at it. Placing it below his red nose he sniffed at it. Then he ran a horny finger round its edges, gave it a bit of dusting with the yellow duster, and put it back.

"Ou, ay," he said, "here 'tis. Ye've gotten it. Daft, that's what we are. . . . Clean daft." and went back to the fireplace.

Judy sat down on the harpsichord stool, enjoying him. She was always completely happy with Angus. "Angus," she said, "do you like me?" She knew quite well that he worshiped the ground upon which she trod, but she loved worming the confession out of him.

"Na," said Angus with decision.

"Angus, that's not true."

He turned round, brandishing his duster threateningly. "Ye're an ill lassie, the Laird should tak' a stick to ye."

"Why the Laird?" asked Judy. "Oughtn't it to be Sir James?"

"Na, the mon's no strength to his arm."

"Angus, say you like me."

"Gr-r-r-r. I like ye well enow when ye keep yer tongue still i' yer head, but a lassie wi' a waggin' tongue ne'er won the likin' o' a sane mon yet. Women were made by th' Almighty to keep the hoose clean, no' to sit chatterin' and catawaulin' and thumpin' on a tin kettle—

He broke off, his head slightly cocked to one side, "'Tis the Laird," he said, "I heerd his step."

"No, you didn't," said Judy, a little sadly. "The Laird never comes now, unless mother asks him."

And instantly the door opened and Ian came in. Judy looked from one to the other, her eyes twinkling. The affection between the two men, never expressed, was yet always amusingly obvious.

"Angus, you blackguard," said Ian, "you ought to have dusted this room hours ago. Lady Cameron might have wanted to use it."

"Na," said Angus, "the woman can bide i' her bed if she no goes gallivantin' i' yon stinkin' car o' yer oncle's. I'll no' put mesel' oot for ony but Mistress Judith." He ambled from the room, poking his head round the door to ask, "Will ye tak' a sup o' usquebaugh?"

"You know perfectly well, Angus," expostulated Ian with some heat, "that I never drink whisky in the morning."

"Ah," said Angus profoundly, "till the day ye've no had to bear wi' a chatterin' woman i' the morning' . . . . Aweel, hae a guid drink while ye can. When ye tak' a wife ye'll no' be able to afford it."

He withdrew, and his chuckle died away with his footsteps.

Ian looked hot. "Forgive him, Judy."

"Nothing that Angus says ever needs to be forgiven," said Judy. "He's inevitable. He's part of the place."

"Were you playing the harpsichord?" asked Ian. "Will you again? I've always wanted to hear it played, but I can't do anything but chopsticks myself. . . . The poor thing has sat there silent for years."

Judy suddenly felt terribly shy. She didn't want him to know about the book inside the harpsichord—not yet. "I'll play to you one day," she said hurriedly, "but not now."

"What shall we do now?" asked Ian. "It's heavenly weather. Shall we go in your car to the coast and look at the islands? We said we would one day."

Judy was astonished, Ian had promised, during that week when they were together, to take her to the islands of the west that lay in the blue strip of the sea that one could see from the top of Ben Caorach, but then had come Lady Cameron's "flat spin," and he had never done it.

And tomorrow was her birthday, and he and Jean and Major Murray were coming to dinner. That he should be prepared to fritter away his time on social intercourse on two successive days, he whom social intercourse bored to distraction, nearly knocked her flat.

"Won't it be a waste of a good day?" she asked mischievously. "If you didn't take me to the islands you could spend the whole morning cleaning out someone's pigs."

"I thought I'd prefer you to pigs on a day like this."

"Very well," said Judy, and slipped off the stool. "I'll go and see about sandwiches. There's hard-boiled egg and ham." At the door she paused, a little wistfully. "Are you getting on all right at the surgery without me?"

"Yes, thanks," said Ian, with that tactless regard for truth which was a part of his character.

Judy departed, closing the door with a slight suspicion of a bang. As she cut sandwiches she wondered miserably if he loved her. When he wasn't there she was sure he did, but when he *was* there she wasn't quite so sure; his remarks were sometimes not all that could be wished for in a lover. . . . But then, of course, poor Charles was here again, blocking the way. . . . Poor Charles, whose expression these days was identical with Sarah's when someone took away her bone. . . . Well, anyway, Ian had preferred her company to the pigs'! That was a cheering thought, and she sang as she tied up the sandwiches.

Angus, when informed of their intention, said there was going to be a thunderstorm, but if they liked to be fules they could be fules. He growled gloomily as he put their mackintoshes and their dogs in the back of the car but, as they disappeared down the drive, was seen to be smiling. Judy had noticed before that it seemed to give him acute satisfaction to see them together.

II

It was a glorious day of alternate sun and shower, with the colors on the mountains shifting and changing as the clouds swept over them, and always the hint of a rainbow across the heather.

The quartette in the car was very happy. Ian, with his worries for once forgotten, looked years younger, and Judy sang as she drove; Lochiel and Sarah, seated side by side on the back seat, lifted their heads and sniffed ecstatically as delicious odors of grouse and rabbit assailed their noses.

Slowly they greeted Ben Caorach and dropped down on the other side. Then, taking a road to their right, they doubled back again, facing the northwest and the sea.

"Now we're on the other side of Ben Fhalaich," said Ian. "There he is on your right. Just over the top is Glen Suilag again."

Judy gazed up at the mountain's great purple flanks. "Extraordinary," she said, "how in this country it takes you all day to get next door. . . . And extraordinary to think that I've never been along this road before."

"It's a good road," said Ian. "From here to the islands is the best bit of country in the world."

"As good as Glen Suilag?"

"Perhaps better. . . . Why haven't you been this way before?"

"Somehow I haven't wanted to," said Judy. "This road never seemed to pull me at all."

Then they settled back in their seats and were silent. Ian was recognizing every landmark in a strip of country of which he loved every inch; but Judy, though she reveled in the beauty all round her, felt a little strange in it. It did not give her that sense of familiarity that Glen Suilag gave her. She had a feeling that Ian belonged here but that she did not, and she felt a little separated from him, a sensation that was to grow stronger as the day went on.

Meanwhile the car sped on past the lochs fringed with their golden weed, through thick larch woods carpeted with brilliant green moss and rocky gorges where the sound of the falling burns echoed as though in a cavern. Every bend of the road brought a view breathtaking in its loveliness, but Judy realized that she was admiring it all as one admires a beautiful stranger, not as one greets an old friend.

"I suppose she never came this way," she said suddenly.

"Who?" asked Ian.

"Judith Macdonald, your ancestress."

Ian looked at her oddly. "No, I don't suppose she did. It would have been too far for her. . . . No cars in those days. . . . But he did."

"Who?" asked Judy in her turn.

Ian looked odder than ever. "Did you remember to bring the sandwiches?" he asked.

"You're holding them," said Judy, and laughed.

They were silent again until Ian cried suddenly, "Stop!"

Judy stopped so suddenly that they nearly skidded.

"It's Glenfinnan," explained Ian. "Where Charles Edward raised his standard and where the clans gathered for the start of the Forty-five."

That touched Judy, and for a moment she no longer felt a stranger. The 'Forty-five had concerned Judith Macdonald very nearly, and so it concerned her too. She shut off the engine of the car and sat looking. In front of her stretched Loch Shiel, shadowed and gray in a sudden scurry of rain; and beside it stood a tall monument crowned with the statue of Prince Charlie. The mountains stood round it in a semicircle, brooding over it and dwarfing it with their great height. Some sea gulls, circling over the loch and round the statue, were crying mournfully. The shadow of Fate that hangs over certain places seemed to weigh very heavily on Glenfinnan and it crept over Judy, too, so that she could have cried with the sadness that pressed on her.

"Is that where he stood when he made his first speech to the clans?" she asked Ian.

"Somewhere there," he said. "The sun was sinking when he arrived and stood waiting with his few friends. He didn't know, you see, how many were going to turn up. He had sent out his summons to the clans, but he could not know if they would obey it. . . . It must have been a bad moment for him."

"And they did?"

"Yes. The little party waiting in the glen heard the sound of the pipes coming nearer and nearer, and then they saw them coming over the mountain, first three men on the sky line, then three more, Camerons and Macdonalds and Macleods, marching in two columns, three abreast. They came winding down from the hills and stood all round him while the Royal Standard was unfurled, and then the blue and gold banner of the Stuarts. He stood under the standard as he made his speech. Someone who was there said it was a 'very short but very pathetic speech.' The last words of it were that with the assistance of a just God he did not doubt of bringing the affair to a happy issue.' When he had finished, the Highlanders flung their bonnets into the air, and they say the sound of their cheering was like thunder."

Judy sighed. "Let's go on," she said. "It's so sad here. That splendid beginning and then that horrible tragedy, and now nothing left of either of them but a stone statue and sea gulls crying in the rain."

"And a story that people don't forget," Ian reminded her.

"Why should tragedies be remembered and successes forgotten?" Judy asked rebelliously. "It just shows how morbid we all are at bottom."

"No, I don't think so. I think it shows that success only stirs easy feelings in us, soon forgotten; but tragedy stirs deep ones."

"Courage and pity and terror?"

"And mystery. One always remembers mysteries, and tragedy is very mysterious."

"Most things are," said Judy, eying him out of the corner of her eye. "Why did you describe the scene of the 'Forty-five as though you'd been there?"

"Shall we go on?" said Ian.

III

They went on, following the coast road. Judy enjoyed herself as the exquisite sea lochs slipped by them with their golden weed and silver sands sparkling in a sudden gleam of sun. Silver was not the right word to describe those sands, but she could think of no other. They did not seem to hold the warmth of the sun in them like the sands she knew in England—they reminded her more of moonlight. She remembered how, when she had driven this same car through England more than two months ago, she had noticed the silver rain and the golden celandines. . . . Silver and gold, the colors of reality.

Ian told her the names of the places they passed through, places with names like music: Borradale where Prince Charles landed, Morar and Mallaig.

The last place was a little sea town, and Ian guided her down to the harbor. "This is where we cross to Skye," he said.

"Oh, are we going to Skye?" asked Judy.

"Yes."

He seemed to have no doubt about it; and Judy, though she was a bad sailor and the wind was fresh and her inside turned right over at the prospect, made no demur. This, she felt, was Ian's day, not hers; and he must do what he wanted to do.

"Is it a small boat?" was all she said.

"Very," said Ian cheerfully. "It's the ferryboat. We're too late for the steamer."

They left the harbor and walked along the stone jetty that ran out into the sea. Judy had a vivid impression of purple mountains, jagged rocks, quantities of sea gulls, and an overpowering smell of fish.

"Look!" said Ian, and pointed out across the green, whiteflecked sea. The streamers of a rainstorm were trailing along the horizon, but as they looked they were drawn aside and a lovely shape appeared very faintly, then parted the veils and came through. It appeared carved out of very pale amethyst with here and there a hint of green that matched the sea.

"Is that Skye?" asked Judy, and instantly did not care how small the boat was, provided it took her there.

"That's Skye," said Ian, "and thank God it's still there."

"Why shouldn't it be?"

"It might have flown away. Its Gaelic name is Eilean Sgiathanach, the winged island, and if you look at it on the map you'll see it's shaped like some flying creature."

He left her abruptly and went slithering down a flight of seaweed-covered steps to find the boat. He was rather excited, she noticed, and seemed to have a certain amount of difficulty in remembering that she was with him. But for the boatman she thought he might have sailed to Skye without her, but that worthy jogged his memory and he came back up the steps to fetch her, courteous but distrait.

The dogs, of course, came too. Lochiel, as always, behaved like a perfect gentleman; but Sarah, who had eaten two fish heads and a half while Judy gazed at Skye, sat her fishy person upon the feet of, and wagged her fishy tail against the legs of, all the other occupants of the boat in turn.

Judy soon ceased to care what she did. The boat, as Ian had said, was small, its sail was inadequate and its little motor engine smelly. It rose high and sank low and rolled from side to side. Some lines from *Othello* said themselves over in Judy's anxious, disordered mind:

> And let the laboring bark climb hills of seas
> Olympus-high, and duck again as low
> As hell's from heaven!

She had never appreciated Shakespeare less. As the minutes passed her mind became increasingly anxious, for what more appalling humiliation could befall a woman than to be seasick in front of the man she loved? Mercifully Ian had apparently forgotten all about her again. He was standing in the bows of the boat, swaying

109

easily to its movement, and watching Skye. Judy closed her eyes and thanked heaven.

Halfway across, Sarah, who never had any self-control, wished she hadn't eaten the fish heads, and howled. The row she made restored Ian to remembrance of his responsibilities, and he came back to Judy, full of penitence.

"Judy, what a brute I am! And you're shivering in that skimpy mackintosh."

He wrapped his mackintosh round her on top of her own and sat beside her, propping her up when the boat pitched and pointing out distant islands to distract her mind.

"Those are Rum and Eigg," he said cheerfully. "You can't see Muck; it's hidden behind Eigg."

Judy didn't want to see it. She closed her eyes again and exercised her will.

And quite suddenly they were in calm water and her strained nerves relaxed. . . . They had taken three-quarters of an hour to cross from the mainland, and by the mercy of Heaven and the strength of her own mind she had not been humiliated. . . . Sarah had; but then Sarah, like most people who lack self-control, lacked self-respect also, and did not care.

"We're there," said Ian. "Look."

Judy looked and experienced one of those rare moments of sheer delight that are never forgotten. What she saw came to her with a shock of surprise that was almost like a blow, delivering her instantly from the burden of herself and swinging her spirit free. The clouds had blown away, and the sun was shining down from a brilliant blue sky upon a rainwashed island where every leaf and blade of grass seemed sparkling. They were entering the crescent of a bay; and in front of them rose a wooded slope, the great trees in their ranks marching right down to the sea. Where Judy expected to see silver sand she saw instead grass of an al-

110

most savage green, with the blue water rippling in and out between the tussocks. The blue and green were pierced by gray ridges of rock where the gulls and cormorants were sitting solemnly, making a pattern of black and white against the brilliant color. The sparkling clearness of it reminded Judy of a Chinese painting of an earthly paradise she had once seen; and it was not until they had landed at the little wooden pier and were walking along a winding road under the great trees, that the familiar smell of ferns and wet earth made her realize that this was still the British Isles.

"I thought Skye was bleak and wind-swept," she said to Ian.

"It is in the north," he said, "but this is the south. This is Armadale, the garden of Skye."

They turned to their left and followed the road until the trees thinned and vanished, and they found themselves in a crofting township. Whitewashed houses stood in gardens protected by thick hedges of fuchsia, and on their right was an old whitewashed inn. "The Ardvasar Hotel," said Ian, "the friendliest hotel in all Scotland."

On the left, between the road and the sea, were fields of flowers. Yellow vetch, yellow daisies, tall grasses, pale lavender scabious, and creamy meadowsweet were swaying in the wind. To the right, behind the crofts, the moors were rolling to the sky line.

"We'll have lunch by the sea," said Ian, and went wading through the meadowsweet.

Beyond the fields were a series of rocky coves with shingle full of green and yellow shells and ledges of rock running out into the water. They climbed along one and settled themselves in the sun with the sea all round them. When they looked up they saw in front of them, across the Sound of Sleat, the great masses of the mountains of Scotland, brilliantly clear; and when they looked down they saw rock pools painted egg-shell green inside and full of frilly anemones like minute scarlet dahlias.

"It's not exactly earthly, is it?" said Judy.

"Not in the least," said Ian. 'It's haunted. . . . You'll soon find out. . . . And be careful, or you'll get an attack of Skye to the head."

It was half-past two and they were very hungry. They ate in a silence caused partly by their starving condition and partly by that queer sense of separation from each other that Judy had felt all day. . . . She was a stranger in this earthly paradise, and Ian was not.

"Now for the moor," he said, when the last crumb had disappeared.

They went up through the crofts and flowery fields until they were out on the moor. It lifted in front of them, ridge beyond ridge, clothed with ling and bog myrtle. There was the murmur of a stream coming down from the furthest ridge, the singing of the wind in their ears and the sound of the sea, and beyond those a great silence.

Judy pointed to a ridge on the sky line. "We'll get there," she said, "right to the top."

Ian smiled. "You never get to the top," he said.

The four of them started off uphill, and very soon they were separated, the dogs going off after rabbits and Judy and Ian drifting further and further apart as they climbed, as though the spirit of the place were affecting them differently, pulling them apart that it might draw them to it in different ways.

Judy panted on and up, splashing in and out of bogs, sniffing the pungent scent of the bog myrtle and the earthy smell of the orange sphagnum moss that squelched under her feet. She did not care how wet she got. A queer ecstasy possessed her. She felt wild and a little lightheaded, and now and then she caught herself singing aloud. She did not look behind her, though she knew that the view behind must be one of the loveliest in the world, for she wanted to get to the top. But Ian was right; she could not. As she breasted each ridge another rose beyond; they mounted up and up forever. Presently a shower swept over the moor, and she raised her face to it, loving the caressing coolness of it against her skin; and then it seemed that sun and shower came to meet her alternately and the world was full of rainbows.

At last she stopped, so winded that she could not go on. She dropped down on a clump of springy heather and gazed. In front of her that eternal moor still climbed to the sky; but to her right, beyond the woods of Armadale, she could see mountains, unreal, fragile things like blown soap bubbles, colored faintest lilac and blue and arched over by a rainbow. For a moment she laughed aloud in her happiness, and then the laugh was cut short by a stab of pain. She could not take in any more. The faculty of joy had been strained to the utmost, like a strung bow, and now it had fallen back. She felt, too, suddenly shut out. The spirit that brooded over this place had allowed her to penetrate so far and no farther into its presence. She was only a stranger. She had gone too far already, and she must turn back. She got slowly to her feet and turned her face to the sea, and the last thing she saw as she turned was Ian's figure still striding on and up. . . . He was not a stranger.

She went slowly downhill, the patchwork of crofts and rocky bays spread out below her like a colored shawl. Before the moor ended she sat down again once more. The sun was out again now and was hot on her back. She was tired, and the sound of the burn lulled her almost to sleep.

Suddenly she flung up her head, her eyes dilating with terror. There was a curious crackling, thudding sound behind her, as though a galloping horseman cracked a whip as he rode at her to drive her away. She jumped to her feet and looked behind her, but there was nothing there, and no sound but the burn. She took to her feet and ran, not stopping until she was down among the crofts again and sitting on a stone by the roadside.

An old, bent woman came along the road with a huge basket of peats on her back. She stopped to smile at Judy and say how fine the day was, but Judy could not answer, not even to say, "God bless the work," her heart was beating so. The old woman smiled a slow, friendly smile and passed on. Judy wondered if she were quite used to terrified strangers flying in fear from that moor. "I went too far for a stranger," she said to herself. "I tried to be too intimate and It resented it."

Presently she laughed. She had been half asleep, she told herself. There was perhaps a shooting party up on the moor, and she had heard the crack of a gun. When Ian came back to her, muddy and disheveled and terribly apologetic, she said nothing to him about it.

They retrieved the dogs and walked toward the hotel for tea, Ian apologizing all the way. "I went too far," he kept muttering. "I did not realize—I struck across country to Loch Dhughaill, where you see the Cuillins —I had to—I'm sorry—it was so far."

Judy could see that he had been far, not only through space but through time.

IV

The hospitable Ardvasar Hotel received them as though their muddy footprints and the muddy paw-marks of Lochiel and Sarah all over the clean floors were a pleasure rather than an affliction. A courteous host greeted Ian as an old friend and scraped the mud off him, while a rosy-cheeked chambermaid, who smiled at Judy as though she loved her, took her upstairs to a white bedroom smelling of the sea and helped her to become moderately respectable.

"I've got to go away after tea," said Judy, "but I shall come back."

The maid smiled. "Yes, miss. That's what they all say."

"And do they come back?"

"Yes, miss, they all come back. They don't seem able to help themselves."

Judy and Ian sat in the cool, dim dining room, where the walls were three feet thick, and ate oatcake and homemade cakes so light that they melted in the mouth like butter. Across the hall Judy could see the quiet parlor with a fire burning. Beyond the windows the sea had turned silver, and the mountains of the mainland, that had been pale yet clear earlier in the day, had turned a deep violet, very sharp against the sky but with the rocks and corries below lost in the depth of color.

"Hullo," said Ian, "look how the mountains have changed. That means a storm tomorrow."

Judy paid no attention; she was too busy enjoying the place where she sat. There are houses that have a special atmosphere all their own, and whether it comes from their past history or from the personality of their owners, who shall say? That of the Ardvasar Hotel was full of friendliness and peace. Anyone who stayed in it on holiday, Judy felt, would be treated not as that hateful thing, a tripper, but as a guest whose happiness would be a matter of concern.

"I could be happy here," she said suddenly to Ian, "couldn't you?"

"I have been, often," he said. "I've stayed here many times." Then he smiled at her. "Don't be low in your mind at saying good-by. . . . We'll come again."

They paid their bill and walked back along the road under the great trees. They re-embarked in the little ferryboat and sailed back over the silver sea, but this time the wind had dropped and the waves had subsided and Judy looked with a favorable eye upon Rum and Eigg and was quite sorry that she could not see Muck.

They found the car still intact, though smelling strongly of fish, and drove off. The sea lochs with their silver sand slipped by them again, and Glenfinnan, and the larch woods carpeted with moss. Judy's demon had been very active all day, and she repeated the result to Ian as she drove, just to punish him for his neglect on the moor. "Listen," she said. "This is what I should feel if I were a sailor and had just seen the sea around Skye:

"Blue are the woods when springtime spreads her mantle,
    Green are the leaves around the throstle's nest,
    Purple the heather-bells that throng the mountains,
    Saffron the clouds when sunset dyes the west.

Yet can no hue of radiant earthly beauty
    Match for one moment with the colored sea,
    Green in the rock pools, purple in the shallows,
    Bluer than bluebells when the clouds go free.

Wide is the sky and sparkling full of wonder,
    Old is the earth and wise in all her ways,
    But yet that shining beauty and that wisdom
    Win not the homage of my mortal days.

No! For the sea has captured all my service,
    No! For the sea has taken of my best,
    I am forever hers through joy and torment,
    Hers though she draw me dead beneath her breast."

"Did you make that up?" asked Ian, astonished and a little alarmed. Verse-making was for him one of the minor and more harmless forms of lunacy.

"It wasn't really me," Judy consoled him. "There's a

116

verse demon in my bedroom, and he's got into me. I think perhaps he was left behind there by someone else. . . . Judith Macdonald, perhaps."

"We're nearly home," said Ian, changing the subject. They had passed the further side of Ben Fhalaich and were creeping up the steep slope of Ben Caorach. At the summit they stopped, pausing unconsciously as one pauses on the threshold of a much-loved home, reveling in possession. The feeling of separateness that they had both been conscious of all day left them, and in its place came a deep sense of unity. They turned and looked at each other, feeling so amazingly at one that it seemed odd they should have two bodies.

"Judy," said Ian urgently, "let's get out a minute. There's a place up there by that rock, to the right, where one can see the sea. . . . You know."

Judy knew. It was the place where she had stood on the afternoon when she came to Glen Suilag, where she had stood by herself in the mist and cried out for someone whom she did not know to be with her. She looked at Ian again and saw that his face had a hungry look that she had not seen there before.

"No," she whispered, 'we can't stop now. We're late as it is." And she sent the car on again downhill. Not even yet, she felt, had their time come. They must understand their love before they could acknowledge it.

As they came up to the house they could see the glimmer of light through the trees, and Judy's heart sank. The others were already having a late dinner, and she had hoped to get back before they did, so as not to upset Charles. The atrocity of her behavior was upsetting her, and Charles more and more. She should, she knew, long ago have given him what their cook in London called the "go-by." It was her pride, she told herself, that prevented her from doing her obvious duty. She wanted to be able to explain to Charles exactly why she, who had always thought herself faithful, was now unfaithful; and she did not know. As she brought the car to a standstill by the front door she felt almost desperate. If she did not find out soon what exactly was the bond that bound her to Ian and Glen Suilag she did not think that she could bear it, and she did not think that Ian could bear it either. Since she had shut him up at the top of Ben Caorach he had sat silently staring in front of him, frowning, and now, with a hasty "Good night, Judy," he called Lochiel and went off through the larch trees without another word.

It was Charles who assisted her and Sarah out of the car, conducting them indoors with a punctilious, hurt politeness that was worse than reproach.

V

Judy was awake most of the night. She had had to bathe Sarah, upon whose person a layer of Skye mud had been superimposed upon a layer of Mallaig fish, before she was tolerable as a sleeping companion, and she was too tired to sleep. Too tired and too miserable. Her longing for Ian, her self-reproach, and her lack of understanding were a torment. All night long it was as though every part of her were beating against some barrier. Her mind was shut out from understanding. Her conscience from rest, and her heart from love. And her body, that longed for the arms of her lover, was turning and tossing in the great bed in the unrest of loneliness. Her misery became a waking nightmare, and the darkness of the night seemed an actual door, built of ebony and reaching to heaven. "Let me in, let me in," she cried, like the Magdalene at heaven's gate, and beat against it with her hands.

But it was not until dawn that rest came to her. With the first chink of light through her curtains the door

swung open a little and she gasped with relief. . . .
today she would be let in. . . . She turned over and
went to sleep.

CHAPTER V

I

JUDY woke up late next morning. Her head ached, and
she felt hot and sticky and miserable. She remembered
that it was her birthday, but she had never felt less
birthdayish in her life. She hoped her head would stop
aching before her birthday dinner tonight; otherwise she
would probably be very cross and everyone would think
her birth had been a great mistake.

Tonight she would see Ian again. She wondered if it
would make her gloriously happy, as she had been yesterday, or utterly miserable, as she had been last night.
It seemed as though, when one was in the passionate
stage of love, one had to be either one or the other.
Poets extolled the state, but personally she didn't think
much of it. . . . Very tiring and unsettling. . . . She
wished with all her heart and soul that she could get
back to her earlier state of tranquillity, when Ian had
seemed like the quiet, steady center of life rather than
like a bursting boiler. She supposed she would get back
to it, and that it would constitute the happiness of all
her life to come. Life, she thought, was always a rounded thing. One came back full circle to where one had
been before. . . . Meanwhile what was she to do about
Charles? . . . And did Ian really love her? . . . And
oughtn't she to do something about Charles now at
once, without waiting for further understanding? . . .
The agonzied thoughts of last night began chasing each

119

other round and round her tired brain again. To stop them she got out of bed and pulled her curtains.

A thick heat mist shrouded the garden and wood and Ben Fhalaich. She was afraid it was going to be a hot, thundery day. "Horrid!" she murmured. She didn't know why, but she had an idiotic fear of thunderstorms. The stupidity of her fear infuriated her, but yet, strongminded as she was, she couldn't control it. It would be too bad if it thundered on her birthday. Up till now nature had never played her such a low-down trick. No. She was sure it wouldn't do such a thing. Those mists would rise, and they could have a glorious day like yesterday. The day was not thundery, she told herself; only hushed and expectant, waiting for the touch of the sun and the wind before it marched out with azure banners and tossing green plumes to conquer one more tract of dark, unknowable time.

Forgetting herself in her thoughts, she leaned out of the window and greeted the day with admiring reverence. . . . Plucky little day. . . . When it had run its course one more particle of time would be bathed in light and draped in beauty; the great darkness ahead would be lessened by just so much stolen away from its horror and stored in the treasury of the past. The future, surely, was much more terrible than the past. The suffering of the past was over and done with, never to be repeated, robbed by its cessation of all its horror, existing only as the foil of joy; but the suffering of the future, that was still to be endured, a dark sea rolling on only to be conquered by the gallant little days that met and accepted it, endured it, and left it behind them robbed of its sting.

What would happen to her today? Judy wondered. There was a feeling of excitement in the hot, still air. The shifting gray mist made her think of the great curtains in a theater shaking with a thrilling tremor, hesitating ever so slightly before they draw softly aside from the love and romance and adventure they have hidden so secretly. Judy tingled with expectancy just as she did when the lights in the auditorium were lowered and the orchestra was hushed. What did the day hold behind those lifting gray curtains and those hushed notes of bird song?

The breakfast gong sounded suddenly, and she scurried to her washstand. At the present moment it held nothing but an aching head and—she sniffed—kippers for breakfast. She hated kippers. . . . How horrid of mother to have them on her birthday.

II

The day began badly. Her father and mother, already oppressed by the heat, assured her rather languidly that they were glad she had been born and gave her a lovely, silverbacked hairbrush that she didn't want. . . . It was not in keeping with that austere west room.

Charles, looking more than ever like a boneless Sarah, gave her a set smile and a lovely little pair of earrings. Overcome with remorse, she kissed him for the first time for days. He draped a listless arm about her shoulders, rather as though she had been a coat hanger, but did not kiss her in return.

Major Murray and Jean had sent her a box of chocolates. Sarah laid a dead mouse at her feet. . . . Ian had not sent her anything. This last omission hurt so much that she refused kipper petulantly and ate toast and marmalade in a damping silence.

When breakfast was over they all separated and went their ways rather disagreeably. . . . It really was very hot, most unusual for the Highlands in September. . . . Lady Cameron went to her morning's employment of bustling about the kitchen and driving Elspeth distracted—she was one of those women who can bustle in

121

a kitchen interminably. Sir James went to the loch, Charles went to the garden, and Judy to the drawing room.

It was sweet and cool and dim in the drawing room. She sat on the stool in front of the harpsichord and put her aching head down on her arms. Before she hid her eyes she had seen Charles striding up and down the lawn with short, irritated strides. . . . Silly boy. . . . He'd get himself into a lather in this heat. . . . Why didn't she *do* something about him? What was the good of this endless waiting? . . . If only Ian had written to her on her birthday. Yet why should he? He was coming to-night and would then have ample opportunity for bowing coldly and stiffly and wishing her many happy returns. . . . Hot, angry tears squeezed themselves out of her tightly closed eyes. The door handle turned, and she clinked them furiously away as Angus came in. . . . How dared he intrude on her!

"Greetin'?" inquired the tactless Angus. " 'Tis a wean ye are, ah'm thinkin'! Greetin' because the Laird no sent ye a letter? Are ye no shamed?"

"I'm not greeeting!" stormed Judy.

"Na, na," said Angus, " 'tis juist that yer face is wet. . . . Ye should be shamed for a' that. A puir weak-minded, soft wee wean!" He fumbled in the capacious pocket in his coattails and produced a little packet. "The Laird was round wi' this for ye at six i' the mornin'—the more fule he."

Judy pounced on it. "Angus! Why didn't you give it to me at breakfast time?"

"I'll no be showin' up the Laird for a fule afore all they foreigners. . . . He to be givin' presents to a woman! . . . Hoots!"

Judy tore the paper off the packet. It was Robert Louis Stevenson's poems. She gave a little gurgle of joy and turned to the flyleaf. "Judith Cameron. September, 1934." How funny of him to put Judith. Everyone called her Judy. She opened the harpsichord and pulled out the other book, laying it beside her gift. She turned to the flyleaf. "Judith Macdonald, August 18th, 1745." There was a queer likeness in the two handwritings, and she closed the book with shaky fingers.

Angus was standing beside her looking over her shoulder. "Ay," he said, and ambled out of the room.

III

The day dragged on, getting hotter and hotter, and no one seemed to have anything to say except: "There'll be a storm before night. . . ." They were all very cross.

Judy's west room, that was so cool in the mornings, was terribly hot as she changed for dinner. Her head still ached a little, and she felt unutterably tired and rather frightened, as though some ordeal lay before her that she had not the strength to face. She wished her birthday party was safely over, even though the end of it would mean another parting from Ian. . . . Well, it wasn't over, and she must get ready for it. . . . She put on her best frock, a pale green one that made her look like a dryad, and brushed her hair round her fingers so that it lay in rows of little curls in the nape of her neck. As she brushed she read R.L.S., propped open on the dressing table in front of her.

> Trusty, dusky, vivid, true,
> With eyes of gold and bramble-dew,
> Steel-true and blade-straight,
> The great artificer
> Made my mate.
>
> Honour, anger, valour, fire;
> A love that life could never tire,

123

Death quench or evil stir,
The mighty master
Gave to her.

Teacher, tender, comrade, wife,
A fellow-farer true through life,
Heart-whole and soul-free,
The august father
Gave to me.

How nice for Mrs. Stevenson to have that said about her. She probably found R.L.S. very trying at times, but one could put up with a lot from a man who said things like that about one. . . . She looked at herself in the glass as, in honor of the occasion, she emphasized the determined curve of her lips with her lipstick. . . . Did *she* look like that? . . . She was dusky and straight, and she hoped she was true. . . . Not to Charles, whispered her conscience, as she screwed in Charles's earrings. . . . But then Charles was not her mate. . . . Honor, valor, anger, fire. . . . Yes, it would be nice to be like that.

She went downstairs before it was dinner time, hoping perhaps that Ian would be early. But he wasn't. There was no one in the drawing room but Angus, prowling round and flicking aimlessly at the furniture with his dirty yellow duster.

She turned slowly round in front of him so that he could admire her frock. "Do you like it, Angus?" she asked.

"Ou, ay," said Angus indifferently, "it's no' that bad. . . . But I prefer yon," and he pointed to the oak chest in the middle window.

"What yon?" asked Judy.

"Hae ye no' found the dress i' the chest?" asked Angus incredulously.

"No," whispered Judy. She never went near the middle window. She had never, since the first day when she

124

sat sobbing on it, so much as touched the oak chest. . . .
Her heart beat. . . . Yesterday the book of songs and
today a dress. . . . It was too much. . . . Judith was
creeping too close. . . . "Don't, Angus," she said,
"please don't."

But Angus took no notice. He opened the chest and
took it out, wrapped up in a soft old linen sheet smelling
of moth balls. "I've ta'en care o' it for ye," he said, and
handing it to her he immediately, according to his irri-
tating habit, turned and ambled out of the room.

Judy undid the sheet, and the little moth balls fell on
the floor at her feet and rolled away. It was what she
had known it would be, a white dress yellow with age,
its stiff silk cracked and stained. It was made in two
pieces, a bodice with panniers and a skirt embroidered
with little yellow roses. Poor dress, so torn and stained
and smelling of damp and camphor; and once it had
been as fresh and sweet as the green dryad's dress she
had on. She held it tightly clasped to her as though it
had been a little child that she was comforting.

Steps sounded in the hall, Major Murray's loud
laugh, and Jean's high-pitched voice. Judy had just time
to lay the dress and the sheet on the chair in the dark
corner by the left-hand window, praying that no one
might see them. . . . Go near that middle window to put
it back in the chest she would not.

They came in, the Major loud and cheerful in immac-
ulate black and white, and the fair-haried, pretty Jean
in a Paris frock, all dressed up to do her honor. And Ian
in Highland evening dress with his hair brushed to admiration and his shoes very nearly clean. She had never
seen him look so tidy, and she was almost more touched
by his efforts to look respectable than she had been by
the gift of R.L.S. at six o'clock in the morning. Then
Sarah came in in a pink bow, conducting Sir James and
Lady Cameron and Charles, all in their war paint, and
the party began.

Dinner was not particularly successful. It was almost too hot to eat, and the conversation would keep veering round to fish, a dangerous topic. Sir James and Major Murray were experienced fishermen and Charles was not; yet Charles that season had been the most successful of the three of them. . . . The favoritism of the gods is hard to understand.

"That fish you landed two days ago—an eighteen-pounder, I think you said?" murmured the Major nastily.

Charles coughed modestly. "Eighteen and three-quarters. I was in the water twenty minutes up to the waist. . . . We're eating it now. . . . Jolly good, too."

Sir James refused it and helped himself to salad only. "Now how much did that fish I landed last week weigh? Nineteen, I think."

"Eighteen and a half," said Charles.

"Nineteen, I think, Charles," replied Sir James in a gentle, but firmly legal, voice.

"Eighteen and a half. I weighed the perishin' blighter myself."

"Ah, but I think there was some slight error in calculation. The kitchen weights are so misleading. Judy thought there was some quite natural confusion."

"You should have weighed the creature yourself," said the Major. "Never trust another man to weigh your fish."

Sir James's manner showed slight signs of asperity. "I had intended to; but Charles, without my knowledge, very kindly saw to it while I was taking a hip bath in my room. Judy told me what he was doing through the keyhole, but by the time I'd got into my bathwrap and down into the kitchen the fish had unfortunately been cut up for domestic purposes."

"I shouldn't let a young man like that into the family, if I were you."

"Perfectly trustworthy," snapped Charles; "Public

School code of honor and all that." Charles's temper, usually beyond reproach, had lately shown distinct signs of fraying at the edges.

"Look at the sunset," said Jean hastily.

The dining room, like the drawing room, faced west. They looked. The sky was a curious molten orange. Ben Fhalaich was a deep purple and seemed to have drawn so near to them that they felt they could have put out their hands and touched it.

"Why, there's another mountain behind Ben Fhalaich!" ejaculated Judy.

"No, it's a storm," said Ian. It was. Great sullen blueblack clouds were gathering behind Ben Fhalaich, stealthily piling up, as though a huge unseen army were casting up earthworks to protect them when the time came to discharge the thunder and lightning of their guns. In the garden there was a deep, ominous, hot silence; not even the twitter of a frightened bird or the rustle of a leaf.

"It's horrible," said Judy.

"It may not come," consoled the Major. "These storms often travel round the mountains for days and never break."

Ian, weather-wise in his own country, looked at the sky with narrowed eyes. "It'll come, but not yet," he said.

Even as he spoke a sudden puff of hot wind scourged the garden like a whiplash. The birds suddenly came to terrified life and fluttered hither and thither, giving sharp little cries of fear. The leaves of the rosebushes, suddenly lifted by the wind, showed their pale undersides. . . . It looked as though they had all turned white with fear. . . . Then, as suddenly as it had arisen, the wind dropped again, and that horrible, hushed silence came back.

They finished their dinner hastily and went out into the garden to look at the strange, beautiful sunset—all but Lady Cameron, who preferred her embroidery to sunsets any day.

They stood in an apprehensive row, watching. The orange sky now had a smoky look, almost like a London fog. It seemed to be pressing down on them so that they gasped for breath. The clouds behind Ben Fhalaich had climbed a little higher. They were inky now, with an edge of pure gold. From very far away came a low mutter of thunder, echoing on and on from mountain to mountain, endlessly.

"Miles away yet," said the Major. "Sounds like the devil rolling his bath tub round hell," and he gave a little uneasy laugh. His facetiousness cheered no one. Judy, hardly knowing what she did, slipped a frightened hand into Ian's and had it gripped reassuringly. Charles saw her. He turned quickly away, throwing his cigarette end savagely at the nearest rosebush, and went to Lady Cameron.

He sat down opposite her, violently, saying nothing, his eyes hot. Lady Cameron, looking at him, pricked her finger and sighed. . . . How very tiring youth was. . . . No sooner had one got rid of one's own, with its fevers and frets, than one started all over again with one's children's. . . . If only dear Charles would refrain from making a scene just now, when it was so hot, she'd be obliged. . . . Well, she'd have nothing to do with the affairs of her grandchildren. . . . Judy, the horrid little minx, should cope with those herself, and then, perhaps, she'd have some sympathy with her poor mother.

"Why don't we get out of this horrible hole?" demanded Charles suddenly.

"Judy and her father like it," sighed Lady Cameron, "and they're so obstinate I can't move them."

"I'd shift 'em soon enough if I was married to 'em," snorted Charles. "They don't know what's good for 'em. We'll all go barmy if we stay here much longer. There's something dashed odd about the place. . . . Look at Judy, now."

He leaned back in his chair and lit another cigarette with a sort of placid bitterness. . . . It seemed the dear boy was not going to make a scene after all. . . . Lady Cameron heaved a sigh of relief and threaded her needle.

"I'm worried about Judy," she murmured. "I'm so afraid of her turning spirtualistic. My sister Adelaide did, and it made her blood pressure go wrong."

"It's my blood pressure that'll go wrong if we don't get out of here pretty soon," Charles informed her. "I shall be doing murder very shortly. . . . That fellow Macdonald! . . . Dragging her up an' down mountains burbling away about the darned Jacobites, an' round an' round his tenants' beastly cottages burbling away about the sufferings of the poor, an' watching sunsets an' burbling away about the equality of man an' what not. . . . It's not healthy."

The entrance of Angus with coffee checked his eloquence, and Lady Cameron turned to the proffered tray with relief, even though Angus's expression as he offered it to her was that of poisoner-in-chief to the Borgias.

"Shall I pour out yours, Charles?" Charles grunted. "Sugar?" Charles grunted. "Sir James and the others are out in the garden watching the sunset, Angus."

"If they prefair sunsets to their drink the mair fules they."

"I wish you to take it out to them, Angus."

Angus glanced gloomily out of the window. "Na, na. They're the yont side o' the garden. I'll no' put the strain on me rheumatics." He banged the tray down on the table. "Let them bide. Keekin' at sunsets at their age! Losh! If their brew's cold 'twill teach 'em a lesson as is sair needed."

He removed himself, growling. The others drifted in

129

from the garden and stood about in depressed attitudes. The oppression of the coming storm was over them all, and, a birthday though it was, no one had the energy to think what to do next. It was Jean who suddenly suggested, "Judy, play to us. That poor old harpsichord never gets played on."

Before Judy could stop her she had flown to the harpsichord and opened it. "What's this?" she said, and held up the book of songs.

Judy suddenly had the horrible feeling that her clothes were being torn off her. . . . They would strip her naked. . . . They would strip Judith naked. . . . They would know everything. . . . They would look with prying eyes at something that concerned Ian and Angus and herself alone. It took all her self-control to pull herself together and think what to do. She took the book gently away from Jean. . . . Come what might they should not read that inscription.

"It's an old book of songs that I found tumbled down in the back of the bookcase in my room," she said lightly, and sat down on the sofa, opening the book for them to see. They crowded round her, forgetting the heat and the storm in their interest. Only Ian stood aloof by the fireplace, not joining in the chorus of exclamations. . . . She was thankful to him for that.

"Fancy Ian not finding it!" exclaimed Jean. "Idiot. Just like him. . . . You didn't know it was there, did you, Ian?"

"No," said Ian. He detached himself from the fireplace and stood in front of Judy. "May I see it?" His request sounded rather like a command, but Judy held tightly to the book and shook her head. . . . He should not see it in front of all these people.

"Well, really, Judy," said Lady Cameron, "let the poor man see it. It's *his* book."

"No," said Judy.

Suddenly she could not bear it any longer. They were

buzzing all round her like a lot of wasps. She got up and broke away from them, going to the harpsichord. . . . She would play to them. . . . Anything to keep them quiet.

"I don't know the songs well enough to sing them," she lied. I'll play you something else. . . . Charles, put Sarah in the dining room. . . . She'll howl."

She played an air of Bach's, her fingers, unused to the harpsichord, going at first stumblingly over the buttercup-yellow keys. The air, formal, precise, cheerful, exquisitely neat and self-assured, stepped gaily out into the room, restoring to all of them but Charles a sense of the ordered continuity of life and its essential happiness. It was a legacy from a world that had been smaller and therefore less confusing, where men had been more certain of belief, and women, their lives and experience restricted, had made of every gesture and every household activity a thing of lovely and paramount importance. While the music lasted they were back in that world, certain, contented, polite, and a little self-satisfied. Then Judy stopped playing and they sighed, overwhelmed again with uncertainties and discontent.

Charles rose to his feet. "How about a rubber in the smoking room?" he asked pathetically. Bach's music made him perfectly miserable. He was not sufficiently musical to enjoy it or sufficiently unmusical to be indifferent to it. He felt exactly as Sarah did, howling in the dining room.

"I hate music after dinner," he said apologetically. "It's so depressing! And there's such a deuced long time to wait before one can have another meal to restore one's morale."

The Major got up with alacrity. "Bridge by all means."

"Who's to make the fourth?" asked Sir James. "Judy and Jean don't care for bridge. . . . Macdonald?"

131

"My bridge is on a par with my shooting," Ian warned them.

"Then it'll have to be you, mater," said Charles decidedly.

Lady Cameron heaved herself up, sighing.

"If you consistently call very low, mother," comforted Judy, "you can be dummy quite a lot and get no end of little naps."

"I found that out before you were born, dear," said Lady Cameron, and led the bridge players gloomily to the smoking room. Jean, with a glance at her brother and Judy, smiled a tactful smile and followed them.

As the door closed behind her it seemed to Judy that the lights in the theater were dimming and the great curtains trembling. . . . The adventure was going to begin. . . . Her heart pounded oddly, and her hands felt sticky and hot. Ian was leaning on the harpsichord, his eyes fixed greedily on the book propped in front of her.

"Is it very old?"

"Seventeen-forty-five," said Judy.

He stretched out his hand for it, a little impatient. "Is the date written in it? May I see? . . . Hang it all, Judy, it *is* my book."

Judy put her hands on it. She didn't want him to take it yet, for she was afraid. "Shall I sing you one of the songs?" she said.

"Please." He went to the window and stood looking out.

She sang a song set to one of the queer, wailing tunes that were like lamenting bagpipes. What he thought she could not tell. His broad back looked stolid and immovable.

The wind that goes whistling a-down the deep corrie
Is one with the pines and the larches he sways,
The clouds that are gathering silently, swiftly,
Are one with the weeping of dark autumn days.

Out on the moor the whaups cry to each other,
Far over the sea the gull calls to his mate,
In the gray croft the babe shouts for his mother,
Each tumbling wee burn loves a river in spate.
Only my soul is bere of its lover,
Let alone in its anguish to mourn and to wait.

The high stars that circle above the steep mountains
Are one with the depth and the light of the sky,
The fish that lie gleaming like silver and opal
Are one with the stream that flows silently by.
In my dim room the tall shadows are leaping
To play with the firelight that flickers and gleams,
Hid in far corners soft colors lie sleeping,
Awaiting the touch of the moon's sliding beams.
I only alone am watching and weeping,
Companioned only in torment of dreams.

She finished the song and sat shivering, waiting, her
eyes on her hands still lying on the keys. . . . They were
in it now, she felt, in it up to the neck.

Ian, without a word, came to her and took the book,
carrying it back to the window to the fading light. She
knew, without looking, that he had turned at once to the
flyleaf. He read the inscription aloud. "Judith Macdonald, her book. Given to her on August 18th, 1745, by
her husband, Ranald Macdonald. Dearest Judith, while
I am away you are to write down all your pretty songs
in this book so that not one of them is lost. When I
come back you will sit at your harpsichord and sing
them to me." He looked round at her, excited. "It's
amazingly interesting. Do you realize who these two
are?"

Judy forced herself to raise her head and look at him.
"Yes. The two you told me about the first day we came.
. . . She blocked up the middle window. . . . He must

have given her that book before he went off to fight for Charles Edward."

"The poor beggar was killed," said Ian.

"Yes. She wrote down her songs as he told her, but she never sang them to him."

Ian looked again at the inscription. "When I come back you will sit at your harpsichord and sing them to me." Suddenly he threw the book aside and swung round, leaning on the harpsichord, looking at Judy. "When I come back."

"But he didn't come back," she whispered.

"Didn't he? Perhaps he has."

Judy looked at him. He was changed. She didn't know him. Some tremendous excitement had taken hold of him, and he seemed hardly to know what he was doing or saying. He was like another man.

"What do you mean?" she asked, her voice sharp with terror.

His voice rang out in the strangely hushed room. "How do the dead come back?"

Judy clasped her hands together tightly. That mounting tide that had so often nearly submerged her in this room was mounting again, and she felt she might fight it, beat it off. If it came right up it would drown her. "They don't," she whispered. "The dead are dead."

Ian was looking at her, his eyes burning her; and she turned her head away. She could not meet his eyes.

"They're not," he said, "they are alive. They possess the living."

Possession! That fear that had been lying at the back of her mind, haunting her, all through her time at Glen Suilag, leaped out now and seized her, just as the first flash of lighting shone out over the garden, showing up Ian's figure black and frightening. She put her hands over her face. "The storm," she cried, "it's coming."

Ian was oblivious alike of the storm and of her terror. "Judy, don't you see what it means?"

"What what means?"

"The compulsion of the past upon us both. . . . When I first came here I felt as though I were possessed, as though some other man had come into me. Ideals and memories that were not my own took hold of me. A dead man laid hands on me. A dead man who planned to build Utopia here and died before he'd built it is finishing his work through me."

"You mean Ranald Macdonald, who wrote on the flyleaf of that book?"

"Yes. That's how the dead come back. They live in the living."

Judy peeped through her fingers, whispering: "And me? What of me?"

"Judith Macdonald, his wife, came to you and took possession of you when you came to the glen weeks ago. . . . Didn't she?"

"No, no," she cried, "it's not possible—the return of the dead—it's terrible."

His words came pouring out in an excited flood. "Why is it terrible? It does away with death. Ranald Macdonald began to build Utopia in Glen Suilag. He must have sickened at the loathsomeness of the world and tried to create a spot of decency in his own place. . . . They must have thought him mad, as they think me mad. . . . And then they killed him, as they kill all madmen. But death couldn't stamp him out. He lives and works in me."

"And Judith?" whispered Judy.

"He loved her as I love you." His excited voice dropped queerly, as though he were remembering words spoken long ago. "She was the sun and moon and stars above the glen, the candle and the warm flame at its heart."

Again came the lightning, pouring a flood of white light over the garden and the wood and Ben Fhalaich, and the thunder, nearer now, echoed again round the hills. The terror of it broke down Judy's last defenses. Her fight was done, and the flood of sorrow pouring over her. She jumped up, letting herself go in a crazy excitement that was deeper than Ian's. "The lightning!" she cried. "I hate it! I hate it! It reminds me of what I did to you. It brings it all back. That ghastly injury I did you!"

As her self-control went, Ian's began to come back. "What injury?" he asked. "Judy, what are you talking about?"

She ran across the room, tearing herself away when he tried to stop her, and dropped down on her knees by the middle window, her head on the oak chest. She began to sob and cry out pitifully, though only fragments of what she said came to him. "O God, O God, let me die in the hilltops where men never come, and only the whaups are crying and the water weeping. . . . Water is sweeter than blood and rain than tears. . . . I can't wash it out! All the water in the world will not wash away the injury I did you. I can block up the window in the wall, but it's open in my heart, letting in death."

He was shocked into complete normality. He was himself again—Ian Macdonald. "Judy! Judy! Good God!" He went to her and pulled her to her feet gently, holding her. He was terrified for her.

The lightning flickered again, and she hid her face against him, crying out, "I can't bear it! I can't bear it! Will nothing stop it!"

"The lightning, Judy?" he asked, and then, in alarm, "Judy! Judy!"

"No." She raised her head and sanity came slowly back to her. The expression of almost crazy grief that had distorted her face slipped away. She was Judy once more. They leaned against each other, exhausted and bewildered, but themselves again.

"What was I saying?" she whispered. "I don't think I

knew what I was saying. . . . Was it me that was talking?"

"You were dreaming," said Ian, "that was all." He comforted her as though she were a child who had just had a nightmare, stroking her hair and kissing her gently.

"What's happening to us?" she asked.

"We don't know yet," he said; "we must wait."

They still stood clinging together till with a sudden exclamation Judy pushed him away and went back to the harpsichord. She sat there, silent and shivering, and he stood where she had left him, silent. Gradually it seemed to them that the world righted itself, as after an earthquake. Ian spoke first. He was his usual rather shy self and spoke in halting, jerky sentences.

"Judy, forgive me. I've frightened you nearly to death. And I had no business to tell you that I loved you. It was unpardonable. I did not mean to. It was as though someone else spoke."

From the other end of the hall a door banged, and they heard voices. The others were coming back, and Judy began to sob weakly, for it seemed to her that they were no further on. They had had a strange and rather horrible experience. and yet they knew no more than they had known before. She could not even remember what were the wild things that she had said. Those great curtains had lifted and then dropped. That tide had swept over her for a moment and then, it seemed, had thrown her back to shore again.

"The others," she sobbed, "and I can't find my handkie."

Ian came to her and knelt by her, finding her handkerchief for her and trying to calm her. "Here's your handkie. . . . Judy, we must leave this. We're running into a maze we don't understand. We'll just wait a little, shall we, till we've found out the pattern of it?"

"Yes," whispered Judy. "Oh, how tired I am! . . . Are you?"

"Yes." He put his head down on her lap for a moment, then got up. "They're coming. I'd better go."

He went out through the window into what was now a stifling, muttering darkness, pierced with zigzags of flame. Judy sat choking down her sobs as the others came surging in, thankful to the darkness that hid her face.

"There's going to be the deuce of a storm," trumpeted the Major. "We must get along back if we don't want to be drowned. . . . Where's Ian?"

"He's gone on," whispered Judy.

"Such a promising rubber!" mourned Charles. "There'd have been plenty of time to play it out."

Sir James went to a window. "Why not wait till the storm's over?"

"No," said the Major, "it'll last all night by the look of the sky. . . . Come along, Jean."

Jean looked at the gleaming, horrible darkness outside. "I'm not going to come along," she vowed. "I shall spend the night here."

"Won't you stay too, Major?" said Lady Cameron, wondering wildly where he was to be put. . . . Ridiculous, the lack of furniture in this house! . . . Dear Charles had better give up his room and go to the box room.

"No, I'll be getting along. Good-by. Such a pleasant evening. Sorry not to finish the rubber. Ian and I will be over in the morning to tell you we're still alive." He trumpeted himself out of the room, followed by Sir James and Charles.

Lady Cameron seated herself on the sofa and became garrulous. "We heard you singing, Judy. So mournful and depressing. It reminded me of that poem of Christina Rossetti's—'Does the road wind uphill all the way, yes, to the very end.' Your father read it to me when we were engaged. . . . I thought it was so tactless of him." A vivid flash of lightning cut her short for a moment, and Judy cowered back. "Pull the curtains, Jean, while I light the candles. Judy's an idiot about storms, has been from a baby. . . . There's nothing more depressing than playing bridge with men. Always asking one why one did so and so. It's bad enough to have to think what you ought to do without having to think why you thought you ought to do it."

While she talked she lit the candles, and Jean drew the curtains, those that hid the scar of the middle window as well as the others. Judy began to revive a little. She felt less frightened with the curtains drawn between her and that horrible storm.

Charles reappeared. "Mater, what induced you to lead the queen of hearts like that?" he asked in an injured voice.

"I thought the king was out," said Lady Cameron firmly.

Sir James reappeared. "But why did you think the king was out, dear?" he asked. "You know it's not enough to think what you ought to do; you must think, too, why you ought to do it."

"Now you go and have a game of chess with Charles in the smoking room, for goodness' sake. . . . Jean will excuse you. . . . Take him away, Charles. . . . I won't be lectured to on bridge in a thunderstorm." They went. "There, now we've got rid of the two darlings for the rest of the evening. It was clever of me to think of that chess; if I hadn't Daddie'd have been the whole evening going on about that queen of hearts. He's so wonderfully tenacious. The secret of his success, of course, but trying in the home."

There was a sudden blinding flash, and almost simultaneously a crash overhead.

"It's here," said Jean.

Lady Cameron got up. "I shall go to bed and put my

139

head under the clothes. I don't like storms any more than Judy does really, only I've got more self-control. . . . Good night, Jean, dear. . . . Good night, Judy. . . . Why, you've been crying!"

Judy held up her white, tear-stained face to be kissed, "Storms frighten me so."

"Little donkey!" said her mother. "Pull yourself together. You're looking exactly like your Aunt Adelaide."

She went, and the two girls were together. Jean crossed to the left-hand window and pulled back the curtain for a moment. "Oh, Judy, you must look! The lightning over Ben Fhalaich is wonderful. Come and see."

"No," began Judy, "I hate it, I——" She stopped. Jean had seen the dress and picked it up.

"Judy, what is it? It's perfectly lovely. Where did you find it?"

Judy was in agony. . . . Again. . . . First the book and now the dress. "It's only an old dress I found in the oak chest," she said.

Jean went on examining it and exclaiming in delight at the little yellow roses and the panniers and the holes and the stains. Judy could have screamed. It was as though someone were pulling about her own little child.

"Put it on, Judy," said Jean at last. "I want to see what it looks like."

Judy shrank back. "No."

"Why not? It'll take our minds off the storm. . . . Judy, don't be such a goat. . . . I'll skin you."

Why not? thought Judy suddenly. Why not be brave and go through with this thing now? The finding of Judith's book and the singing of Judith's songs had carried her a little way into the adventure that she knew was coming to her. Perhaps if she put on Judith's dress, if she put her body inside the silk folds that had once draped the living body of Judith, perhaps then their two

140

lives would merge and the flood would roll over her again and would carry her, this time, right out beyond the confusions of time and space to a place where she would understand.

She stood up, very straight and slim, and held her arms up while Jean pulled the green dryad's dress over her head. Then, taking the skirt with the little yellow roses from Jean, she stepped into it, and slipped her arms through the sleeves of the bodice that Jean held for her. The strong, acrid smell of camphor was in her nostrils. Jean pulled and patted and hooked, and the stiff folds fell into place. She stood there—Judith Macdonald.

"It's a perfect fit," cried Jean. 'It might have been made for you. . . . You look adorable, Judy."

The patter of thunder rain began. The storm was on them in good earnest now. The fierce drops came louder and faster, and mingled with them Judy heard the sound of footsteps on the terrace outside. . . . It was Ian. . . . Ian coming back. . . . She knew it was Ian. "Be quiet, be quiet!" she whispered to Jean, "I must listen."

"What for?" asked Jean, round-eyed.

"Oh, can't you be quiet!" cried Judy. "Didn't you hear him?"

"Who?" asked Jean, scared. "I only heard the rain." She gripped Judy's arm. "Judy, Judy, what's the matter with you?"

Judy shook her off. . . . She had heard the steps again. . . . They were halting and dragging. . . . "Let go of me!" she cried to Jean. "Why can't you go?"

Jean, terrified, went. Judy stood still, listening tensely. She could hear nothing now except the pouring rain outside, but she was conscious again of the mounting tide creeping close to her and of the great curtains trembling.

She looked at the middle window. Its curtains were closely drawn; but as she looked they, too, trembled a little. Terror seized her. . . . Was there someone outside trying to get in? . . . But no one *could* get in, the window was blocked up. . . . But they were moving. . . . Oh, God, what would she see through that middle window?

In a moment she knew. The curtains were dragged aside and he stood there, leaning against the window frame, gasping, the lightning flickering behind him. His kilt was torn and muddy, his hair, tied back in a queue, matted and untidy. One hand was pressed to his side, and a red stain was creeping through his fingers over his tattered shirt. His face looked white as death. As she looked it seemed as though life drained away from it, leaving it like those sightless faces that had marched by her in procession on her first night.

Then the tide rolled right over her, and it was all dark. She could not see anything any more. When Jean came back with Lady Cameron she was lying on the floor in a faint, a tumbled heap bunched up in faded white satin starred with yellow roses.

The middle window was as usual.

BOOK II

Union

All that is not One must ever
Suffer with the wound of Absence,
And whoever in Love's city
Enters, finds but room for one
And but in One-ness, Union.

—JÁMÍ

CHAPTER I

I

On an August day in 1745 Judith Macdonald was riding up the further slope of Ben Caorach on her gray mare. It was a lovely evening. The sun, dipping behind the mountains, threw up their peaks and ridges into the likeness of a stark, midnight sea of toppling, frozen waves. Dark they were, and a little ominous, waiting as though held back in leash. But the sky was tender and gentle, pale green like a bird's egg and scattered all over with little clouds like curling golden feathers. Earlier in the day it had been very hot, but now there was a delicious freshness in the air and heavenly scents of cooling earth and green things refreshed and grateful. The crying of the whaups and the clip-clop of the horses' hoofs on the rough path stood out sharp and clear against the deep silence.

Judith straightened her tired back and pressed her lips together to keep herself from crying with the pain of her aching limbs. All day long she had been riding side-saddle up and down mountain paths, and it had been much too hot for her beautiful, new, dark-blue riding habit with the flowing skirt, and her wide-brimmed hat with the white plumes had got tighter and tighter as the day went on until it made her head ache. When she had ridden off that morning she had thought it didn't matter much if her lovely clothes were uncomfortable provided that she looked a dream, but now she wasn't quite so sure. . . . She didn't feel a dream. . . . Her stays hurt her, and her belt was too tight. . . . She would have liked to ask Ranald to stop a little and let her rest, but she didn't like to. He was so very anxious to get home before dark. . . . And she didn't want him to think he had married a weakling.

"Is it tired that you are, Judith?" he asked.

"No," she lied, "I feel as fresh as when I started. Mountain air is like wine, only nicer. . . . Is it not beautiful now?"

"Yes," he said, and was silent again, his eyes taking in every shadow and every flush of heather and verifying every landmark of lichened rock and crag. For he had been away from Glen Suilag for a very long time and to return to it was a satisfaction too great for words; and he was returning to it now, for the first time, as its master. While he was away his tyrannical old father had died. He was now the Laird and could do with his inheritance what he wished. . . . And he *would* do what he wished. . . . He would show them!

Judith stole a glance at him. He looked a little grim and determined. Though she worshiped him she was sometimes just a tiny bit afraid of him. He could be exquisitely gentle sometimes, and at other times a little bit fierce. He was a man of almost savage loyalties and of an idealism that could, she knew, be ruthless at need. What he cared for—the Jacobite cause, the Highlands, Glen Suilag—he cared for very deeply; and now that he had married a wife he cared for her, too, very deeply, but the wife in question knew quite well that she would have to be utterly at one with him in all his loves and work or else their life would be a misery. For such an individualist as Ranald Macdonald there would be no room for two in the house of love, but only one. Judith, a very individual person also, must so submerge her life in his, like a drop of wine poured into water, that she enriched while she was lost in him. This she knew. This sacrifice of herself she had made joyously and deliberately, when she had married him that morning.

Joyously but a little apprehensively, for how should a bride of eighteen not feel a little frightened? She was a

146

Lowland girl, and she was marrying a Highlander who would carry her right away to a life of which she knew nothing in a strange new world behind the barrier of the mountains. Moreover her family, of Hanoverian sympathies, did not like Ranald Macdonald. He was odd, they thought, with queer ideas and questionable politics, and an air of arrogance that exasperated them. For though Ranald, unlike most Highlanders, was a traveled, cultured man, who had met Judith in the course of his travels, nothing in their opinion could alter the fact that he was a Highlander and a Jacobite, and therefore a barbarian and traitor, with no reason whatever, that they could see, for giving himself airs. Ranald had disliked Judith's relations as much as they had disliked him, and said so. She knew, when she married him, that she had cut herself adrift forever from her old life. . . . The doing of it had taken some courage.

Her final rift with her own people, the cutting of the knot that bound her to them, had been the manner of her wedding. That had infuriated them and had nearly given her uncle and guardian, a man of portly habit, an apoplectic fit. Ranald had insisted that his wedding night must be spent in his own home. Having captured his Judith, he was not going to spend a moment longer in her depressing Lowlands among her fatiguing relations. . . . He had expressed himself more prettily, but his meaning had been clear. . . . So the entire wedding party had ridden north, at great fatigue and expense and acerbation of temper, that the wedding might take place at the house of a relation of Ranald's own, a lady who lived a day's ride only from Glen Suilag. Judith and Ranald had been married in the early morning, in their riding clothes, and had mounted their horses immediately afterwards. . . . An exasperating performance altogether, Judith's relations had considered as exasperating as Ranald himself.

Arrogant, odd, barbaric, they thought him. Judith

147

looked again at this man for whom she had left her home and outraged her kindred. Arrogant? He was a person of importance in his world, knew it and accepted it, and she loved the look of dignity that his knowledge gave him. He looked what he was—prosperous, happy, and self-assured. She was infinitely proud of him as he rode beside her, tall and strong, sitting his horse as though he were a part of it, in his tartans and bottle-green coat, with the Jacobite's white cockade in his bonnet. . . . He had said he wore the cockade as a wedding favor, but she had her suspicions that he had put it in his bonnet to annoy his relations-in-law. . . . Yes, she was very proud of him, and very proud to be his wife; but she did wish she hadn't worn her stays under her habit, they did stick in so dreadfully; and she did wish they could stop for a minute, her backache was something wicked.

They climbed on and on, the path growing rougher and steeper, for there was no road over Ben Caorach in 1745, only a rough track strewn with stones and rutted by the water that raced down it in bad weather. . . . Surely they were nearly at the top. . . . Yes. . . . Looking up, Judith could see the path end abruptly against that lovely background of golden, feathery clouds.

Her horse, as tired as she was, stumbled and nearly fell; and but for Ranald catching her arm she would have pitched over its head. He had been lost in his dreams, but now he was suddenly aware of her fatigue and jumped off his horse.

"Judith! It's a brute that I am! Off with you for a moment, and it's a rest we'll be having." He lifted her off her horse. "It's half dead that you are."

"I am not!" said Judith petulantly, and clutched his arm to keep herself from sitting down suddenly on the path.

He picked her up and carried her a few paces to the right over the turf and heather. He set her down and sat beside her, holding her against his shoulder. He took off her tight hat and she loosened her belt and tugged at her stays with sighs of relief. Their abandoned horses shook themselves, the equivalent of sighs of relief, and turned their attention to the refreshment of the inner horse.

Ranald was overcome with penitence. He kissed her and petted her. "It's a brute that I am. I was not thinking. I was dreaming of Glen Suilag," he said to her in his soft, lilting Gaelic.

Judith smiled placidly, her eyes shut. She loved it when Ranald petted her in Gaelic; it more than made up for all her aches and pains. "Is it far to Glen Suilag now?" she asked.

"Only a little way. It's down below you in the valley, though you will not be seeing it from here. But you will be seeing other things. . . . Look!"

Judith opened her eyes. They were right on the summit of Ben Caorach. It seemed as though they were on top of the world. All round them were mountaintops, peak beyond peak and ridge behind ridge, azure and amethyst and topaz, scarred with black rocks and pierced with silver spears of falling water. They could look through miles of limpid air, north, south, east, and west, with no barrier to check the outward flow of their minds. Space was theirs, with the full glory of the sky over their heads and the glory of the earth a carpet beneath their feet.

"If you stand up you will be seeing something else," said Ranald, and helped her to her feet, turning her toward the west. Far away she could see a straight blue line drawn between earth and heaven. It was the sea, cold and lovely, like a slab of sapphire pavement paving the door to paradise. It was so overwhelmingly lovely that the faculty of sight seemed to faint and die. It could not take in any more. Judith shut her eyes and listened instead. There was no sound at all. The ringing of some sheep bells and the tinkling of falling water were far away below her, so faint that their murmur was only the silence talking. The humming of the wind in her ears was not sound; it was the harp music that her heart gave out in gladness as the fingers of beauty plucked at it.

Suddenly Ranald turned to her and flung his arms round her. They stood together silently. It was the loveliest moment of their lives, lovelier than anything that had gone before or anything that came after. To Judith there came a deep sense of the joy and reality of union. They were one with all the beauty around them, and they were one with each other in a way that they had not been before. They had achieved something, she felt, that would never come to an end, and the physical union for which their bodies longed was unimportant compared to it. It was this that mattered, this unexplainable thing that was linking them not only to each other but also to this particular spot of earth in which their lot was cast, and through that to the reality of which it was a symbol.

"It is life," said Ranald suddenly.

"What is?" she asked.

"This that is born of union, this eternal thing."

So he felt it too? They stood still a moment longer until slowly and reluctantly they felt their moment creep away from them, creep away perhaps never to return; then Judith stirred and sighed a little, slipping back again into the world of her body.

"Let us go home," she said, "I am so hungry."

"Home?" said Ranald, and laughed. . . . The word sounded so sweet on her lips.

II

Half an hour later Judith stood in the big west bedroom taking off her dusty riding habit. She looked round at the big paneled, austere room. How bare it was! But she loved it. It was so cool and spacious. She looked at the big bed with its stiff, flowered chintz curtains, and her heart beat a little. . . . Ranald's father had died in it. It would be her bridal bed. She would bear her children in it. Perhaps she would die in it. Perhaps Ranald would die in it. . . . Really, beds bulked very large in life and were best not thought about too much. She turned her thoughts to less alarming subjects.

She noticed that there wasn't a single picture in the room. She and Ranald had had their portraits painted in England, and she would hang his in this room, over the mantelpiece, where she could see it when she woke up in the mornings. He could hang hers where he liked, but she wasn't going to have it here, not if she knew it. One was obliged, several times a day, to look in the glass and wish that one's nose was different, but there was no need to have one's nose on the wall as well.

Out in the garden she could see Ranald prowling round the lovely, trim, flower-filled beds. He seemed to be examining each individual petal and blade of grass. How he loved this place! And no wonder—it was perfect. How happy they would be, living out their lives together in this paradise.

She brushed out her dark curls and tied them at the nape of her neck with a yellow ribbon. It wasn't a very matronly style of hairdressing. She should, of course, now that she was Mistress Macdonald of Glen Suilag, have powdered her hair and dressed it high over a cushion, so that six inches were added to her height and miles to her importance, but there wasn't time tonight.

Ranald was waiting for her.

She slipped gleefully into her very best frock, one that Ranald hadn't seen yet. She hoped he would notice it, but there was no knowing. He wasn't always very good at noticing the things he ought to notice. She looked at herself in the glass and was obliged to own that, in spite of her nose, she looked quite lovely. The pearly white satin bodice of her dress tapered to her waist and then billowed out into panniers like full-blown roses. Creamy lace frothed round her shoulders, and her full skirt was sprinkled all over with little yellow roses. She clasped her pearls round her throat, slipped her feet into white satin slippers with high golden heels, and pattered across to the door, holding her skirts up on each side in case the floor should be dusty. . . . She had her suspicions that Ranald's servants were not all that they should be. . . . A mistress, she could see, was required in this establishment. . . . She set her jaw and tilted her chin as she pattered down the dark, shallow stairs to the parlor. . . . They would soon see they had a mistress to be reckoned with. . . . Lazy sluts! . . . She would show them!

But at the door she encountered Angus and didn't show him anything. Instead she twisted her hands together and looked at him appealingly. She was dreadfully afraid he didn't like her. When he had opened the front door to them, the funny, crusty old thing, with his red nose and thicket of beard and disreputable tartans, she had loved him on sight; but she feared the emotion was not reciprocated. He had looked at the Laird with doglike devotion, and even smiled a little at the sight of him; but when he had looked at her he had merely growled and snuffled in a very peculiar way and then ambled off. Ranald had translated these sounds and movements into an expression of esteem, but Judith had her doubts.

"Angus!" she said softly, and gave him a look that would have melted a heart of stone.

"Yer dinner's set i' the parlor," he growled. "I've no' put the eatin' parlor to richts the day. Tis no' worth the trooble for so wee a while," and he disappeared down the dark hall. . . . What did he mean? . . . A tiny shadow seemed to fall on her.

Then, forgetting it, she went into the parlor and stood

152

exulting over it. Lovely, lovely room! Its three long windows faced west and let in a flood of golden sunset light. The lovely brocade curtains and the brand-new harpsichord that they had had sent on ahead of them from Edinburgh were in place, all shining with newness. The new green paint was beautiful, though it still smelled a little, and the chairs and writing table had been polished till they shone like glass. Over the mantelpiece hung her portrait. . . . So Ranald had sent orders about that on ahead, had he? . . . She really looked quite nice, she thought, though she was simpering a bit, in her rose-pink satin with her hair powdered and a spotty spaniel with a ribbon round its neck lying at her feet.

Their dinner table was set in the middle window. It looked lovely with its glass and silver, its decanter of red wine and bowls of red roses and fruit. Through the window she could see Ranald pulling groundsel out of the rosebed, and she ran across to it to scold him. "Do not do that, Ranald! You will make your hands dirty. Come in to dinner."

He came, smiling very sweetly at her but making no comment on her frock. . . . Tiresome man! . . . As a husband he would need a lot of educating.

III

The dinner was perfect. They were too hungry at first to talk much; they merely absorbed with great rapidity whatever Angus put in front of them; but gradually as the meal went on they began to drift into one of the intimate talks that crop up at sunset when the wine and food are good and have stolen away weariness. By the time Angus left them to their dessert they were hard at it.

Ranald held up his glass so that the sunset light set

little golden sparks twinkling in the red wine. "I drink to you, m'eudaill."

Judith clinked her glass against his and smiled at him over the top of it. "And I to you, and may you never regret your wedding day."

"And may *you* never regret."

She smiled, stretching her aching limbs. "I must not drink any more toasts, Ranald; my legs feel vastly peculiar as it is. Think what we have done! Riding hell-for-leather all day long to get here by night."

Ranald leaned forward, looking at her. "Was it not worth while? Do you not think one's wedding night should be spent in one's own home?"

She met his intense look unflinchingly. The intimate things that were still to come between them had seemed unimportant on top of Ben Caorach; but now they did not seem so. She wanted them. She wanted to be one with him in every way possible. "Yes," she said, "I do. . . . They say a woman's wedding night is the most important in her life. . . . They say it changes her and sort of—roots her. . . . If that is true she ought to be rooted in the home that is to be hers for always, ought she not?"

"It is not afraid that you are?" he asked.

"Afraid of anything that could happen to me with you? . . . No!"

They were silent a moment until he pushed the dish of fruit toward her, speaking lightly. "I am thanking you for that. . . . You'll not be finished? Have another of these; they will be off the south wall."

"I could not. I have eaten too much as it is, and I want you to show me the garden before the light goes." Ranald took a peach, his third, from the dish, and her tone turned to disgust. "Oh, Ranald, hurry! . . . How men do go on eating!"

"This is my last, I promise you. . . . Sing to me, Ju-

dith, while I eat it. You said you had written a new
song."

"I have. A song for you and me." She went to the
harpsichord, fingering the spotless black and snow-
white keys lovingly. She fancied herself as musician,
composer, and poetess; and the harpsichord was Ranald's wedding gift to her. "Now do not dawdle, Ranald,
or the light will have gone off the garden. . . . Swallow
in time to the music," and she gave him a strong-mind
ed, bracing frown to counteract the suggestion of yielding in her conveyed by the words of her song.

Today there is sunlight caressing the dew,
Today clouds go chasing all over the blue,
Today echo answers the cry of the dove,
Today there is laughter and singing and love.

And now I have tasted the fulness of bliss,
And now I have given my heart with a kiss,
And now I hold heaven close clasped to my breast,
And now my whole being is hushed and at rest.

My life is now given for weal or for woe,
My life is your own now wherever we go,
My life is your vassal, your child, and your slave,
My life your possession through death and the grave.

God shield us from partings, hobgoblins, and tears,
God save us from demons and dangers and fears,
God keep us together the length of the day,
God grant we keep laughing the whole of the way.

Ranald obediently swallowed twice during the first
verse and then, entirely forgetting his peach, came and
stood behind her, his hands on her shoulders. She felt
that he had become suddenly grave. "Thank you, Judith. . . . Are you as happy as all that?"

155

She flung out her arms. "Dhé! There is not a glen in Scotland holds a girl with a happier heart than mine."

"The deil knows I would give him my soul to burn in hell if I could be sure you would say that every evening of your life until the end."

"And why should I not? Why should we not be happy for ever and ever? . . . How serious you look, Ranald!"

He turned back to the table. "One must not be too happy; they say the gods are jealous."

She felt, as she had felt when Angus had spoken to her before dinner, that a tiny shadow had fallen. She jumped up and ran to the table, trying to ward it off. "Oh, la, la! We will propitiate them!" She poured wine into her glass and raised it. "To the jealous gods!"

They drank the toast standing. The shadow was still with them when Angus returned looking intensely disagreeable.

"Hae ye no' finished?" he ejaculated. "Dod! Ye've eaten an' drunk ower muckle."

"Not quite finished, Angus," said Ranald. "Our wedding day. You must forgive us if it is a little slow we are."

Angus pointed disgustedly at the harpsichord. "When I heard yon tin kettle clatterin' I hoped ye had done. . . . Singin' i' the middle o' yer food! Hoots!"

Judith smiled sweetly at him. "The Laird told me that you do not like music, Angus. . . . I am sorry."

"I'm fond o' the pipes, but yon tin kettle—when I heard ye singing at it I just spat an' gied ower. . . . Now finish up yer vittles and yer drink. I'll no' be kep' up till all hours to help the Laird to his bed."

Ranald grinned. "Hold your tongue, Angus! Now that I have a wife I shall go to bed at the proper hour and proceed thither unassisted."

"Gr-r-r-r," said Angus nastily.

"Will you not wish us happiness, Angus?" said Judith wistfully.

He looked at her dourly, pityingly, as though she were a little robin dead on the garden path. "I can no' wish ye happiness. I had a seein' ower the fire the morn an' I seed a biodag wi' bluid upon it."

He ambled out and Judith turned to Ranald, clutching him. "Ranald! . . . Has he the two sights?"

He put an arm round her. "Not that I know of—though it is needing it he is to balance his complete lack of one brain. . . . Do not be heeding him. . . . It is old that he is and queer sometimes. No one ever takes notice of what he says. . . . Do not look like that, Judith!"

She laughed a little, trying to push the shadow away from her. "I do not believe he likes me; that is what makes him so gloomy."

"Oh, yes, he does. He will be liking you very much. He always spits when he sees newcomers, but he did not when he saw you. . . . A prodigious compliment to you, Judith."

She was still not satisfied. "Well, I hoped he would love me at sight. . . . *You* did. . . . Do I look nice in this dress?"

"You look enchanting."

"Then why could you not have said so before? It cost a fortune. My poor guardian! Well, he has got rid of me now. You will have to pay for them in future. . . . Ranald, you are not looking at my dress, you are looking out of the window."

Ranald had gone back to his seat, and his eyes were on Ben Fhalaich, purple against the golden sky. He held out his hand to her. "*You* come and look out of the window."

She came and stood behind him, her hand on his shoulder. The shadow had gone now, banished by the wonderful golden light, and they were intimate and happy again as they had been before.

"Do you think," she said, "that at evening, in paradise, they open the door and spill some of it out into our glen? That light is not earthly."

"Do you like this home that I have brought you to?"

"Why is this tongue of ours so inadequate?"

"It is not," said Ranald hungrily. "It is you that are lazy. Try."

She tried, longing to give him what he wanted. "People dream of a little country, not of this world, but enclosed in it a magic place lost and hidden in the mountains. They dream of it, but you and I have found it. . . . When you brought me home this afternoon, when we turned the corner into the glen road and I saw it for the first time, I knew I had come home. This is what I have hungered for, this sound of running water in the mountains, this scent of bog myrtle and wet earth. I am myself now that I have found it. It is all mine. I belong to Glen Suilag for ever and ever."

"And Glen Suilag belongs to you.'

Judith went back to her seat. "And its Laird?"

"And its Laird."

"Do you love me?"

"What a foolish question."

"How much?"

"Judith! You should have asked me that before dinner. That sort of thing is so much easier to do on an empty stomach."

"Ah, that must be why lovers always turn from food. . . . But try, please, Ranald. . . . You are being lazy. . . . I tried."

He leaned forward, searching for words speaking in English that she might completely understand him. She knew that he was thinking of their great moment up on Ben Caorach. "It is difficult. . . . People give the word love to so many different emotions, to affection and liking and even to lust, so that there is no word now to describe that thing that comes to only the favored among human beings, that thing that goes on and on."

"Will what you feel for me go on and on?"

"Yes. Today is its flowering time, but it has roots and it will have a fruit. It stretches back into a past we cannot remember and forward into a future we cannot see."

"Do you mean that we have loved before on this earth and that after we are dead we will come back and love again?"

"But we shall not be dead. We shall not come back as ghosts, child of my heart; we shall come back as living, immortal creatures."

"That sounds lovely, but it makes me feel very unbecomingly elongated, as though the past were pulling at my toes and the future at my head. It makes me feel very thin in the middle." She laughed and put her hands on her slim waist. "Here. . . . Even after all that dinner. . . . No, I will not think of the roots and the fruit, I will just think of the perfect flowering in our paradise of a glen."

Ranald's tone changed quickly, in a way that was characteristic of him, from gentleness to fierceness. "The glen is not a paradise yet, but it will be."

"I think it is now."

"You have only seen the heather and the clouds lying on the mountaintops; you have not seen the human beings, my crofters."

"Are they *so* disagreeable?" asked Judith apprehensively. There was a note of fanaticism in his voice that scared her.

"It is sin and misery and filth that there is in this glen, but now I have inherited the place there will not be for long." He paused, grim and challenging. "There will not be for long."

"Ranald, you alarm me. Are we to go out every

159

morning with a scrubbing brush and a pail and clean up our glen?"

He answered with a fierceness that made her jump. "We are. The world will never cease to be the filthy plague spot it is till every man has cleaned out his own stinking stable."

Judith, though finding their prospects alarming, smiled at him. "I will help you. I do not think it sounds very nice, but I will help."

He seized her hands, carried away. "Judith! Judith! Our home shall be Tirna nOg, the land of heart's desire. . . . We will build Utopia here. . . . Shall we?"

"By all means, dearest. I have always heard it is very difficult; people do not always want to be Utoped, but there is nothing like trying."

"Trying to Utope is the only thing worth doing in life."

"And loving? Loving me, I mean?"

"Yes. It is for two things that I love: to love you and build Utopia in Glen Suilag—and one day to help to build it in Scotland."

Judith stirred a little uneasily. She feared that politics were about to be mentioned. When Ranald was her ardent lover she adored him; when he was a fierce idealist she admired and respected him; but when he was a politician she simply did not like him at all. She had swallowed his politics whole, as a good wife should; but it had taken a good hard gulp to do it, in spite of the pill's jammy coating of love, and she preferred not to think about it.

"Why?" she asked anxiously.

Ranald answered with alarming intensity: "When the King comes to his own again we will all of us, with him at our head, build a new Scoutland on the old foundations of romance and chivalry that are still alive in these mountains."

"Ah, but that is all so far away," said Judith hastily. "We will not think of that now."

"But one day, Judith, it will come. . . . And it is not far away either. . . . There have been rumors lately."

"Do not talk about it, do not!" She waved her hands, trying to push him back to his former topic. If she couldn't have the lover, she preferred the idealist to the politician, any day. "What you want to do in Glen Suilag, my dear will take you all your time."

She was successful. He was back again in his dreams for his glen. "Time? What's time?" he demanded. "Only a picture frame that fit round the existence of a body, giving it a beginning and an end. Time has nothing to do with a life and its work."

"Then does work go on and on, like love?"

"A man living a life is like a man writing a book. He may break off after a few chapters, but he comes back to his work again and again until the book is finished."

"And will you and I come back again and again through the centuries until we have built paradise in our glen? Faith, but Glen Suilag will grow mighty tired of us."

"No! We are as much a part of it as the bog myrtle and the heather. It does not tire of its children."

Judith suddenly began to laugh. Really, he was too absurd! "Ranald, you madman!" She paused. "Or do you believe what you say?"

He laughed back at her. "I believe it. My creed is as good as another's. I did not learn it out of books; the hills taught it to me, and the whaups crying and the burn in the corrie. All these things go on and on. Living in the shadow of mountains makes one feel rooted in eternity. . . . Do you not think so?"

"Yes, there is nothing transitory about mountains," said Judith. "It is a lovely belief. I wonder if we shall prove it true?"

They were interrupted by Angus, even more dour

than before. "Hae ye no finished fillin' yer bellies yet?" he growled.

"No, Angus!" said Ranald, annoyed. "Go away!"

Judith made another attempt to win him. "No, do not go away, Angus. Stay and tell me that you like me. . . . Do you?"

"Gr-r-r-r," said Angus.

Ranald tried to rally him. "Angus, you have just been presented with the loveliest and most charming mistress in Scotland, and you have not even told her how much you like her."

"Do you like me, Angus?" asked Judith again.

"Ou, ay," said Angus vaguely.

Ranald tried again. "That, Angus is not sufficient praise. It is you who must learn to understand women. They like to be told how charming they are. They like to be told it all the time. It is not enough to say it once; you must go on saying it. When they do their obvious duty you must praise them for their virtue, and when they do not do it you must praise them for their charming waywardness. When they are passable to look at you must praise them for their incomparable beauty, and when they are as ugly as sin you just praise them for their intellect."

"Oh, la, la!" interrupted Judith. "*Do* you like me, Angus?"

Angus turned in complete silence and ambled to the door. There, with his back turned to them, he paused.

"It is no good," said Ranald; "it is oiling that he needs." Suddenly he became aware of something unusual in Angus's attitude. "Is anything the matter, Angus? . . . Angus!"

Angus turned round again, his eyes blazing, his ramshackle old figure vibrating with passion. "Ay. . . . There's been doin's i' the glen, ay, throughout the length an' breadth o' the Highlands. Hae ye no' heard? Ay, we've been throng i' the glen. Targes an' claymores

162

an' skeans that hae no' seen the licht o' day since Bob-
bin' John hae been unearthed by the score this twa
weeks past. The clans are ready." He paused for breath,
shooting out a finger fiercely. "Ay, they hae all been to
Glen Suilag after ye, Drummond o' Achnabar an'
Mackay o' Glen Eil an' the lave o' 'em; but I told 'em as
ye were occupied wi' a woman." He ambled to the door,
where he shot out a finger again. "I've packed all ye'll
need in readiness for ye."

A chair crashed to the ground as Ranald leaped to
his feet, beside himself with excitement. "Angus!"

"Ay?"

"Has the Prince landed? Why the devil did you not
tell me before?"

"Ye were occupied wi' a woman. . . . Drummond o'
Achnabar will fetch ye the nicht." His voice rose to a
shout. "The clan is up. Ye will ride wi' it the nicht."

He turned and went out. Ranald, still wild with excitement, turned to Judith. "Judith, it has come!"

Judith sat perfectly still at the table, her hands
clenched and her eyes blazing. A sick rage possessed
her. "War!" she said, "on our wedding day!"

"At last!" shouted Ranald. "After all these years of
waiting! I have dreamed of it, thought of it, planned for
it; but I never dreamed it was so near. Dhé! Dhé! And
I have been away from Glen Suilag for months! Good
God, Judith, if we had stayed away longer we might
have missed it all!"

"Yes," said Judith, "if we had stayed away longer we
might have missed it all. . . . Do you mean to go tonight?"

Something in her tone penetrated Ronald's excitement. "Judith? . . . But, of course."

She jumped to her feet, her cheeks scarlet, her cruel
rage tearing at her and mounting beyond her control.
"Why could he not have stayed where he was? Why
must he come back again to ruin Scotland? Was not the

last time enough? Was there not enough blood poured out then to satisfy these Stuarts? What right have they to climb to their thrones on broken bodies?"

Ranald seized her hands. "Judith! Judith! You do not know what you say!"

She pulled her hands away furiously. "And will you go tonight? Will you leave me on our wedding day?"

"Judith, I must."

"Must? No! You can follow them tomorrow."

"Judith, how can I? The clan marches tonight. I must be with it."

Desperately she tried to get control of herself. It was no good to be in a rage. That would not move him. She must think of arguments. If she could keep him for one night then he would have been hers and by tomorrow, perhaps, something would happen to stop this terrible thing. In the morning he would be cooler. "You can follow them tomorrow," she said; "you are the fastest rider in Scotland. . . . I am not asking you to stay behind altogether, Ranald. You are a Jacobite; you have been bred for this. I am only asking you to wait til tomorrow. I am only asking you to give me my wedding night. . . . To have something to remember."

"Judith, you know I cannot do that."

"Why not? You are being cruel, Ranald. You are going to have, perhaps, twelve months of fighting, and you will not spare me twelve hours out of it. You have so much in your life, your work and your wars; but I have only you."

She had touched him very deeply, she saw; but she had not moved him. With a sick heart she realized that where his loyalties were concerned she would never move him. He was like iron.

"Judith, Judith," he cried, "you will not be thinking I do not want our married love as much as you do, you know I do; but this must come first. Our love and work

164

are only postponed a little. Loyalty to the King over the water comes first."

"Only fools are loyal to a dead cause," said Judith. "The Jacobite cause is dead everywhere but in the Highlands. . . . You know that is true. . . . It is doomed, it is hopeless. Five years ago you may have thought success was certain; you cannot think that now."

He was sobered by this. "I do not think that is true, Judith; but if it is it should make no difference. When one is very young one's delight in a cause is like a great flame burning, and one does not see death behind; but when the flame dies down, the ashes that remain must hold loyalty to the cause that set the flame burning."

"Loyalty!" said Judith bitterly. "You speak as though it were the only virtue."

"It is," said Ranald. "It comprises all the others."

Anger surged up in Judith again, and she blazed out at him: "Ten minutes ago building Utopia was the only thing in life for you. Now it is something else. In five minutes it will be something else again. You idealists! Running after will-o'-the-wisps over the hearts of those who love you! You are the most cruel people on earth."

He flung his arms round her. "Judith! Judith!"

"Let go of me," she cried, struggling.

Into the midst of their quarrel came the sound of tramping feet and the clip-clop of horses' hoofs. The noise came nearer until it seemed to Judith to fill the whole world. Then it ebbed a little, dying down to the shuffling of feet and the murmur of men's voices and the clanging of the knocker on the front door.

"They are here, Judith," said Ranald. "Drummond of Achnabar has come. . . . And the clan is ready. . . . I must go a minute."

He took his arms away from her and went.

She stood quite still, sick with misery. At the sound of those tramping feet her rage had nearly died away. All that was left of it was directed now against herself.

... What sort of woman was she to rage so at a man who thought he was doing his duty? ... This morning she had given herself to him and now, in fighting against his loyalties, she was fighting against the man himself, trying to break the bands that bound them together. ... Was she mad? ... Up on Ben Caorach she had felt their union to be a thing of the spirit. If that were so the separation of their bodies would not harm it, but the bitterness and anger of their hearts would wreck it utterly. ... She was mad, mad. ... And perhaps he would not come back to her before he went.

The door slammed and she turned eagerly, but it was only Angus.

"You need not go to the door, Angus," she said dully. "The Laird has gone."

Angus came close to her, furious with her. "Will ye behave yersel' as a woman should who is wife to the Laird? Or shall I tak' ye i' my twa hands an' twist the life oot o' ye?"

"You listened at the door," cried Judith, indignantly.

"Ay. I heard ye. Are ye no' shamed?"

"Have you no pity, Angus?"

"For a brave woman, ay; but no' for a squeakin', cowardly wean."

He glared at her. She felt his anger, like a flicking whip, scourging her along the path of righteous wifely behavior. She turned away from him and went to the left-hand window. From there she could see the road winding down Ben Caorach. An hour ago they had ridden down it so happily, but now she hated it, for it linked their little hidden country with the outside world. If it had not been there, she felt, the sorrow and the turmoil of the world beyond their mountains would not have broken in upon their peace. She stared out of the window, fighting with herself, her hands gripping the edge of the little writing table that stood there. When Ranald burst into the room again she swung round, completely mistress of herself, holding a little book that she had picked up unconsciously from the writing table.

"Prionssa Ban has landed!" he shouted. "He landed at Boradale on July 25."

Judith tilted her chin. "How wonderful."

Ranald was overcome with admiration at the change in her. "Judith, you are marvelous!"

"Are the clans rising?"

"Most of them. The Prince is raising his standard at Glenfinnan tomorrow, and we march in ten minutes." He swung round on Angus. "Angus, you blackguard, where are my things?"

"Packed," said Angus stolidly.

"Get them out then. Do not stand there like an owl. And tell Jock to saddle Mactavish."

"Mactavish is saddled. Jock was runnin' to the stable door afore Drummond o' Achnabar had hammered the front door open. *Ye* may hae been haverin' i' the Low-lands wi' a woman, but we i' the Highlands hae had the sense to mak' ready." He snorted contemptuously.

"Go away, Angus," said Ranald. Angus went, and he turned to Judith. "Judith! Judith! Whatever can I say?"

Judith stood rigid. "Now do not be nice to me! I am good now, but if you are too nice to me I might disgrace myself."

"Judith, I do not know what to say. . . . Forgive me."

"Yes, yes. Forgive *me*."

"Judith, you must go back to your guardian."

"No!" cried Judith. She was near losing her temper again. If she and Ranald were to be separated she was not going to be torn away from this place that was a part of them both. Moreover she was now the mistress of a household, with some prospect of having her own way in things; and she was not going home again to do what she was told.

"But, Judith, you must. You cannot stay here alone."

"I can and I will. . . . I am not going to leave Glen Suilag."

"But, Judith . . ."

"There is no but about it. Here I am and here I stay till you come back again."

"I shall not be long. It will all be over very soon. I will be back again before you have had the time to turn round, but—"

Judith interrupted, lifting her chin and setting her jaw in the way that her family, from painful experience, had learned to dread. "I am not going to leave Glen Suilag ever again as long as I live unless you are with me. What is the good of arguing? You know you always get the worst of it."

He put his arms round her again; but her stiff, determined little figure, bound now in iron self-control, was unyielding in his arms. They both of them knew, with misery that all the softness and sweetness of love that they had enjoyed for so short a time, was over. Ranald went on talking for the sake of talking, longing to get away and have the parting done with, yet agonizing over leaving her, this obstinate, passionate girl the worth of whose love was, he knew, immeasurable.

"It is obstinate that you are!" he said. "Angus will look after you of course. . . . Will you be happiest here?"

"Yes." She was standing pressed against him, rigid and unresponsive, the hard edges of the book she held sticking into them both.

"Then I give in. You shall stay."

"I would have stayed whether you gave in or not," muttered Judith to his waistcoat. Then she pushed him almost savagely. "Take your arms away or I shall cry!" He dropped them, and she looked confusedly down at the leather-covered book she held. "What is this? . . . I must have picked it up off the writing table. . . . I did not know I had."

He seized on it, thankful for something to do to fill up time and ease their misery. "Why, it is a little gift that I meant to give you. It is for you to write your songs in. . . . I will write your name in it now."

He crossed to the writing table and sat down, Judith looking over his shoulder. "How dear of you, mo chridhe," she said. "Scores of blank pages. Could anything be more inspiring to a budding composer?"

"You must write the song you made for me upon the second page."

"What are you writing on the first page?"

"A dedication excellently composed by Mr. Ranald Macdonald upon the spur of the moment." He read aloud with pride. "Judith Macdonald, her book, given to her on August 18th, 1745 by her husband, Ranald Macdonald. Dearest Judith, while I am away you are to write down all your pretty songs in this book so that not one of them is lost. When I come back you will sit at your harpsichord and sing them to me."

"And so I shall," she said. "Thank you, Ranald. . . . Do not smudge it. . . . Be careful."

She broke off. From outside came a terrible wailing. . . . The bagpipes. . . . She had not yet learned to love them, and their music seemed to her now like the lamenting of all the betrayed, frustrated creatures who had broken their hearts since the beginning of the world.

Ranald jumped up. "Drummond's pipers! They are ready to start. . . . Judith!"

They clung to each other awkwardly, finding nothing to say, hurting each other with the pressure of their arms.

"Go now," said Judith at last. "There is nothing to say. . . . We know it all."

"Yes. Good-by, child of my heart."

"Good-by."

He had gone. The trample of horses' hoofs and men's

169

feet, the shouting of commands, and the screaming of the pipes rose into a hideous din and then lessened as they marched off through the larch wood.

Judith went to the window and watched the hated road that wound up the side of Ben Caorach. Presently they appeared, Drummond of Achnabar on his gray horse heading the pipers, and then Ranald sitting straight and arrogant on his black horse Mactavish, the white cockade in his bonnet. After him came his men, wild-looking, wiry Highlanders, armed with ancient rusty weapons or with nothing at all, men who knew little about the cause for which they were to fight, and who cared less, but who were prepared, for any reason and at a moment's notice, to go to hell for the Laird.

Judith watched them as they wound away up the mountain into the shadows, their tartans indistinguishable against the heather and bracken, the music of the pipes growing fainter and fainter. . . . And all over the Highlands it was the same. . . . Ranald's sacrifice of work and love was typical of many another. From every glen trails of men were winding up the bridle paths over the mountains, converging upon that spot in the west where the blue and gold standard of the Stuarts would be unfurled in the wind from the sea and young Charles Edward stand to receive the homage of the clans, kneeling to do honor to a hopeless ideal.

For that it was hopeless Judith knew. She had come from the Lowlands, and she had heard them talking there. Only in the Highlands was loyalty to the Stuart cause a real thing; only in the glens ringed round by the mountains with the beauty of it still protected and alive . . . What waste, thought Judith, what hideous waste. . . . Or would something imperishable flower out of this tragedy, something imperishable both for her and Ranald and for Scotland? . . . Would it?

And now the last notes of the pipes had died away and the last man disappeared. The glen was silent and empty and growing dark. The sense of her own loss overwhelmed Judith, but it was at the moment a loss too bitter for tears. When Angus came in to clear away the last of their wedding feast she was standing very straight in the middle of the parlor, stiff and unapproachable.

"I shall go to bed now, Angus," she said coldly; "good night."

"Good night, mistress," said Angus, and bowed to her. There was respect in his eyes and the first glimmer of his great love for her.

Holding up her flowered skirt on each side, and with her head held high in the air, she crossed the room with short determined steps. He heard the whisper of her silks and the clack-clack of her high-heeled shoes going up the uncarpeted stairs and along the passage, and then the clang of the door as she shut herself into her big, empty bedroom.

Because of the very pity of it all he began to curse softly.

CHAPTER II

I

NEXT morning Judith embarked with great determination upon her duties as Mistress Macdonald of Glen Suilag. She must work hard, she determined, so as to try and forget the disagreeableness of fate. She got up at dawn and hung her pillow out of the window, for a large, wet, salt patch in the middle of it must dry up while she dressed and tell no tales. Then she went downstairs and told Angus what she thought about the dust in the hall while she tried to eat some breakfast. Both these activities were difficult, for she still felt a little afraid of Angus, and after crying most of the night her throat felt swollen and sore and it was difficult to swallow; but they were her duty and she did her best. If her domestics thought that a mistress of eighteen, with no husband to back her up, was going to give them an easy time she'd soon show them that they were mistaken. . . . And she showed them.

She went on showing them until they were reduced to a state of nervous prostration bordering on hysteria. Day after day she pattered upstairs and downstairs, in and out of the kitchen, up to the attics and down again and round and round the garden, scolding and ordering and exhorting, scrubbing, and polishing and dusting, with an enormous bunch of keys at her waist and the exhausted Angus plodding at her heels. When she could think of nothing else to do she changed round all the furniture in the rooms and then changed it back again. In the evening, when her legs ached too much to march round and round and up and down any more, she sat alone in the parlor and darned the linen. She went on sewing sometimes until very late at night, so as to put off as long as possible the moment when she had to go up to that great bedroom and put herself to bed in the great bed, and lie awake most of the night listening to the mice and longing for Ranald.

At the end of a month the house and garden were in applepie order, and Judith's reputation as a martinet of a mistress was firmly established, never to be shaken; but Judith herself was pale and hollow-eyed and listless, with the freshness of her girlhood tarnished.

And then, quite suddenly, her body rebelled against overwork and lack of sleep, and she was ill. She had never been ill before, and she formed a low opinion of the whole business and grumbled loud and long. It was terrible to her to be dependent upon other people, and even more terrible to lose the narcotic of hard work.

Yet when she got better she was grateful to her illness, for it seemed to have won for her the devotion as well as the respect of her servants. Janet, the elder of the maidservants, and Angus had looked after her between them; and the love that her helplessness called out was deep anl lasting. Between herself and Angus the bond was strangely strong. He seldom gave her a kind or even a polite word, self-expression and courtesy not being among his gifts; yet she felt that no one on this earth, except Ranald, loved her as much, and she was grateful and comforted.

In the morning he would bring her her gruel and stand over her as she ate it, growling if she did not finish up every drop; and in the evening he would pick little bunches of flowers in the garden and thrust them at her without a word; and betweenwhiles he would fetch and carry unweariedly. He was exactly like a dog, and she felt that, doglike, his love once won, nothing she could do or say would ever shake it; however she treated him, whatever she became, it would make no difference.

In other ways, too, her illness helped her. In the pause and quiet of convalescence she was able to adjust herself and come to terms with life. Things had turned out badly for her, but it was no good making a fuss; she must make the best of things as they were and find happiness where she could.

So she set about the task of preparing a perfect home for Ranald's homecoming in a different spirit. She tried to love and enjoy where before she had only scrubbed and scolded; and gradually she became as happy as it was possible for her to be without Ranald. She loved Glen Suilag more and more. She had loved it at first sight; and now, as it companioned her day by day, she made her impress on it as it made its mark on her. She fitted into it as a body slips into a new and shapely garment made to measure, and went on her way warmed and protected and subtly changed.

For it altered her, as a garment can alter personality,

giving fresh confidence. The quiet dignity of the house, now that she was attentive to it, taught her patience, while from the green things in her garden, storm-shattered yet never destroyed, she learned her courage. Above all, the constant beauty of the glen, as the changing seasons flowed past her windows, was like a stream running over the sore places in her mind and bringing her healing.

And she had her music. In her odd moments she wrote gay little songs about the glen, and about her love for Ranald, and wrote them down in her book to amuse him with when he came back.

II

And the time wore on. The purple of the heather gave way to the russet and gold of the dying bracken, and they in turn to the grays and browns of winter. At first news came often, handed on from glen to glen or brought by traveling peddlers, contradictory and confusing but always good.

They heard of the march south of the gallant little army, the occupation of Edinburgh and the victory of Prestonpans, and then of the gay doings of the Prince's court at Holyrood. Many of the Jacobite ladies, encouraged by success, now went south to join their husbands; and Judith too, had she wished, could have danced with Ranald in the great gallery at the palace, and curtsied to the Prince as he stood on the dais with the lights blazing behind him and flowers flung at his feet.

But she did not go. It was her part, she felt, to care for Ranald's home in his absence, and she would not leave it. It was hard not to go, yet her sense of union with him was sometimes so strong that his physical presence could hardly have increased it.

And then, in November, the army marched out of Edinburgh on its way to England, and they heard no more. Judith now began to feel tormented. She had had no faith in the early success, and she had thought the dalliance at Holyrood a crazy waste of time; but this invasion of a great country by an army so small seemed to her the crowning madness. She thought it would never be seen again, and when no news came she had hard work not to see terrible pictures in her mind of Ranald and his men dead in the flat fields of England.

It was at this time that it suddenly occurred to her that she was not the only anxious wife in the glen. She had been so absorbed in her house and garden that she had paid no attention to the world beyond, but now her heart reproached her. The whole of the glen was Ranald's and he had wanted to make it perfect for those who lived in it. Well, she couldn't do that, and she didn't intend to try, having at this stage no faith in his heroics; but she could at least be polite.

So she put on her scarlet cloak and mounted her pattens and splashed about the glen visiting the crofts, with Angus following behind carrying her basket and growling horribly. It was uphill work, for though Ranald had been teaching her she did not know very much Gaelic yet, and her remarks, passing through Angus and translated by him, sometimes seemed, if he did not approve of them, to come out of Angus quite different from what they were when they went in. And then she was fastidious, and the inside of the dark, smoky, mud-floored little houses was almost more than she could endure with patience. But she persevered, and gradually, bit by bit, she conquered the language, accustomed herself to the smells, and won the love and confidence of her people.

Just before Christmas she had a brilliant idea. There was at the northern end of the loch a crofter's house that was always empty. Someone had been brutally murdered there, they said, and no one would live in it. Judith had a wholesome contempt for ghosts, in daylight, and the house took her fancy. The walls were built of unhewn, mortarless stone and sloped a little inwards, and it was thatched with rye thatch. She determined to have it for herself and make a sort of little office of it, where she could go one day in the week, in broad daylight only, and see any of her people who liked to come there to ask her for news or for help. The rougher, wilder people, she had discovered, were afraid to come to her at the house. They did not like the servants or the dogs, and the height of the rooms, they said, made them feel queer. And she could not always go to them. The weather was often so bad that not even her pattens and Angus pushing behind could get her though the mud.

The plan worked well. Angus made the little house clean and respectable for her, and every Friday morning she went there with him and sat in judgment. She would sit very upright on a stool, hoping she was looking like Portia and afraid she wasn't, because of her nose, and hear complaints and settle differences and give advice to the mothers about their children and tell the grandmothers what to do about their ailments. The advice that she gave was extremely startling and would have given a modern district nurse a fit, but there were not more deaths in the glen than there had been before her arrival, and the good food that she sent by Angus to a house where she was told there was illness nearly always counteracted the effects of the bottle of medicine, mixed by herself, that she sent with it. Sometimes, of course, it didn't; but on these occasions any misfortune that might occur was always put down to the hand of Providence rather than to Judith's medicine, and her reputation did not suffer. And she comforted them. She, too, had a husband swallowed up in a foreign country and she, too, had no news; and yet she could sit there, composed and smiling and deliciously pretty, and discourse on the colic and the megrims as though nothing were the matter but the colic and the megrims. . . . She gave them great confidence.

But at last they heard rumors. The invading army was back again in Scotland. Nothing had happened, it seemed; they had simply turned round and come home again. Judith's heart sank. Surely it could only mean one thing; they had realized the hopelessness of it all and they were making for home. If only she could know more, but it was midwinter now and they were utterly cut off from contact with the outside world. Wild weather, with whirling snow and bitter winds, swept down on them from the northeast. The glen road was impassable, and even the rumors stopped. She could do nothing; she could not even get through the snow to the little house at the other end of the loch; she could only sit indoors and wait and shiver, the cold eating into her very bones. . . . That January and February lasted ten years.. . .

III

But they ended, and March brought the first hint of spring. The long dark nights, when Judith, try as she might, could never get warm in her big bed, shrunk a little and became less terrible, and the gray dawns came in with a twitter of birds and a stronger wash of light behind the hills. At the height of the bitter cold there had always been black streaks down the snow-covered mountains, for the larger burns ran too fast to freeze; but now there was more and more of this delicate, twisting tracery upon the white, as the melting snow fed the smaller streams and woke them to life again. On the rocks in the glen green mosses appeared, and in the larch wood fat salmon-pink toadstools grew in the moss, and scarlet fungi like scarlet cups perched cheekily on the fallen, decaying twigs. Primroses appeared in sheltered, sunny nooks, and Judith even found one or two violets. Color was creeping back into the world again, and her heart sang at the sight of it.

She went out one late afternoon in early April into the larch wood to gather moss and some of the little scarlet cups. She liked to arrange them in a bowl in the parlor; they reminded her of the red roses that had stood on the dinner table on her first night. When she had gathered them she went through the wood to the loch and stood there looking at it. It was sunset, and the glen was a cup filled with amber wine. Through the haze she could see that each little ripple had a golden crest and the orange weed at the loch's edge burned like a fire.

She was so lost in wonder at the beauty of it that she did not see a short, wiry figure get up from the grass by the water and come toward her. She started and nearly screamed, thinking of warlocks and bogles, when a hand was laid on her arm. Then she saw that he was a human being, a disreputable, tattered Highlander, and she smiled at him in relief. He smiled back at her, his teeth flashing in his tanned, bearded face, and slipped a sealed packet into her hand. Then, without a word, he turned and padded off.

Judith gave one glance at the packet, where the words "Mistress Macdonald" in a neat handwriting were dimly discernible through the dirt that stained it, and then ran like a hare back through the larch wood into the house and up the stairs to her own room. She flung herself down on the floor by the window, where the sunset light was pouring in, and tore open the package. It was a letter from Ranald, pages of it, the very first she had had since he went away. Her heart pounded, and she felt warm and rosy all over. Her eyes, blinded by the sunset, seemed full of golden dust, and she had to rub them savagely with her knuckles before she could see to read.

*I wonder, Judith [wrote Ranald], will you ever read this? I have tried to send you letters before, but I doubt if you got them. But I think that you may get this. AEneas Macmillan is weary of war and is going home to Glen Suilag. Were he not my foster brother I should shoot him for a cowardly deserter, but seeing that he is I will let him go with no worse than a clout on the head and a letter to you in his hand. If he gets home alive to Glen Suilag he will not fail to give you the letter, though I fear he will be long upon the way, he being the finest dawdler ever created by the devil. May the Good Being give him a safe journey, though he does not deserve it, for the sake of that which he carries.

Are you lonely, child of my heart? Sometimes I have a nightmare that you are crying in the dark night because that bed is too big and you are cold, and frightened of the mice, and you want me with you. And then I remember that you are a brave child, and sensible, and that when the dawn comes you will laugh again. Sometimes I have had bad moments too, when there seems nothing in the world but waste and mud and despair, with death at the end to round off the uselessness of it with destruction. And I have thought that there is no use in living at all since youth is gone so quickly and one works and loves only to fail in the work and see love quenched at death. And then I say to myself that we should believe in that which we felt when we were strong and happy rather than in that which we feel when we are sick and sad. Do you not think, Judith, that one is more truly oneself in times of joy than in times of sorrow? "I was not myself," we say, when some weakness has led us to behave badly. If that is true, then it is that which we think when we are ourselves that is true, and not the other. Things were well with us the night that we came home, Judith, and we were our-

* The language and spelling of the letter Ranald wrote to Judith are modernized.

179

selves. "I am myself," you said to me, and fair were the things that we thought. Love. Unity. Eternity. Perfection. We flung down the words like golden coins, and they rang true. I have tried, since, to fling them down again, and they seemed to me to be dross, not gold. Yet I must have been wrong, Judith, because I was not myself then. So have faith, little darling, in the dark nights. That unity that we achieved on the top of Ben Caorach was a true thing, and the things that I said to you later were true in their essence.

It is as though I were talking to you. It is midnight and very cold, too cold to sleep, and I am writing to you by the light of a tallow candle, so forgive me if my writing is not easy. We are near Inverness and not far from the moor of Culloden. Cumberland and his army are very close to us, slowly pushing us to the place where they want us to be, and out at sea are the English warships, sailing parallel with the line of march. Behind them, where they have been, they say that the houses and churches are all burnt. We know now what hunted animals feel like when they are driven into a corner. It is so strange to think that, as the crow flies, you are not so very many miles away. But I cannot get to you.

Forgive me, Judith. I begin at the end when I had meant to begin at the beginning. I mean to try and tell you, in outline, all that has happened. Perhaps I shall never see you again, or only for so short a while that I can tell you nothing, and you are an active-minded child, one of those who say: "Why? How? Where?" and do not rest contented with no answer. So I will try and tell you.

It began so well. It has been all along like the life of a man, so strong and gay and hopeful in youth with the shadows darkening as time goes on. After I left you, Judith, we marched all night long. We lost our way a little in the darkness and it was sunset of the next day before we reached Glenfinnan. I wish I could make you see the scene that followed as I saw it. When we came over the top of the moor, marching three abreast with our pipes playing, we could see the valley of Glenfinnan down below us with a company of men standing on the shores of Loch Shiel. As we came nearer we could see who they were, three companies of Clanranald's men and the Camerons nearly eight hundred strong, who had got there just before us. They were drawn up in their ranks round the Royal Standard and under the standard stood the Prince. It is impossible to describe him. He is dangerously attractive—one of those men who can win devotion by just existing. There have been quarrels, treacheries, cowardice, all through this war; yet our feeling for him is so strong that it has held us together. It is a miracle to me. I think it is because he is more than himself to us. I think he stands to us for our very existence. You know, Judith, we in the Highlands do not belong to the modern world, that hateful world of eighteenth-century London that seems to me both insincere and indecent. The mountains have kept modernity away from us, though it creeps always a little nearer. We are mediaeval, Our chivalry is mediaeval, and our customs and sometimes our savagery. And Prince Charles seems to belong to our world. He is a romantic. In fighting for him we have been fighting not only for our rightful king but for the way of life that we know and care for, a way of life that is threatened. I love that way of life, Judith, and it was on that foundation that I had planned to build Utopia.

But I am wandering again, and you will complain that this outline is very far from being clear. He made us a short speech. He said that he was here to secure the welfare and happiness of his people and that with our assitance and that of a just God he did not doubt of bringing the affair to a happy issue. He spoke well, and he meant every word that he said. We cheered him until it sounded like thunder in the valley.

After that all went magnificently. The clans came pouring in, and we dodged the enemy and marched on Edinburgh. We had a good start, you see. Cope, the English commander, was still without reinforcements from England, and in any case the English are poor fools in our mountains. We took Edinburgh. One of the gates was opened for a coach to pass out, and we just yelled and rushed in. Our army was only three thousand, ragged and ill-armed, and the inhabitants of Edinburgh were sixty thousand. They could have slaughtered the lot of us had they wanted, but they were so astonished that they did not seem able to get their breath. . . . And they say the ladies were all Jacobites, because of the Prince's looks, and their husbands all henpecked. . . . And we had, in those early days, a great reputation. They thought of us all as wild savages, scarcely human, and they were terrified of us. They said that we ate babies and spit fire. And the Prince, too, with his beauty and his charm, seemed to them scarcely human. I think they felt they had against them Lucifer, Son of the Morning, leading the fiends of hell. Their fear had something superstitious about it.

And then Cope came after us, and we went out to meet him. I do not suppose that the victory of Prestonpans will ever be explained in military terms. We were ill-equipped and ill-trained, and we had been given to understand that the British infantry were invincible. But what one is given to understand is not always so. We charged them, just a ragged line of running, leaping, yelling devils, and they turned and ran. They did not wait to see us close, so we never heard the clash of our basket-hilted swords against their bayonets, a sound we had been longing for. The actual battle took just fifteen minutes, and it was comical. It was not really a battle at all; it was an exhibition of superstitious fear.

We marched back in triumph to Edinburgh, and they

gave us a wonderful welcome. It had, I believe, been prepared for Cope, but it did just as well for us.

And then we made what, I think, was our first mistake. Two courses were open to us. Should we march straight away into England with our ridiculous little army, and try to get to London before English reinforcements could be brought back from the Continent, or should we wait at Edinburgh until our army was larger and we could make a braver show? I thought, and many others with me, that we should have struck while the iron was hot, while we were still drunk with victory and while they were still afraid of us. When success depends upon certain attitudes of mind delay is dangerous, for an attitude of mind can change so soon. But the Prince and his advisers took the other view, and we waited at Edinburgh for six mortal weeks.

I hated those weeks of revelry at Holyrood. From Glenfinnan to Prestonpans the days had been too crowded for me to think too much of you and Glen Suilag; but at Edinburgh, with no work to take my thoughts, the longing for you was unbearable. The dancing and the music and the shimmer of the lights on women's dresses and powdered hair all reminded me of you, and at night I could not sleep because I wanted you. And I felt crazy with remorse. What I was feeling then you perhaps had been feeling for weeks. And you had begged me to stay with you one night and I would not. If I was cruel to you then, Judith, I was punished during those weeks at Holyrood. I wrote a letter to you and sent it by a messenger I trusted, telling you to come to me; but I had no answer and you did not come. I was angry with you, Judith. Even if the letter never reached you I thought that you should have come without. And then, one night, I knew why you did not come. You thought, you darling, that you should not leave Glen Suilag because you must look after it for me. I saw right into your mind. I had again that strange sense of unity with you that I had on the top of Ben Caorach, and you could not have been nearer to me had you been lying in my arms. After that I felt easier and the scent of the flowers, and the women's perfumes in the great gallery at the palace, did not torment me any longer.

On November the fourth we marched for England. Our numbers had swelled, and we had five thousand foot and five hundred horse. And again all went well. The fear of us was not, perhaps, as great as it had been; but it was still there, and queer things happened. There was no fighting. There was an English army waiting for us under Wade, but we dodged him, as we had dodged Cope, and marched on, and one by one the English towns opened their gates to us. I wish you could have seen the Prince as he made his entry into Carlisle. He rode a white charger, and a hundred pipers played before him. He was wonderful in those days, when he still believed in himself and in us. He never rode a horse on the march, or used his coach; he tramped on foot with the clans. What we did he did, and it was his personality that inspired us. "A grave or a throne," he said. God in heaven, what a king he would have made!

And so we came to Derby, with our flags flying and the pipes playing and the bells pealing in welcome. The Prince was in wild spirits, talking and laughing and cheering us on. He was in sight of the goal at last, and he could scarcely contain himself. He kept asking us what he should wear when he entered London. The next morning he called a council to decide the best route for marching on London, and they let the blow they had been preparing for him fall.

I was not at that council. It consisted of the Prince and the seventeen chieftains whom he had appointed to form his council of war and by whose decisions he was bound. While they talked I was in the street below with the men. We had caught the infection of enthusiasm from the Prince, and we talked of nothing but London, and as we talked we sharpened our swords. How could we know that up in the room above our leaders had refused to go on? They were cowards and worse. I think they were mad. Surely they knew that our only hope lay in swiftness and unhesitating cheek? We were playing the game of David and Goliath. If David's hand had faltered as he took the stones from his sling he would never have sat upon the throne of Israel.

On the sixth of December the retreat began. They say that the worst is still in front of us, but nothing that comes can be as bad as that retreat. We had marched into Derby singing and shouting, but we marched out of it in silence. An army is like a man, Judith; nothing takes the heart out of it like effort for no purpose. To be asked to die for a cause, that is nothing, that is easy, if the end be attained with the death throes; but to be told to go back with the thing undone after all the labor and sweat, that is an insult to the spirit of man that is hard to bear. I think that to be able to bear it is the final courage.

After that, though a great deal happened, there does not seem to be much left to tell. We had destroyed, by our own act, the legend of our supernatural powers, and that destruction was the beginning of the end. The Prince knew it. He never marched on foot with the clan again. All through the retreat he rode on horseback with the van, where he could not see our faces or hear our silence.

Once back in Scotland again there were weeks of mistakes and indecisions and disloyalties and treacheries. Numerically we were stronger than we had ever been. Help from France had come at last, and the whole of Aberdeenshire had been carried for the Prince; but war is an odd thing and the spirit of an army incalculable. When we had been ludicrously at a disadvantage we had been successful; but now, with so much to help us, everything went wrong with us. Fear had got

185

in like a canker, and was eating the heart out of us. We had victories, but our leaders in their cowardice seemed to turn every victory into a retreat, and the spirit of the army began to change. I think that behind all their councils and their tactics and their quarrels they had but one idea: to be as near their homes as possible when the end came.

At the end of January we heard that the Duke of Cumberland himself had arrived at Edinburgh with an army to make an end of us. The Prince was glad. He wanted to attack the Duke at once, and surely he was right. He alone now had the will to win and we should have obeyed him. But again our leaders were cowards. The men were deserting and the weather was bad and their hearts failed them. They urged instead instant retreat to the north. The Prince had no choice but to yield; but he said, "I take God to witness that it is with the greatest reluctance, and that I wash my hands of the fatal consequences which I foresee but cannot help." And so we marched away up north to Iverness by the Highland road through the most appalling weather I have ever endured. We could not see for the wind and the hail in our faces, and men fell exhausted in the snow.

And now we are just waiting, with Cumberland creeping after us, heavy and ponderous like fate. The Prince is sick and the men are mutinying and our pay is in arrears. I hope that the end will come soon because this waiting is very difficult. By the time that you get this, Judith, I think that the end will have come and you will know more than I know now. I wish that one could see a little into the future. I think that I shall see you again, but I do not think that we shall live together as we had planned. At least not in this life. There will be another. I believed that when I was happy, and so it must be true. It has taken me till the dawn to write this letter because my brain is so dull and my fingers are numb with the cold. Good-by, Judith. I do not know how to finish this letter because for the things that I feel about you, and for you, there are no words. Forgive me that my love has brought you sorrow, and believe that one day it will bring you joy again.

The last sheet fluttered down into Judith's lap. The sunset had passed, and she was numb with cold, numb right through, as cold as Ranald had been when he wrote that letter. She had lived so intensely with him as she read that the tide of her life seemed to have run dry, and she had no feeling left. She was like a dead woman, cold and lifeless. "When you get this you will know more than I do now," he had said; but she knew nothing. The man who had brought this letter was a dawdler, Ranald said. He had been Heaven alone knew how long upon the way. What had happened meanwhile? Outside was the blue dusk and the still garden and no answer to her question.

IV

She sat crouched on the floor until it was quite dark. So drained of life was she that she would have sat there all night had not a tap on her door roused her. She got to her feet and stumbled across the floor to open it. Outside was Angus.

"They want ye at the haunted hoose," he remarked.

"Why?" asked Judith crossly.

"The laddie sent wi' the message gave no reason. 'Tis maybe sickness at ane o' the crofts. Bestir yersel', woman, an' pit yer cloak aboot ye. Are ye the wife o' the Laird or are ye no' the wife o' the Laird?"

He wrapped her red cloak about her and led her down to the hall, where he hoisted her onto her pattens and pushed her out into the night to do her duty. He followed her, carrying a peat from the fire that the wind blew into a torch as they walked. Judith did not care who was ill or who died or what happened. She clanked along the glen road in her pattens, her cold hands pushed under her armpits for warmth, and every now and then she stopped for very weariness. When she so far forgot herself Angus growled and prodded her gently in the back, and she went on again.

They came in sight of the crofter's house at the northern end of the loch, and Judith saw a faint glow from the doorway, as though someone had lighted a peat fire inside. That was strange, for the crofters were always afraid to be at that house after dark. She walked dully up to the doorway and stood there looking in. In spite of the fire it seemed pitch dark inside and she could scarcely see the floor of trampled earth and the smoke wreathing up toward the hole in the roof. She heard no sound at all, but the thick, smoky shadows were full of huddled figures.

She stepped over the threshold and walked to the fire, standing there and looking about her. As her eyes grew accustomed to the dim light she saw that the room was full of her people, silent, rocking themselves. One figure detached itself from the shadows and came to her, seizing her cloak and thrusting a wild face close to hers. She drew back from him in horror, for he was terrible. He was half naked and his body had patches of dried blood on it. He held her, pouring out a flood of Gaelic in a hoarse, exhausted voice. She did not understand a word; she wanted only to get away from him, to get away from his mad, bloodshot eyes so close to her face and from the sight of the blood on his body. Suddenly his hands seized her shoulders and he was cursing her, cursing as men do when they turn in madness on the men and women in high places who control their fate and lead them to disaster.

With an exclamation Angus lurched forward and

dragged him off Judith, pulling her out of the house and away from the lamentation and wailing that had started inside it. They went together down the road the way they had come, stumbling over the stones. It was pitch dark now, and they could not see each other's faces, for Angus's torch had been left behind.

"What did he say, Angus?" whispered Judith ,shaking his arm. "I could not understand. What is it?"

Growling and stumbling over his words, Angus told her. The end of the rebellion had come in a battle on Culloden moor. It had been a massacre of the clans, and the man in the crofter's house who had cursed her had barely escaped with his life.

"And the Laird?" said Judith. She said it over and over again like a parrot. Her cloak had fallen half off and kept twisting round her feet so that she stumbled, but she did not seem to notice it, nor the cold of the April night.

"The mon no kenned what had come to the Laird," said Angus. "If he is livin' he'll tak' to the heather an 'turn west for Glen Suilag. A hunted beast aye gangs hame. We mun wait."

And they waited while spring turned to summer and summer to early autumn and once more the mountains wore the heather that had greeted Judith as a bride. All over the Highlands the victorious Hanoverians were engaged in burning and pillaging and murdering, with a calculated cruelty unknown in those parts before; but little Glen Suilag, hidden in the mountains, escaped. It waited with its beauty unimpaired.

CHAPTER III

I

IT seemed to Ranald Macdonald, in the days that followed the writing of his letter to Judith, that of all the nightmare horrors created by man for his own undoing the beast of war is the most unmanageable. The beast seemed to him to control the man far more than the man controlled the beast. In the early days of the war Ranald had felt that they had the upper hand, that they had let the beast out of his cage for a good purpose; but now it did not seem to be so. It had got loose and was trampling them under its feet, and God alone knew what destruction there would be before the thing was caged again. He tried to console himself by thinking of those moments in the past history of war when the spirit of man had been momentarily triumphant over the beast, moments whose poignancy of tragedy or grandeur of courage had lifted them above the welter of war and made them immortal. Termopylae. Salamis. Syracuse. They were such small affairs that the beast, as he sprawled over them, probably thought them negligible; yet, looking back, they shone out quite clear of his slime.

Yet Ranald had not the slightest idea, as he stood on Culloden moor in the driving rain on the morning of April 16, 1746, that he himself was about to play his part in one of those very moments. He had not much idea of anything, nor had the shivering men around him. They were soaked to the skin, hungry and exhausted, and their minds were blank.

Everything that could go wrong had gone wrong. For weeks Cumberland had been bearing down on them,

190

but now that the crisis was actually here they were not ready. The Prince and his chieftains, struggling with shortage of money and food, mutiny and sickness, had not been able to get the whole army together in time. More than two thousand clansmen were absent, and they were appallingly outnumbered.

The day before, a night march and a surprise attack at dawn had been planned. It was a return to the bold tactics of the earlier days of the war, and they set off with relief and a glimmer of hope. But it was pitch dark, and they had twelve miles to go. The men were exhausted and the rear could not keep the pace set by the head of the column. Halfway through the night they realized they could not do it in time and turned back. It was dawn when they returned again to Culloden moor. There was nothing to eat, not even oatmeal, and they flung themselves down to sleep on the sodden ground.

They were still sleeping two hours later when a message came with the news that Cumberland's cavalry were in sight. Ranald staggering with fatigue, had only the vaguest idea of what was happening. Drums were beating, pipes playing, chieftains on their horses galloping backwards and forwards in wild confusion, yelling their orders. Hardly knowing where they were going or what they were doing, the men, still half asleep, fell slowly into line across the narrow strip of moor. On one side of them was the border wall of some estate, on the other the sea. They were boxed up in a narrow corridor.

Ranald, mechanically obeying orders, found himself with his men on the left of the frontline. The Macdonalds stood all around him in their ranks in a sullen silence. In every other engagement they had fought upon the right wing, the post of honor, which they always occupied when they fought for the house of Stuart. How they came to be where they were no one knew; but they resented it with savage bitterness. As they stood they hacked viciously with their claymores at the heather at their feet. Ranald, from where he stood, saw one lovely bush of white heather slashed utterly to pieces, and he watched with the curious fascination that trivial events sometimes have for one in moments of strain. He did not know that forever after the fraoch-geal, that brought luck to everyone else, was to be called "the curse of the Macdonalds."

When the heather was all gone he raised his head and looked in front of him. Through the driving rain he could see a gleam of red at the other end of the moor. It crept nearer, as it had been creeping all these weeks, advancing with a sort of contemptuous slowness.

A sudden burst of cheering lightened the tension of the terrible silence. The Prince was riding down the lines. Dressed in the Highland dress and mounted on a splendid gray gelding, outwardly gay and confident as ever, he affected them as he never failed to affect them. Even the sullen Macdonalds flung their bonnets into the air and yelled, as he turned his horse and rode back to his position in the second line, just as Cumberland's guns opened fire.

The Jacobite army had scanty artillery, and their only hope lay, as always, in the Highland charge. They were told, therefore, to stand where they were and wait until the distance between the two armies was sufficiently small to let it loose. It seemed to be the business of no one to tell them to fling themselves on the ground, and only some of them did so. The rest stood upright and were shot down.

It was a kind of warfare that they could not understand. Magnificent in attack, utterly confident in hand-to-hand fighting with the sword, they hated firearms. The grapeshot that ploughed great swaths through their ranks, hurled at them by an enemy they could scarcely see, filled them with terror. They were used to fighting on their emotions, the "crith gaisge," the tremblings of valor, leading them on to the "mire chath," the frenzy of battle; but in this terrible inhuman slaughter there was nothing to rouse in them either valor or frenzy.

After nearly an hour of endurance they began, some of them, to fling away their muskets and run. It seemed to Ranald as he looked round him that all his men were either dead or deserting. He yelled and shouted at them. He went up and down the shattered lines encouraging and cursing and even, in his fury, striking them with the flat of his sword. But the ordeal was too terrible to be borne, and he could do nothing with them. Once, as the smoke and mist parted like a torn curtain, he saw the Prince, who should have been in a place of safety, riding up and down in a desperate effort to strengthen his men. That he was not killed as he rode was a miracle, and the greatest misfortune that befell him that day.

At the end of an hour the enemy were quite close to them, and a murmur ran along the lines. Now, at last, they were near enough, and the right wing was commanded to charge. They went forward as they had gone forward at Prestonpans, a running, leaping, yelling line of devils. Ranald watched with sick rage. The right wing should have been the Macdonalds, but instead of that the men who had come into their own at last were Murrays, Gordons, and Stuarts who had no right to the post of honor, while the Macdonalds on the left stood still to be shot to pieces.

But this time the charge failed. They broke through the first line, still yelling and leaping, and hurled themselves against the regiment of the second line. It was Wolfe's regiment, and something of the personality of the fighter of Quebec seemed to inform the regiment also, for it received the terrible charge with calmness and resolution. The Highlanders, once checked, began to give ground, and in a very few moments they were in flight, and not even the Prince could rally them, though he rode up and down among them, the tears streaming down his face.

Those of the Macdonalds who had stood their ground stood it still, sullen as ever, the Hanoverian horse circling round them. The command to charge was given at last, and Ranald as he dashed forward shouted to his men to throw away their hated muskets and draw their swords. He was happy now, that ghastly immobility over, stumbling and staggering over the rough, boggy ground, with those hated redcoats only a few yards away. Once, as he fell and picked himself up again, he saw to his astonishment that he was practically alone; his men had not followed him. The Macdonald charge was being carried out by a handful of officers only. He felt a moment's bitter shame and then had no more time for feeling or thought, for a plunging black horse with a scarlet rider was on top of him before he had regained his balance. He struck upward with his dirk and then fell, a mountain of black flesh descending on him.

He felt it roll off him again, but he still seemed in darkness, a night shot with stars; and from the pain in his head he judged confusedly that his skull was cut in two. He felt hands dragging him, heaving him up and then the night seemed rushing by him in a hideous din of shouts and cries and the sound of rushing water, with the drenching cold of it on his body. Presently he found himself on his feet and running, soaking wet and lurching drunkenly while hands gripped his arms on either side. The wind was singing in his ears, the heather was under his feet, and he was conscious again of the gray daylight and of a tinkling burn quite close to him. The pain in his head was still agonizing, and he was thankful when the hands that gripped his arms suddenly let go and he fell forward into a heather clump.

Someone seemed to dip his head in the burn, and in a few moments he was almost himself again and astonished, as he gingerly felt his skull, to find nothing wrong with it but a lump the size of a hen's egg. He would have liked to lie where he was, but he was pulled to his feet and dragged on again. He found he was one of a small band of fugitives who had crossed the river Nairn and were making for the hills. On each side of him were two Highlanders, not his own men, grinning at him rather sheepishly. Had he had breath he would have sworn at them for dragging him away to share in this headlong flight, but he was still half winded as well as half stunned. They stumbled on and up, making for the friendly clouds that came rolling down the mountainside to cover them.

II

By the order of His Grace the Duke of Cumberland, every Highlander upon whom hands could be laid was instantly massacred. His Grace's mercenaries spent an exhausting day and perhaps it was as well for the fugitives in the hills above that what went on in the valley below was hidden from them by the driving clouds.

All night they toiled westward, their instinct to put as much wild country as possible between them and their pursuers driving them on. By good luck they overtook what was left of the right wing of the army, those Murrays and Gordons and Stuarts who had fled before them. The next day found them at Ruthven, not far from Fort Augustus, a little force of perhaps two thousand, all that remained of the Jacobite army. They heard that the Prince had escaped, and they waited here to learn his will for them. Some of them hoped that even now they might rally again.

But the message from the Prince, when it came, was the ominous one that he desired every man to take the steps that seemed best to him for his own safety. They had no supplies of any sort; and the Prince, who alone had the power to hold them together, had left them. Bitterly and sadly they parted from each other and took to the heather, little groups of threes and fours wandering forlornly away up the mountainside, the clansmen as they went raising wild howlings and lamentations.

Ranald found himself alone. The men who had saved his life were not Macdonalds. It was thought, they told him, that those of his own clan who had not died on the moor had fled in the direction of Inverness. If so, by this time they were either prisoners or massacred.

He supposed that he ought to try and get home to Glen Suilag, but in spite of his longing for Judith he did not want to do this. He was obsessed by the thought of the Prince. The last glimpse he had had of him, trying to rally the men with the tears streaming down his face, haunted him. The Prince stood to him, as he had told Judith, for more than the house of Stuart; he stood for the way of life that he cared for and for the Utopia that he had hoped to build.

But that was all over now. He knew quite well what the kind of life that he hated, now that it was victorious, would do to the kind of life that he loved. It would crush it out utterly. There is no vengeance in the world so cruel as the vengeance of a new age that has been checked and hindered in its progress by an older age that will not die without a fight. The old Scotland was dead, and his own Utopia was dead too. Nothing was left but the Prince, the symbol of them.

So he turned toward the sea. He would not go home until he had paid the last possible service to this last remnant of what he cared for. When the Prince was either dead or in safety, it would be time enough to go home to Glen Suilag. He thought he knew where he would find the Prince. He would be sure to make for the coast, for his only chance of escape to France would be by sea, and he would choose the part of the country that he knew and where he had friends. He would make for the Glenfinnan country.

The journey there was easy. Cumberland's men were

still engaged in massacre at Culloden and had not yet begun their systematic murder in the Western Highlands, and fugitives like Ranald could find sympathy and help at every croft they passed. As he drew near to the coast he was not so many miles from Glen Suilag, and his heart reproached him. He wrote a letter to Judith and gave it to a crofter's wife, who promised faithfully to send it to Mistress Macdonald. She had a pleasant, open face and he believed that she would keep her word. . . . And so she would have if a sheep dog puppy had not eaten the letter when her back was turned.

Ranald made straight for the beach at Borradale, that very same beach where the Prince had landed. Instinct took him there, and his inborn knowledge that life is always a rounded thing that swings full circle back again. It was probable that where the Prince's adventure had begun, there it would end.

It was the night of April 26 when he reached the beach, a dirty night with promise of worse to come, and he could not see the silver sand and the golden weed that edged it; but he saw the outline of a boat and the light of a lantern that dimly illumined a group of muffled figures. He silently joined the group, and the light of the lantern was swung on his face while hands gripped him.

" 'Tis Ranald Macdonald!" said a voice in relief, and a dirk that had been uncomfortably near his throat was withdrawn.

He took stock of the party. The Prince and five of his friends, one of whom was Allan Macdonald, a cousin of his own, and six boatmen. He bowed to the Prince. "You will need a seventh boatman," he said.

"Since you say so!" said the Prince, and laughed.

He looked ill and exhausted, yet at the same time Ranald thought he was enjoying himself. It was a relief to him, perhaps, to get away from the jealousies and follies that had tied his hands and marred all the latter

197

part of his adventure, and an unspeakable relief to get away from the endless playing of a part. He could be himself now, an ordinary man dodging death. . . . And he was of the type that finds such a dodging fun.

They climbed into the boat and pushed off. Their immediate object was to put the sea between the Prince and his pursuers, and they were bound for the islands.

III

The weeks that followed were the strangest that Ranald ever spent in his life, stranger even than the early days of the war with their uncanny success. Their object was always to keep moving. That first night they rowed through the storm past Rum and Eigg to Benbecula, but they dared not stay there. They went from island to island always, it seemed to Ranald, in the most terrible weather. Looking back later he could remember very little of those days except the surging of waves, and gray rocky islands half hidden in driving rain. He was so numb with fatigue that he scarcely noticed the ceaseless discomfort of wet clothes and insufficient food. He seemed to himself to be always swinging and tossing. Even on land, when they lay down to sleep in some fisherman's hut or even in the open fields with the boat's sails spread over them, this tossing sensation went on. Judith and Glen Suilag seemed so far away as to be almost unreal; his one and only longing was to stop still.

June found them in South Uist, in greater danger than they had ever been, for the hunt was narrowing down. The sea was full of English ships, and there were redcoats now on most of the islands. It was obvious that their party was too large for safety and that they must break up. The Prince decided to keep only two men with him, and Ranald was not one of the two.

The little party said good-by to each other on the shores of Loch Boisdale, and to Ranald it was the worst moment of the whole war. The Prince was playing out the game as cheerfully as ever, and he went from man to man, smiling and confident, holding out his hand to each in turn. He had a little money with him, and he parted it among the seven boatmen, taking no refusal. Then he turned and walked away with his two companions, striding easily over the rocks and turf, his tattered kilt swinging. On the sky line he stopped and looked back, waving to them, and then disappeared; and only Ranald of that little party ever saw him again.

IV

A few days later Ranald and two of the boatmen, both of them natives of Skye, found themselves in North Uist. They had made their way north with some vague hope of hiring a boat with the money the Prince had given them and crossing to Skye. The two men left Ranald by the sea, where the fields with their June flowers ran down to a little bay, and went off to look for a boat.

It was nearly eight o'clock, brilliantly clear with the luminous clearness of a northern summer night and the added clearness of bad weather to come. Across the sea Ranald could see Skye, a lovely shape carved out of amethyst. In all their wanderings they had not yet been there, but on clear days they had always seen it appearing and disappearing through the webs of mist that it seemed to spin round itself. It had always had a curious attraction for Ranald. It had seemed not of this world, an earthly paradise where a man could both dream his dream and realize it.

For Ranald thought now that on this actual earth there was no such thing as fulfillment. He believed in nothing. Even the Prince, the symbol of what he had hoped for, had gone; and he doubted if he would ever get back to Judith and his home. Life was a pointless, useless thing, and man a soulless animal differing from other animals only in a greater capacity for suffering. When he remembered his old beliefs and the things that he had said to Judith, he cursed himself for a fool. He was, though he hardly realized it, on the verge of illness and more dismal than he had ever been before.

As he sat there, glowering at Skye, he heard the splash of oars, and a boat rounded the rocks and came gliding into the bay. He slipped round a rock and crouched hidden, for the militia were everywhere on the island and his hold on life was still strong enough to make him want to avoid hanging as long as possible.

The boat drew into the shallows and seemed waiting, the men in it resting on their oars. Presently a little group came down the beach, two women and a man. The latter Ranald recognized instantly as MacEachain, one of the men the Prince had taken with him and who had relations, Macdonalds, living on the island. He had hoped, Ranald knew, that they might in some way be able to help the Prince.

The two women were evidently a lady and her maid. Ranald looked at them with burning curiosity, illness and gloom for the moment forgotten, and raising himself on his hands and knees gazed at the maidservant with his mouth falling open. She was tall for a woman and strode down the beach with long, inelegant strides. Every now and then she seemed to be kicking savagely at her long, flowered linen gown as though it incommoded her beyond endurance. The shawl that she had wrapped round her head and shoulders hid her face, but as she held out a hand to help her mistress into the boat she gave a sudden crow of rather reckless laughter. Ranald had heard that laugh over and over again, and always at moments of rather exciting danger: at Prestonpans, on the march to England, before Culloden, during the height of a storm at sea. He did not need to see the woman's face to recognize her, and he sat back on his heels, grinning.

Then he looked at the face of the other woman, now standing bareheaded in the boat, and he caught his breath. She had an unforgettable face. A broad forehead under straight black hair, a large nose and resolute lips, a firmly molded, obstinate chin, and dark, brooding, somber eyes. She stood in the boat with her head thrown back and a hand on her hip, her whole attitude courageous and purposeful. When her companions were safely in she sat down, with her hands calmly folded in her lap, and seemed to be issuing orders. Ranald could not hear what she said, but all the men in the boat, including her maid, were obeying her with the meekness of lambs. . . . Judging by her face, Ranald gathered that it would be the worse for them if they did not.

The men bent to their oars, and the little boat glided across the bay and out to sea. They seemed to be making for Skye, whose pale amethyst was now almost extinguished by the violet storm clouds that were creeping up behind it. It was going to be a bad night, and that woman would need all her courage before she got to her journey's end. So thought Ranald, and wasted a good deal of pity on her, not knowing that the only effect that storm had on the iron nerves of Flora Macdonald was to soothe them so that she slept right through it.

Ranald, as he crawled out from behind his rock, felt almost lightheaded with relief. He felt convinced that the Prince was saved. That woman's face convinced him. She had made up her mind that he should escape, and therfore it would be so. She was obviously one of those who can control the destinies of others through sheer force of will, and feel the better for it. In the privacy of the domestic circle, thought Ranald, she was probably a terror; but as the savior of a prince it might be that she would never be forgotten.

V

Five days later Ranald, too, was in Skye. They had hired their boat, though it took their last coin to do it, and fought their way there through the usual wind and drenching rain. They had wanted to land in the north of Skye, where were the homes of the two boatmen; but the wind swept them right out of their course, and they landed at last, at sunset, by a sheer miracle, in Tarskavaig Bay in the south. They beached their boat and came ashore where a few fishermen's huts stood round the bay, backed by a half-circle of blue, dreaming hills.

Here they separated, the two boatmen turning toward the north and Ranald following a path to the east. If he were to follow it for only a few miles, they told him, he would find himself at the coast with only the Sound of Sleat between him and Scotland.

The wind and rain had vanished with the suddenness that distinguished all weather changes in the islands, and the evening was blue and fragrant and still. Ranald had reflected grimly, as he rolled up over the rocks, that the storms always got up when they took to the sea and vanished when they landed. Ever since Culloden the weather had been on the side of the enemy.

Beyond the rocks he found a grassy path that wound upward in a hollow of the hills beside the delectable stream that is now called Gillean Burn. On each side of him the slopes were covered with green bracken and ferns, and the bright pink roses of the north were everywhere.

Ranald did not notice them. The last terrible journey from North Uist, short of food and water and soaked to the skin for the hundredth time, had been one journey too much, and pain had built a wall all round him that completely shut out the beauty of the world. He lay in the bracken beside the burn and was conscious of nothing but a vague wonder as to what he was to do. He could not breathe without pain, and his head spun round when he stood, and his legs moved in opposite directions when he tried to walk. It was obvious that this body of his would not carry him to the coast. He had worn it out, and it was useless. He looked longingly at the cool water in the burn and wished he could drown the thing.

But the queer pressure of the will to life, so much stronger than the wish of the mind for death, drove him to his feet and on again, staggering like a drunken man. The path entered a wood, and all round him stood birches and rowan trees, their trunks and the floor of the wood covered with deep, rich moss. Earlier in the year the place must have been carpeted with bluebells, and even now there were a few stray patches of blue lying like pools of water in the green moss.

The path sloped more steeply, and Ranald realized sudenly that he could not get up it. He had the horrible feeling that he was disintegrating where he stood. His body seemed to be separated from his mind, only the pain of it still a part of him. It would be humiliating to collapse on a public footpath, like a rat that had been run over, and he swerved to the right, toward a pile of gray stones that might be a wall one could die behind in private. It was a crofter's cottage, with the reek of peat smoke drifting out through the open door to meet him, and he collapsed headlong across the threshold.

VI

The amazing generosity of the poor to each other was as remarkable in Skye in the eighteenth century as in an English slum in the twentieth. The old fisherman and his wife who lived in the cottage, faced with the problem of an unconscious vagabond blocking up their front door, tackled it with promptitude and resignation. They towed the obstruction inside and searched it for silver. Though intending to be merciful in any case, they felt strongly that virtue should be rewarded if reward could be found. But there was nothing on Ranald but a gold ring on his finger and his dirk in his belt. The old man laid the dirk aside for future use on a dark night, bit the ring to make certain that it was as true as it looked, lost interest in the case, and went out to his night's fishing.

The old woman remained, staring down at Ranald with her arms akimbo. Her heart was touched, and moreover she felt that the burying of one so large would be a problem. She therefore decided that he should live and took instant steps to that end, rolling him onto her own bed of heather, taking his wet clothes off him, and wrapping him in a dry sheepskin.

Then she went out into the twilight wood and gathered an armful of rowan branches and a bunch of St. John's wort. The latter she found accidentally and was overjoyed, for to find it without looking for it was to increase its potency tenfold. Returning to the cottage she fastened a branch of the rowan over Ranald's head to keep off the evil eye and placed the St. John's wort under his armpits, for thus worn it had the power to keep even death at arm's length. The blessed Columcille himself had always worn it so, and it was well known that death did not touch him until he left off his St. John's wort in a fit of absent-mindedness and promptly caught a cold. Outside the door she piled the rest of the rowan branches and set fire to them, for a fire of rowan is three times sacred.

Then she came inside again and set about the ceremony of smooring the fire. She spread the embers on the hearth in a circle which she divided into three parts, one part for each Person of the Trinity. Then she laid a peat upon each pile of embers. The first she laid down in the name of the God of life, the second in the name of the God of peace and the third in the name of the God of grace. Then she piled sufficient ashes over the peats to lessen without quenching the fire and knelt down to say the prayer that ended the ceremonial.

> The sacred Three
> To save,
> To shield,
> To surround,
> The hearth,
> The house,
> The household,
> This eve,
> This night;
> And every night,
> Each single night,
>   Amen.

Finally she went once more to the door and looked out to make sure that the sacred fire of rowan was still burning. It was night now, though in June in the islands there is practically no darkness. A few stars shone faintly in the still bright sky, and the night birds were calling. The sound of the sea came to her very clearly in the utter stillness. She nodded her head in satisfaction. Death and his demons might be lurking in the shadows of the wood, but here in the cottage she had seen to it that only holy things should help her in her fight for a life.

Going inside again, she found Ranald stirring and muttering in fever. She poured a draught of cold spring water down his throat and piled the cooking utensils and the furniture on top of his legs to keep him from rolling about in the night and disturbing her. Then she lay down beside him and went to sleep.

VII

She was entirely successful. In spite of, or because of, the rowan and the St. John's wort, Ranald recovered. His strong constititution helped him and the absence of a doctor was, no doubt, very beneficial indeed.

But his recovery took a very long while, and by the time he was able to crawl out of the cottage into the sun the wild roses were over and the heather was just beginning to spread a lavender mist over the world. He asked how long he had been ill, but the old couple had no idea. He asked what month it was, but they did not know that either. They said it was the time of the dragonflies, and the canna-bawn, the mystic flower of the Gaelic singers, was blowing on the hills.

Ranald felt mad with impatience. His one longing now was to get back to poor Judith, but between him and the sea was a steep path up the wooded hillside and several miles of moorland; and, curse at them as he might, and did, his legs still obstinately refused to belong to him or take any responsibility whatsoever for his weight. Day after day he set himself to crawl up that hill, getting always a little further but never reaching the top. The old couple watched his efforts with amusement. They had got used to him now and were in no hurry to part with him. There was plenty of fish in the sea for him to eat and plenty of water in Gillean Burn for him to drink, and he was clever with his fingers and made himself useful to them in the cottage. Each morning they waved to him as he set out on his crawl, and later they fetched him back from wherever he had got to.

The day when at last he got to the top of the hill was a great day for him. He had lived so long in a wood that it was a relief in itself to climb up out of the trees onto the bare moorland above. It was a fine, calm day with a thin veil of gray clouds hiding the sun. All round him was the moor covered with the heather in full bloom, and at his feet lay Loch Dhúghaill, its surface so still that it looked like a sheet of dull silver. Raising his eyes from the loch, he looked to the far distance and caught his breath at his first sight of the Cuillin hills. They were many miles away, and their splintered peaks appeared only very faintly against a background of pearly clouds. In color they were pale lilac and blue and gray. They did not look like mountains; they looked like the spires and turrets of a fairy city.

Ranald sat down in the heather and looked at them bitterly. He remembered how he had looked at Skye from North Uist and thought of it as an earthly paradise where ideals could be realized; yet when he had landed on it it had only been an island, possessed of a haunting beauty, it was true, but still only a part of the earth like other islands. And now there were those hills looking like the city where dreams come true; yet if he journeyed to them the city would vanish and he would be left with the hard rock of material things. Even as he watched them the pearly clouds descended and the pinnacles and turrets disappeared into the mist.

He saw his city vanish with an intolerable heartache. It took with it, he felt, his old beliefs, his love, his youth, and his very life. He had a touch of the second sight of the Highlander, and he did not think he had very long to live. That he did not mind particularly; he had seen death at close quarters too often to fear it. It was the loss of his own faith that made him wretched.

He had told Judith that death could not touch their love or their souls or their work, but now he thought that that belief was only a mirage seen by the eyes of youth and hope. He did not even think now, as the had thought when he wrote to Judith, that the thoughts of the happy were more likely to be true than the thoughts of the unhappy. He thought now that only when every joy and treasure have been stripped away can a man see truth; and the truth that he thought he saw was just nothingness.

He was tired by his walk uphill, and he fell asleep in the heather. When he woke up again he went on drearily thinking, and he wondered what he would do supposing that after all his life was not over. How would he face life with beliefs, the mainspring of it, broken. One lived the life of an animal, he supposed; one just went on mechanically eating and drinking and taking one's pleasure where one could. . . . He supposed he would do that. . . . Then he suddenly sat up, his eyes on the mists about the Cuillin hills. No, he would not. It was a way of life he could not endure after the other. He was a man and not an animal. He would live out his life as though the belief he had once had was his still. Though the holy thing seemed gone from the shrine he would continue to care for the empty walls and sweep the floor, however dreary and useless the work might seem. He remembered what he had said to Judith about loyalty to a cause. The same was true in a deeper sense of belief. Flames might die down, but nothing could rob one of the ashes.

The warmth went out of the day and the west darkened. He did not want to get wet, and he got up to go back to the cottage. He took infinite care of his dilapidated body in these days, for it was all he had to rely on to get him back to Judith, and his longing for her during this time of inaction was a torture, as it had been in Edinburgh.

As he paused for a moment for a last look at the moors before he went downhill into the wood, the Cuillins reappeared through the clouds and stood out, their pinnacles lit by a gleam of sun. He looked at them almost maliciously. That city of dreams had tricked and betrayed him.

Halfway down the hill he stopped dead, struck by a sudden idea that came to him like a lightning flash. What *was* faith? Was that easy, happy belief of the old days, that had added so much to the pleasure of life, perhaps not faith at all? He wondered if he was now, for the first time in his life, actually experiencing faith. This fighting with no certainty that there was anything to fight for, this going out into the night with no belief that the dawn would ever come, was it perhaps the real thing of which the other, easier, thing had been only a foretaste? Standing still in the wood with the dragonflies darting about him, he felt certain that it was so. Yet of what use was this faith, either to himself or to the world? Like another flash came the thought that not to know its use was the very essence of it. Faith was a charge in the dark by blindfolded men, urged on by instinct only. Of that instinct one knew nothing except that it was the greatest thing in life.

He lay awake most of the night, awed by the knowledge that comes perhaps only once in a lifetime—that a great change had taken place in him. These last weeks of mental and physical pain had been the birth-pangs of some new advance.

When the dawn came he got up and went out into the wood. He looked at it with new eyes. What the miracle of beauty meant he did not know, but he loved it with a new love that was in itself a justification of life. He knew that he would never know happiness again, as he had known it in the old days; but he now knew peace. . . . He thought that as long as memory was his, till death or beyond it, if memory lasted so long, he would never forget the island that had given it to him.

VIII

Some while later he climbed the hill, took his last look at the Cuillins, and then tramped over the moor and down through the Ardvasar woods to the bay that is now Armadale Harbor. A kindly fisherman, a relative of his old friends in the wood, took him out in his boat for the night's fishing and under cover of the darkness rowed him across to the mainland. He was put ashore at a little rocky fishing hamlet that then, as now, smelled abominably of fish, and is now called Mallaig.

He turned south along the coast road in a dawn that turned even the silver sand of the little bays to molten gold and lit flames in the sky. He traveled so slowly that he did not reach Borradale until evening. He went down to the shore, hoping to find a warm corner between the rocks where he could sleep. It had been a beautiful September day, but now a mist was creeping in from the sea and it was cold. He slept a little, the fitful sleep of exhaustion, and then woke up with a start. He peered over the top of a rock and saw a blurred shape out at sea, only faintly visible through the mist. It was a ship, and a large one. He wondered if it was a French ship. A rowboat with men in it had come quite close to the shore.

He felt interested and watched intently. He heard the scrunch of feet on shingle, and a little group of men came down to the small boat. They walked quickly, and they did not speak. At the water's edge they stopped, and a tall figure detached itself from the group. He went from man to man, as he had done in South Uist, and they bent to kiss his hand. Ranald could not see his face, but there was desolation in his attitude as he turned abruptly away from them and got into the boat. There was the soft rattle of oars, and it glided away into the mist. Both Ranald and the group of men on the shore stayed quite still, waiting. They none of them moved until the ship weighed anchor and passed out of their sight.

So he had got away. Ranald wondered at himself that he did not feel the elation he had felt when he saw the Prince escape to Skye. He felt nothing but a heavy sorrow, and he even wondered if he, with death perhaps not far off, was not the more fortunate of the two.

The group of men broke up. They did not speak to each other, and they crept off up to the moors in different directions. Their hurry and their secrecy gave Ranald his first hint as to the state of things in the Highlands.

IX

Two nights later he was close to Glen Suilag, with only the great pile of Ben Caorach between him and home. He sat down by a little tarn that lay there in the valley and wondered what to do, for it was very late and already the stars were blazing in a clear sky. Now that he was so close to his home he felt in deadly terror of what he would find there. Judith, hearing no news for so long, would perhaps think he was dead. Perhaps she had gone away. Perhaps the house was burnt. He had passed several ruined homes in his journey from the coast, and the sight had sickened him. Perhaps his home was like that. Perhaps, even, Judith was dead. It had been a long hot day, and he was worn out; his mind began to paint horrible pictures against the darkness.

To dispel them he got to his feet again and looked at the sky, trying to tell the time by the position of the moon. It was too late, he decided, to go home that night. If Judith were there he would frighten her, and she must have had enough to frighten her, poor little darling, in the black year that had passed.

He decided that he would try and get to the cave of Ben Fhalaich and spend the night there. From it, perhaps, he would be able to see if the house was still standing.

It was a long, hard climb in the dark, and when at last he got to the black tarn he fell flat on his face in the heather beside it. He lay there for a long time trying to get his breath, and trying to face looking at the valley below. At last he sat up and looked. A thick ground mist lay like smoke in the glen, and he could see nothing at all. He would have to wait till the morning to know what had happened there. He rolled over in the heather again with a groan, for God knew how many hours must pass before dawn came and dispelled those mists. Sleep would be impossible, he thought; so he closed his eyes and prayed for patience.

Presently something prodded him, and he opened them again, thinking some animal was pressing against him. The moonlight showed him a small, ragged, dirty boy with a round black head. He stared at him, wondering if he was Glen Suilag child, but the brown face with the completely circular black eyes was strange to him.

"Who are you, child?" he asked in Gaelic. "Where is your home?"

"Achnabar," said the child, pointing over the hills; and, taking a dead frog from somewhere about his person, he held it out for Ranald to see. The frog was very precious to him. He had had that frog for days and days. His action was sweetly courteous and showed plainly that he was friendly disposed toward Ranald and was anxious to share his pleasures with him. . . . Ranald shared them, very politely.

"What is your name, little son?" he asked.

"Duncan," said the child.

"And why are you not in your bed?"

Duncan sniffed contemptuously and drew his forefinger under his nose. His gesture implied that his home was not what it might be and he preferred the life of a free man in the hills.

"Tell me, Duncan," said Ranald hoarsely, "is the house of the Laird of Glen Suilag still standing in the glen?"

Duncan nodded, and the stars seemed wheeling and falling round Ranald.

"And Mistress Macdonald of Glen Suilag, is she still there?"

But here Duncan was only puzzled and shook his round black head. He knew nothing of Glen Suilag, he said, except that the house still stood and the Laird had not returned from the wars. Then his black eyes traveled slowly from the torn tartan that Ranald wore to his face, where they remained in an unwinking stare. " 'Tis yourself is the Laird," he said.

Ranald acknowledged it, and instantly the child's whole bearing changed. He removed himself from Ranald's chest, where he had been sitting, and sat himself down at a respectful distance. . . . Clansmen did not sit upon the chests of chieftains. . . . His eyes were still fixed on Ranald, and he seemed to be thinking what he could do.

Presently inspiration came. He got to his feet and began rooting up handfuls of heather which he carried to the cave. He trotted backward and forward for a long time, much absorbed, his tongue protruding at the corner of his mouth; and then he came to Ranald and signified that the Laird's bed was prepared.

"God bless the work," said Ranald, and followed him to the cave. The little stream was bubbling up and seeping over the pebbles just as it had always done and always would do; and beside it, where the ground was dry, Duncan had prepared a heather bed.

" 'Tis yourself is a good child, Duncan," said Ranald, and sank upon it gratefully.

Duncan squatted at the mouth of the cave and thought a little longer. Then he dived about among his underclothes and produced a bit of oatcake which he presented to Ranald with the air of a butler handing venison. It had probably been keeping company with the frog, but Ranald was starving and was not particular.

There seemed nothing more that Duncan could do, and he knew his place. He got up and vanished like a sprite into the night.

Ranald was amazingly comforted. He lay for a little longer watching those glorious stars and then, in spite of the impossibility of sleep, slept for hours.

CHAPTER IV

I

THE stars that had shone so gloriously over the cave of Ben Fhalaich were dimmed with a heat mist as the night went by, and dawn saw the mountains muffled in a thick pall. Their summits, that seemed so often to be holding up the sky at arm's length, had apparently crumpled up and disappeared, letting the sky hang down on the earth with an oppressive, stifling weight.

Down in the valley on the far side of Ben Caorach there was not a breath of wind and not a whisper of sound. Young Duncan, coming down from the heights to get a drink at the tarn, marveled at the silence. Standing on a spur of rock just above the tarn he looked up at the misty sky and down at the dulled and brooding earth. . . . There would be a storm before night. . . . Then according to his habit, he looked long and curiously at the road that wound away to his left to the great cities and the world of men. For Duncan had imagination. He had never left his mountains and never would, but he liked to wonder what it was like outside them. It was flat, he had heard, and the sheep and cattle were different and the people so daft that they could not understand a word of the Gaelic. A poor sort of place, obviously; but it was interesting to wonder about it.

As he was wondering about it he saw something else to wonder at. At the far end of the valley a red ribbon was threading through the gray morning and wriggling along the road like a scarlet snake. With a beating heart Duncan dropped like a stone behind his rock. He knew what it was. . . . Sassenachs. . . . They had come like that, he had heard, up the road to Achnabar, and burnt his Laird's house to the ground, the Laird being dead at Culloden and not able to express himself on the subject. . . . But the Laird's young son had expressed himself, and had been hanged on the rowan tree by the front gate for his pains. . . . The fear born in Duncan by that memory made him want to run away, yet his curiosity, the strongest thing in him, kept him where he was. He had never seen a Sassenach close to and he wanted to see if it was true, as had been stated, that their ears grew upside down. They would not see him where he was; they would pass up the road below him.

As they came nearer all his fear was lost in amazement, and his eyes and mouth formed themselves into three completely circular discs. Never had he seen such amazing creatures. Gods, obviously—a dozen minor gods marching on their sacred feet and two major gods riding magnificently on two bay horses. All wore scarlet coats with gold facings and curious tight-fitting garments on their legs and weapons that clanked as they moved, but the two on horseback had in addition white hair. This puzzled Duncan, for though the elder of the two was perhaps old, being stout and red-faced and kindly looking, with a tendency to burst at the seams, the other one was quite young, slim and straight and arrogant, with a curling lip and an insolent eye. Their ears, to his great disappointment, were right way up.

They came jungling along the road until they reached the tarn when, to Duncan's horror, the fat god shouted a command and they all stopped, the lesser gods flinging themselves on the grass to rest and the other two dismounting and standing talking together exactly under Duncan's rock. . . . He hardly dared breathe lest they should hear him.

He knew no English, but he guessed by their gestures and by the words "Glen Suilag" coming again and again in their talk, that they were hunting for it and did not know if they were on the right track. So they were after the Laird of Glen Suilag, were they? They would do to him what they had done to his Laird's son, would they? Duncan's heart seemed beating all over him, and the palms of his hands had prickles in them, and he prayed hard under his breath to the holy St. Bride that they would turn back the way they had come.

He could not see so very well where he was, and so anxious was he to know which way they went that he wriggled on his stomach a little way up the rock, and in doing so dislodged a little bit of earth that fell with a plop right on the cocked hat of the younger god. There was a sharp exclamation below, and the deity in question came scrabbling up toward him. Duncan did not stand upon the order of his going. Leaping up, he ran like a hare and did not doubt that in a moment the friendly mountaintops would have hidden him. But unfortunately the younger god, a young ensign in his nineteenth year, could run too. He came bounding up the mountainside with huge long strides and seized Duncan by the left ankle just where the bracken left off and the heather began. Duncan bit and scratched and kicked with all his might and main, but the young ensign, hold-

216

ing him under his left arm and cuffing him vigorously, carried him back triumphantly to the party below.

"Here is a young spark who will tell us the way," he said, and set Duncan on his feet, holding him firmly by the left ear. They all closed round, barring the way to freedom, laughing and staring at him. The memory of the Laird's son emptied his whole being of everything in the world but sickening fear. He stood there abandoned to fear, looking pitifully like a little rabbit caught in a trap, his eyes dilating with terror and his breast lifting and falling in agonized pants under his ragged garments. The red-faced officer with the bursting seams, a kindly Londoner risen from the ranks, took Duncan's face between finger and thumb and tilted it up. "The lad is scared to death," he said. "Leggo his ear, Thomas."

Thomas, the ensign, a sprig of the aristocracy with none of the tenderness to be met with in the sprigs of nature, let go of the boy's ear, but put a hand round his neck from behind, pinching it nastily. It seemed to Duncan that the noose was already round his neck, and he nearly fainted with terror.

"Tell us the way to Glen Suilag, lad," said Jenkins.

Duncan stared stupidly, the sweat starting out on his freckled forehead.

"It appears to have escaped your notice that the local savages neither speak nor understand English," said Thomas in the superior way that always exasperated his senior officer beyond words. "This is obviously a typical specimen of the species," and he gave Duncan's neck a nasty twist to the left.

"Leggo that child's neck," said Jenkins. " 'Ere, you, Fraser, come you 'ere and gabble to the infant in its damn double Dutch."

A man in the rear came forward and bent down, thrusting a blotched, cruel face almost against Duncan's. . . . The child was too terrified even to scream. . . . Was this the road to Glen Suilag, he asked? Duncan nodded. Was the Laird at Glen Suilag? Duncan shook his head. Where was the Laird? There was no movement at all from the little round black head except that it trembled with the agonizing tremors that were shaking the whole body.

"The boy knows," said Thomas. "Threaten him, Fraser." And he put both hands round Duncan's throat, squeezing it, while Fraser poured out a flood of Gaelic threats. Duncan lifted a dirty, shaking finger and pointed toward Ben Fhalaich. "Is it in the mountains that he is?" demanded Fraser. Duncan nodded.

"Then we'll get him tonight," said Thomas with decision, and letting go of Duncan he vaulted into his saddle.

Jenkins pushed up his periwig and scratched his sandy hair despondently. "I'll tell ye out o' my experience, Thomas," he muttered, "as chasin' a flea in a pigsty on an 'ot day is 'eaven in comparison with catchin' an' 'ighlander in the 'ighlands. No sooner do you think you've got 'im in front of you but 'e's 'opped it a couple o' mile be'ind."

"Why hop in the mountains at all on a day like this?" demanded Thomas. "A hopeless task. 'Twill be vastly cooler to ride first to Glen Suilag and threaten information out of the relations," and he rode off up the path. Jenkins, shouting a command to his men, heaved himself on to his horse and followed him, muttering something about, "Badgerin' women an' children an' callin' it war; a bloody business, too bloody by 'alf to be called war, and 'e didn't like it, damned if 'e did."

The scarlet ribbon wound up the side of Ben Caorach, paused for a moment on the top, glimmering like flame in the mist, and then disappeared.

Duncan, who still lay flat in the bracken where he had fallen when Thomas let go of him, sat up and stuck his knuckles into his eyes, trying not to cry. His breath came easier now, and he did not feel so sick. But with the ebbing of his fear his wits returned to him, and with the return of his wits came the knowledge of what he had done. . . . He had betrayed the Laird of Glen Suilag. . . . He jumped to his feet, palpitating now with a new sort of fear, almost worse than what he had endured when the Sassenachs had surrounded him—the deadly fear of the result of his own baseness.

Running like a hare, he crossed the path and struck up the mountainside beyond, making for the cave of Ben Fhalaich. That the Sassenachs were making for Glen Suilag he had not understood; he only knew that he had told them the Laird was hiding in the mountains and that they were now going to look for the Laird. On and on he ran, up and up, trampling through the bracken, falling headlong over brambles, and cutting himself on stones. It was a scratched, bleeding, breathless small boy who came at last to the tarn and ran round it to the cave, creeping inside with words of warning and pentence tumbling out between his gasps. . . . But there was no one there. . . . The little stream was seeping softly through the pebbles, and the heather that Duncan had pulled for the Laird's bed was dented where he had lain on it, but there was no Laird.

Duncan ran out of the cave and round the tarn again till he came to the flat ledge of bracken where he could see the whole of the glen laid out at his feet. There was the loch and the Laird's house and the crofts beyond, and there, just turning off the glen road into the larch wood, was the scarlet ribbon of the marching Sassenachs. It was quite clear to Duncan what had happened. The Laird, waking in the morning and making for his home like a rabbit for its burrow, had arrived there too soon. . . . They'd got him.

Duncan turned and scrambled blindly up the mountain behind the cave. He climbed higher and higher until he was right on the top, hidden by the clouds.

Here, in a little hollow filled with bog myrtle, he flung himself down. Somehow he was too passionately ashamed even to go back to his home. He didn't want to go anywhere or do anything. He didn't want even the daylight to see him; he wished he could die. With the passion of his race he abandoned himself to grief as he had before abandoned himself to fear. All the long, hot day he lay hidden in the hollow, and again and again during the next week, night after night, he haunted the cave of Ben Fhalaich like a little ghost.

II

The daylight that same morning woke Judith out of a hideous dream in which she stood paralyzed in a stifling, dark room. From somewhere outside the room footsteps came nearer and nearer. She knew they were Ranald's footsteps; and she knew, too, that Ranald must not come into the room or something terrible would happen to him. She tried to cry out to him, but she could not. She tried to move so that she might go to him, but she could not. There was a terrible constriction round her throat, and her legs felt held down. Then there came a blinding flash in her eyes, and she woke up to find herself lying in a twisted heap in the middle of her great bed. One of her hands was against her throat, and her night-shift was tangled round her legs. The horror of her dream was still with her; she could not shake it off. She told herself that the nightmare had been caused, like most nightmares, by her physical position. Her own touch on her throat and the twisted night-shift had made her dream that she was bound and helpless, and the flash had been the daylight in her eyes. She told herself this over and over again, yet she could not free herself of the feeling that some harm had happened, or was going to happen, to Ranald that was her fault. . . .

Yet how could that be? . . . He was not even with her. Perhaps he was dead.

With a great effort she sat up. The curtains of her bed were drawn all round her so that she sat in a dim tent so big that it was like a little room. The blue and yellow flowers on the chintz twined round her as though to protect her from the outside world. She loved these faithful, unfading flowers that never deserted her even on January mornings when the garden was hard and black with frost and the bare branches of the trees were like interlaced prison bars.

Like all lonely people, she had in her thoughts endowed her possessions with personalities. The harpsichord, the brocade curtains in the room below, the furniture in her bedroom, the book that Ranald had given her to write her songs in, the dress she had worn on her homecoming night and that she kept now in the oak chest in the parlor as in a cradle—these were all her conforting and kindly friends; she could not now imagine her life without them, and it would, she thought, be horrid to have to leave them when she died. They would be lonely without her, surely, and want her to come back again.

Her bed would miss her the most of all of them, for it was the best of her friends and did the most for her, carrying her when she was tired and sick, cradling her dreams and watching her visions and knowing all her miseries. All these last months it had held her up through the horrible hours when she had lain looking at terrible pictures painted on the darkness—pictures of Ranald a hunted fugitive, Ranald in prison, Ranald executed at Carlisle, and most dreadful of all, Ranald's body as it would look now if he had been killed at Culloden. It had held her and comforted her and, on the rare occasions when she cried, it had received her tears and told no tales of her afterward. She was grateful to it, and she loved it very much.

Now she scrambled down to the bottom of it and drew the curtains at its foot so that she could see Ranald's portrait. Always when she had terrible dreams it comforted her, when morning came, to look at it. It was so impossible to connect death with anything so radiantly alive as Ranald was in that picture. His youth and strength seemed so secure there, the brilliantly clear, rain-washed background was so undying in its loveliness that the whole picture seemed vibrant with immortal life.

Judith thought sometimes that it was that sense of eternity that made the creations of art so satisfying. The men who painted great pictures died and were dust, and the people who loved them passed by in procession and vanished, but the pictures went on. The ears that listened to great music listened only for a little, but the music was always there. Actors, each in his turn, played Romeo, Orlando, and Ferdinand until their youth was gone from them and they were not heard again; but Romeo, Orlando, and Ferdinand lived on. These things, created by the immortal in man, were, it seemed, themselves immortal. They were apparitions from another world, messages from another order of life.

Ranald's portrait was, Judith felt, symbolic of the something in him and her and their relationship that time could never touch. "Time?" Ranald had said, "what's time? Only a picture frame." That was all very well, but a picture frame could be a horribly constricting thing, as unscalable as a prison wall. While it thrust itself between her and Ranald she could have nothing of him but that invisible something symbolized by a square of canvas enclosed in four gold bars. . . . If only, somehow, she could smash those bars so that the man in the picture walked out of it and came to her. . . . If only she knew some alchemy that could dissolve time and give her again all that had been.

But she did not and she must get up, for there was a

222

great deal to do today. She wanted to try a new recipe for syllabub, a very economical recipe that only needed a pint of cream and twelve eggs, and then all the furniture in the parlor needed polishing, and one of the brocade curtains was a tiny bit frayed at one of its edges, and she must mend it. She had got into the bad habit of always holding it back with her hand so that she could watch that bit of road down which news came, or did not come. . . . Somehow that bit of road had got on her nerves; she was always watching it. . . . She must break herself of the habit, or by the time she was an old woman the poor curtain would be quite worn out where her hand held it.

She pulled back her curtains and jumped out of bed, pattering across the floor on her bare feet to inspect the day. The thick mist shrouded the garden and wood and Ben Fhalaich, and already, early as it was, it felt hot and thundery. She hated these stifling days; they destroyed all that made the beauty of the Highlands. They enchained the austere winds and the sweeping, cooling rain; they breathed their defiling breath over the colors of the world so that they were dimmed as a mirror is dimmed by the hot breath of one who thrusts his face too close to its beauty. They were evil things, she felt, and one almost welcomed the great storms that ended them, tearing the chains from the wind and the rain so that they raged like mad things over the earth and in the wake of their passing color and refreshing coolness were born again.

There would be a storm before night, Judith felt sure, one of the rare September storms. . . . Yes, it was September again. . . . Ranald had been gone more than a year.

She turned to the washstand and began to dash cold water into her face to stop herself from crying. By this time, if only Ranald and King James and Prince Charles and all the men who had combined together to ruin her life had had a little sense and not done it she might have had a little baby. She wanted her baby dreadfully; no one knew how she wanted it.

She dried her face and hurried savagely into her clothes, pulling off two buttons and breaking a tape. She put on her oldest and shabbiest frock and tied back her hair just anyhow. What did it matter what she looked like? What did anything matter? Her lover had left her, and there was no one to say that she looked pretty, and perhaps she would never have a little baby to gurgle into her neck when she tickled it and clutch at her curls with its fat hands.

She clattered down the stairs in the way that warned Angus in the kitchen that she was in one of her rages. When he brought her some breakfast she refused it petulantly, and when he suggested a dose of rhubarb cordial she threw her slipper at him. His aggrieved growls could be heard all the way down the hall as he withdrew with the rejected breakfast.

Judith went to her harpsichord. When she was in one of these moods her music was the only thing that helped her. It seemed to draw the sting out of her misery. That was another thing that art did. It gave the artist the power to express in symbol all the deep feeling that, unexpressed, would have driven him mad. It was a merciful thing for the community at large, Judith thought, that art had been devised by a merciful Creator. A man standing at his window and hurling his crockery into the street in the misery and rage of his heart would merely get himself disliked; yet the same man expressing himself, as an alternative, in the fury of a great symphony, was a blessing to society.

Her fingers moved softly over the harpsichord. Yesterday she had composed the music for a song she had written that embodied Ranald's ideas about the past and the future. She was not sure, really, that she believed a word of Ranald's nonsense, but it was comforting to

224

imagine that she did. She sang very softly, the notes of the music falling like tinkling drops of water into the silence of the room.

I have known maytime,
And flowers of the springtime,
And caroling bird songs of April's high noon.
I've laughed in the sunlight,
And sung in the starlight,
And danced like an elf in the light of the moon.

I have known pleasure,
And youth's careless leisure,
I have been loving, beloved and gay,
If thoughts of the morrow
Brought shadows of sorrow,
I hid them away 'neath the joys of a day.

Now that the sunshine
Is dim as the starshine,
And now that spring flowers are withered away,
I'll even remember
In barren December
Nor heaven nor hell can my memories slay.

Safe is my treasure,
Filled up to full measure,
Locked secret and safe in the heart of the past.
I look to the future
To give back my rapture,
Untarnished and perfectly mine at the last.

As she sang Angus came in with a basket of peats and stood regarding her with sour disapproval. His attitude toward her music was that of a dog. He loathed it, yet whenever he heard it he would come hurrying from the other end of the house to protest. Judith thought that both he and dogs regarded all music as a dirge and were anxious, out of a sense of kindly fellowship, to join in lamenting the cruelty of fate to dogs and men.

"Gr-r-r-r," said Angus, and thumped his basket of peats down by the fire.

"I shall not want a fire this evening, Angus," said Judith; "it is much too hot. . . . The heat makes one tired."

"Who would not be tired an' hot," said Angus disagreeably, "thumpin' all day long on a tin kettle."

"It's no more tiring than walking backwards and forwards all day long with peats that nobody wants," snapped Judith. Then penitence seized her. She and Angus loved each other dearly; yet lately, somehow, they did nothing but bicker and scratch like two cats on the tiles. "Forgive me, Angus," she cried, holding out her hands to him, "I am so tired. . . . You are so tired. . . . We must do something all day, you and I, to keep our minds off Culloden."

It was the first time she had spoken so openly to him. They had both of them, he with his intense reserve and she with her courageous assumption that all was well, hidden their anxiety from each other. Her remark had a disatrous effect on Angus. He began to snarl as savagely as an animal will when a cruel hand touches a sore.

"Culloden! A year ago today we had no' heard the word Culloden. Curse yon Hanoverians! The deil tear 'em limb from limb! Let 'em fry in hell! The flower o' the Highlands dead upon Culloden moor! May the deil tak' Prionssa Ban that he brought 'em to it."

He went on cursing in Gaelic, his eyes blazing and his whole figure quivering, all his pent-up fury pouring out. If Judith had not been so scared by this alarming spectacle of a controlled man losing control she would have thought of her gentleman hurling his crockery out of the window.

"Angus!" she cried, "hold your tongue."

226

As suddenly as he had begun he stopped. He stood there trembling and blinking at her. He looked so shaken that she went to him and patted his arm gently. It was terrible, surely, to be so very old and yet to have the capacity for grief of someone who was very young. Life, that in passing dulls the power to feel so that it is commensurate with the power of the body to bear, seemed to have forgotten to deal so with Angus. . . . It was pitiful.

"Do not be unhappy, Angus," she pleaded.

"Ye fule o' a woman!" said Angus contemptuously, and she was obliged to agree with him. . . . As well might she request the sun not rise and the flood of life to stop still.

He shook off her hand and ambled to the door, pausing to remark indifferently, "There's been redcoats seen i' the mountains the morn, so they say."

"What?" said Judith sharply.

"Ou, ay. The sumphs tell that tale every day, but the redcoats dinna come. They've coombed oot every glen but ours. They hae burnt doon every hoose but ours, but they miss oot Glen Suilag."

"One day," said Judith uneasily, "they may find us." Beside the fear of Ranald's death the fear that her home might be destroyed was a very minor anxiety; yet it was a real one. . . . If all her friendly treasures were destroyed she would have nothing at all left to comfort her.

"Aweel," said Angus, " 'tis no matter. If they came they would no find the Laird. The Laird is dead at Culloden wi' the lave. Dead at Culloden or hanged at Carlisle, one or t'other."

Angus's sudden collapse into hopelessness seemed to Judith so pitiful that she forced herself to fight it. She would recite Ranald's creed to him. What did it matter if she did not really believe it? One must act to live. Life was a drama and human beings the actors who must

227

play their chosen parts willy-nilly or the curtain would go down upon confusion. What one really felt was often too contemptible to express, and one must act the self one should be. . . . She ran to him and seized the lapels of his coat.

"Angus," she said, "it is not all over. Do you hear? You and I and the Laird are bound together like three twisted strands, and those three strands together make a strong cord, and that cord is life that goes on and on."

"Eh?" said Angus.

"The cord seems all unraveled and broken now, but it will get straightened out again. Only you and I must believe that it will, believe with all our might. To have faith in happiness is to put out hands into the dark of the future and drag it to you. . . . Did you know that?"

"Ye're daft," said Angus. "Hands i' the dark! There are hands i' the dark at Culloden that will ne'er lift claymore again."

"You know, Angus, time has a queer trick of putting the victor's crown on the defeated."

"After the worms hae eaten 'em," said Angus.

"Angus! Angus!" cried Judith, and pushed him away from her. All her carefully built up edifice of courage came tumbling about her ears. How dared he say a thing like that? When the door clanged behind him she flung herself down on the sofa more abandoned to grief than she had ever been. Why must the whole world be so ghastly? Why must everything in which was the breath of life, from a splendid young body such as Ranald's had been down to a blue butterfly dancing in the sun, suffer this same horror of decay and ugliness? She sobbed despairingly into the sofa cushions while her friends, the curtains and the writing table and the harpsichord and the room itself, breathed out their essences to comfort her. The flowers on the curtains, unfading even in midwinter, showed her the wisdom in their hearts; and the writing table, so shiny whatever hap-

pened, uttered a remark very much to the point. As for
the harpsichord, it sang a little song that it had once
heard and that had stuck in its memory.

> Of his bones are coral made;
> Those are pearls that were his eyes;
> Nothing of him that doth fade,
> But doth suffer a sea-change
> Into something rich and strange.

Judith, her eyes hidden, heard. So death was a sea-
change, they said. Its bitter, salt water divided what it
engulfed into its elements; spirit was divided from matter and each was absorbed into its right home. . . . Dust
to dust. . . . If the change was terrible it was soon over,
and out of the earth flowers sprang.

III

"Judith!"
She looked up. He was standing in the middle window, clinging to it for support yet laughing at her. She
had never seen such a deplorable sight as he looked,
lean and hungry-looking as a wolf, his tartans torn and
stained, and his shirt hanging in rags. She scrambled up
the back of the sofa, tumbled off it, picked herself up,
and fell into his arms as he staggered through the middle window. They swayed about the room gripped together and talking like lunatics.

"Do not you touch me!" gasped Ranald, holding her
so tightly that she could not breathe. "I am filthy. . . .
Get me something to eat. . . . Dhé, it is sweet that you
smell!"

"Ranald! . . . I knew you would come back. . . . Are
you hurt? Mo chridhe, are you hurt?"

"No. Starving. Get me something to eat."

"How can I when you will not let me go?"

"Dhé, it is sweet that you smell."

"Let go, idiot," cried Judith, clinging to him. "Mo chridhe, let go, I tell you."

"Call Angus. Let the old fellow kill the fatted calf."

"Angus! Angus!" she cried.

Their knees gave way, mercifully at the sofa, and they sat down with great suddenness.

"Dhé! How soft!" cried Ranald. "What luxury! It is in the heather that I have been since Culloden. Darling, darling Judith, do not come so near."

"Let go of me then," she gasped.

Angus, entering disagreeable, remained rooted to the spot for a full minute. Then he staggered to the sofa and stood leaning on it, gazing at Ranald with a madness of intensity. "Dhé!" he shouted, "Dhé, Dhé!"

Ranald stretched up a hand and seized him by his beard. "Good old Angus! Pleased to see me. Get me something to eat."

"How can he?" said Judith, on the verge of hysterics. "Let go of his beard."

Ranald let go, but Angus remained where he was. "I' the name o' the Good Being!' he ejaculated; "i' the name o' the Good Being!"

"In the name of the Good Being get me something to eat," implored Ranald, punching him feebly in the chest.

Angus staggered out, looking like an ecstatic scarecrow and ejaculating, "Dhé! Dhé!" all the way down the hall.

"Quite an exhibition of feeling from the old blackguard," said Ranald, and they leaned against each other weakly.

"Ranald, how thin you are."

"Exquisitely sylphlike," he murmured sleepily. "Been living on berries. Not fattening, though nutritious. Always wanted to live close to nature. Did not think much of it. Nothing to eat. No soap. . . . Oh, meudaill, how sweet you smell."

"How you do keep harping on that!"

"Sweetness and cleanliness seem so wonderful. . . . Oh, Judith, I spent last night in the cave of Ben Fhalaich. Nice it was, but nothing much to eat there. . . . I am thinking it will have to be called Macdonald's cave now."

"Did you? . . . Oh, there! Now I have got the hiccups with laughing and crying together!"

Angus came back with hastily collected food and drink on a tray. Every trace of emotion had disappeared from his manner.

"Sit up an' hae yer vittles," he said sourly, and banged the tray down on a little table by Ranald, who fell on it like a wild beast.

"Angus!" cried Judith with a sudden terrifying memory. "The Sassenachs! The redcoats!"

"Eh?" asked Angus.

"You said they had been seen in the mountains."

"Naught but talk."

Ranald, for whom at the moment the fact of food was the only fact in the world of any importance, took not the slightest notice.

"But it may be true," cried Judith.

"Na, na. Each morn I hae been told there were Sassenachs i' the mountains an' no' a sight o' 'em hae I seen, no' so much as a glimmer o' their red hell fire i' the heather."

But Judith, the memory of her waking dream vividly with her, was now in an agony. Everything she could do for Ranald's safety she must do. No harm should come to him through any mistake of hers. She must think for them both. She seized his arm. "The Laird must go. He must not stay in the house. . . . Ranald!"

"What?" he asked, his mouth full.

"There have been Sassenachs seen in the mountains."

"I came over the mountains and did not see 'em. . . . Angus, get me some more of this."

"Na, na," said Angus, "ye must no' o'erfill an empty stomach, or the consequences are to be regretted."

"Ranald!" cried Judith, "what if it is true? You must not stay here. They will search the house and take you if they find you. You must go back to the heather."

Ranald tore the wing from the cold chicken on his tray with a most inelegant action and poured out his third glass of wine. "No. I am not going back to nature. I have had enough of the bosom of nature to last me for a lifetime. I prefer yours."

"Just go back to the mountains till night, Ranald. Perhaps by then they will have come and gone."

"They will no' come," said Angus crossly. " 'Tis naught but a rumor. . . . Stop the Laird eatin'. He's ta'en ower muckle for a starvin' man."

Judith was frantic. Brutally tearing his food from him she knelt on the floor by Ranald, pleading with him. . . . He looked at the chicken longingly over her head.

"Ranald, Ranald! Listen!"

"Good God, Judith!" he interrupted savagely. "Can I not stay in my own home? . . . Even the rats have holes."

"You do not know what they do to rebels . . . they . . . they——"

"Hanged, drawn, and quartered," interrupted Angus with gloomy unction.

Ranald turned to Judith gently, giving her all his attention. "Child of my heart, do you think I do not know that? But 'tis I who am staying here. Glen Suilag is hard to find—a little country lost in the mountains. The devils have missed us. On my way through the mountains I passed ruined homes, nothing left of them but blackened heaps, and I thought our home would be like that. . . . And then . . . it was not . . . it was still here."

232

His voice trailed away and Judith put her head down on his knees, fighting her tears. Angus felt with exasperation that emotion was once more about to engulf them all, and spat out of the window. "G-r-r—" he growled, "sit ye up an' behave yersels."

"You don't understand, Ranald," said Judith feverishly. "They have the names of those who died at Culloden, and they have the names of those who are still free, and they are tracking them down and down like hunted animals." She broke down completely, crying as she had never cried all the long year past. The two men looked at each other despairingly over her head.

"Ye had best gie in," said Angus firmly, "or we'll hae the mistress i' a fit. An' I tell you, I can put up wi' a guid deal, an' hae done i' yer service, but a squeakin' woman turns me vitals inside oot."

Ranald lifted Judith gently off his knees and got up reluctantly. "I will go, Judith, till this darned rumor of yours dies with the sunset. . . . Do not cry any more, Judith."

"No," she whispered, "thank you, Ranald." And she choked back her sobs like an obedient little child, rubbing her eyes with the back of her hand and sniffing pathetically. He looked ruefully down on her tumbled brown curls. . . . And she was only nineteen. . . . What a world!

"Judith, darling, I will be back by night. Get immense quantities of warm water ready for me to wash in, and clean clothes, please, Judith, and then we will have a little dinner, shall we? Like the night when I went away. . . . We will have our wedding night, Judith, we will have it yet."

"Yes, we will, we will."

"I will be in the larch wood at the bottom of the garden when dark comes. How shall I know the coast is clear?"

"You can see the middle window from the larch wood. I will put the little dinner table in the window with the candles lighted on it and pull back the curtains. When you see the light you will know it is all safe." She pushed him gently. "Good-by, m'eudaill."

He kissed her tousled hair and wet, disfigured little face. "Good-by till tonight. . . . Tonight we will be in paradise, darling. . . . Could I take anything to eat with me, do you think?"

"Ye may tak' the butt end o' the loaf wi' ye," said Angus graciously, "but dinna spoil yer appetite for yer dinner."

Halfway out of the window Ranald paused, his eyes going hungrily round the beautiful, beloved room and finally coming to rest on Judith. "Mo chridhe, all this last year I used to dream of Glen Suilag and wonder if it was real . . . and if you were real. . . . You seemed the sun and the moon and the stars over the glen, the candle and the warm flame at its heart. . . . Something that shone out of my reach. . . ."

"Hoots! Hold yer tongue, mon, an' go on wi' ye," growled Angus.

"It is all real," sobbed Judith. "I will be here when you come back tonight. . . . Only till tonight."

She pushed him out of the window and watched him as he went slowly and reluctantly across the lawn, his feet dragging. What a brute she was to send him away! . . . But she must. . . . And she must not go with him because of the Sassenachs. If they came she would have to be here and to use all her wits. "Oh, please, God, do not let me make any mistake," she prayed distractedly. "Let me have a little sense."

" 'Tis needed," said Angus.

Quite suddenly, childlike, her mood changed, and she went quite mad with joy, jumping up and down and flinging her arms round Angus. "Angus, the Laird has

234

come back! I told you he would! I told you! We have got him again! Oh, Angus!"

Angus, outraged, struggled furiously in her arms. "Dod! The woman is mad! Let go o' me, Mistress. Hoots! I will no' be strangulated like a wean." He extricated himself and put the table between himself and Judith.

"Oh, Angus, Angus, tell me that rumor of the Sassenachs was false."

"I hae been tellin' ye that this last half-hour till me tongue aches."

"Thank God! . . . Oh, Angus, I am so happy!"

"Ye need not scream aboot it an' squeeze the life oot o' a puir mon's body."

"Are you happy, Angus?"

"Ou, ay."

"Angus, Angus, the dinner tonight! What have we in the house?"

"Port. Canary. Whisky. Burgundy. Claret."

"Yes, but to eat?"

"A bird. Bread. . . . Na, the Laird has ta'en the bread."

"Angus, it must be a perfect dinner. Go and see about it. Tell Janet. I'll come in a moment. See that there are all the things the Laird likes best. Get out my wedding china and the silver. . . . All our pretty things."

She pushed him out of the room. Left alone, she cried a little, laughed a little, danced a little, and finally caught sight of herself in the glass. She was immediately rooted to the spot in horror. What a dreadful dress! And her hair looked like a last year's bird's nest and her eyelids were swollen and her nose—her dreadful nose —was red with crying. . . . What a sight for a man to come home to!

She darted to the corner of the room where the oak chest was. Here, laid away with lavender, was her very best dress, that she had worn last more than a year ago.

235

She took it out. The yellow roses seemed laughing at her; she could almost hear them giggle. She ripped off her faded old print dress, tearing it and wiping her eyes and nose on its fichu as a sign of contempt, kicked it into a corner, and put on the other one. The lovely silk folds fell round her, whispering softly, the panniers billowing out like full-blown roses and the lace frothing joyously round her shoulders. When Angus returned she was pacing up and down the room, Mistress Macdonald of Glen Suilag, a lady of beauty and importance with a real live husband somewhere in the vicinity.

"Gie me the key o' yer siller," growled Angus. Then he saw her. "Guid sakes! Hae ye stripper yersel' i' the parlor? Hae ye no decency, woman? Are ye crazed?"

"Yes, crazed with happiness. . . . Oh, Angus, have I grown old and ugly this last year?"

"Ay."

"Angus, I hate you! . . . Do I look so very old?"

"Ay, but the Laird is no' obsairvant."

"Angus, you are simply detestable. . . ." She broke off. "Listen! Angus, listen!"

He listened. The sound of horses' hoofs approaching through the larch wood was unmistakable, accompanied by the jingle and rattle of accoutrements.

"Sassenachs!" said Judith.

"Ay," said Angus, and disappeared out of the window.

Judith stood perfectly still, her head high and two red spots burning in her cheeks. . . . Her fight was beginning. . . . Angus was back in a moment, his face disfigured with rage.

"Ay," he said, "a dozen an' more, dressed i' hell's color."

"And the Laird only just gone. . . . Could they have seen him?"

"Na, na, they came by the road. He'd hae been halfway up Ben Fhalaich afore they turned the corner by the hoose." The knocker sounded loudly. "Noo, Mistress, there is nought to scream aboot."

"Certainly not," said Judith. "They will not find the Laird. . . . Open to them, Angus, for goodness' sake. If we are unfriendly they will think we have something to hide.

"They will burn the hoose," warned Angus.

"Let them. . . . So long as they do not find the Laird."

Angus went out and she heard him opening the door and letting them in. In spite of an undercurrent of agonizing anxiety she felt almost exhilarated. She adored a fight. She was keyed up to fever pitch and tingling all over, and in the excitement of the moment she had quite forgotten her dream of the morning. Glancing round the room, like a general surveying his battlefield, her eyes fell on Ranald's tray of food. She had only just time to push it under the sofa and seat herself above in in an attitude of superb calm, before Angus reappeared ushering in Jenkins and Thomas.

"Sassenachs," he said, and the scorn in his voice was unutterable.

Judith rose at Jenkins's awkward bow and stuttered introduction of himself.

"Captain James Jenkins, beggin' your pardon, marm, your 'umble servant. No wish to intrude on you, but I am sent to capture the person of Mr. Ranald Macdonald, whom I 'ave reason to think is 'ere in the neighborhood."

Thomas bowed gallantly. "A darned unpleasant duty, marm, all deuced awkward."

Jenkins scowled at him. "Hold your tongue, Thomas. Am I conducting this affair or are you?" He turned to Judith, indicating Thomas. "Thomas Arbuthnot, marm. A good 'eart but no 'ead."

Judith curtsied superbly. "I am sorry you should

have been put to such unnecessary trouble, sir. My husband was killed at Culloden."

"Now ain't that interestin'?" said Jenkins. "The retainer told me in the 'all that 'is master 'ad escaped to France."

"These little inaccuracies will occur," murmured Thomas charmingly.

For a terrible moment the eyes of Judith and Angus met. . . . The first mistake. . . . Then she quickly recovered herself, tilting her chin. "I think I should know, sir."

Jenkins glanced admiringly at her dress. "You will forgive my mentioning it, marm, I am sure, but those are the prettiest widow's weeds I ever set eyes on."

"You look like a rose, marm," chirped Thomas.

"Hold your tongue, Thomas," snapped Jenkins.

Thomas was unquenched. "Exquisite. . . . It has been our painful duty, marm, to set a guard round the house, so that it will be impossible for you to communicate with Mr. Macdonald and impossible for him to come to you without running straight into our loving arms. After searching the house we will turn our attention to the mountains and apply the patient eye to each fragrant heather bell in turn. . . . I trust you will not find yourself inconvenienced?"

"Not at all, sir," said Judith stoutly. "I have no wish to communicate with a man who is not there. . . . Will you require refreshment?"

"Marm, you are too good. We have the usual digestive organs."

Judith turned to Angus. "Angus, tell Janet to prepare food for the gentlemen, and bring some wine. . . . You are doubtless thirsty, sirs?"

Jenkins mopped his brow. "Well, marm, it *is* uncommon 'ot." Angus went and he turned to Thomas. "Take a couple of men and just take a look round the 'ouse. And see those fellows outside don't fall asleep in the 'eat. All doors and windows must be watched, mind you."

Thomas bowed gallantly to Judith. "If you will excuse me, marm. . . . I detest myself. . . . The path of duty, to a man of feeling is frequently deuced unpleasant."

" 'Is majesty don't pay you to stand still and talk, Thomas," interrupted Jenkins, and assisted his subordinate's exit. Then he turned back to Judith. "Might I sit down, marm? I am not so young as I was, and all this 'unting of rebels in the 'eat of the summer is uncommon trying to a man of my size."

"By all means, sir," said Judith coldly, and they sat down.

"Now I'd like a little conversation with you, marm."

"By all means, sir." She looked at him. Pity was written large upon his broad, red, perspiring face and she felt a little stirring of fear. . . . She did hope he was not going to be kind to her. . . . If he were kind the playing of the part that she had set herself would be doubly difficult. . . . Pity was so unnerving.

He cleared his throat, leaning forward. "It ain't no use, marm, 'idin' the truth. Your 'usband escaped from Culloden an' went to the islands. We've been on 'is track some time but could not seem to lay our 'ands on 'im. These rebels, marm, they are very nippy in their 'ills, very nippy indeed; and in their tartans the color of 'eather you can't seem to see 'em."

"You must be very fatigued, but I do implore you not to exhaust yourself looking for my husband. . . . The Laird is dead."

"Yes, marm. . . . Well, as I was going to say when I interrupted meself, the game is up, marm. If you was to tell me where the Laird was 'idin' you'd save 'im and me a lot of runnin' up and down."

"The Laird's grave is at Culloden."

239

He made a gesture of despair. "Very well, marm, 'ave it your own way."

"I suppose, sir," said Judith wistfully, after a little pause, "that you will burn the house?"

"Such are my orders, marm."

She looked round at her darling friends, the harpsichord, the curtains, and the writing table. "Am I—could I——am I allowed to save any of my belongings?"

He smiled at her with great kindness. "When I am 'ospitably entertained at an 'ighland 'ome I sometimes find it sufficient to light a bonfire of damp wood at the bottom of the garden. The smoke, seen from afar, informs my superiors that I am performing my distressing duties."

Judith was breathless. "You mean— you will not burn the house?"

"It's a pretty old 'ouse, marm, an' I can see you're fond of it."

"Oh, sir, you are good."

"Yes, marm. As an infant I understand my virtue brought tears to me poor mother's eyes."

His kindness had the effect on Judith that she had feared. She was quite suddenly no longer a general on the battlefield but a terrified girl in deadly fear for her lover. If they caught him what would they do to him? Were the rumors that she had heard true? She twisted her hands together. "Oh, sir, I thank God that my husband died at Culloden, for I understand that you Hanoverians treat your prisoners with intolerable cruelty."

"Did they tell you that, marm? 'Twas unkindly done. Do not believe all that you are told, my dear."

His eyes were on her hands, which somehow she could not stop from twisting together, and by the pity in his voice she knew that she had now given herself away utterly. . . . She had made her second mistake. . . . She jumped up, losing control of herself. "Am I mad to talk to you like this? If my husband were here you would take him prisoner. You would send him to England to be hanged and—and—and I sit here talking to you as though you were my friend! Oh, God forgive me!"

Jenkins had three young daughters at home, Polly, Jemima, and Sue; and this baiting of the species was almost more than he could endure. He went to her, taking her twisting hands in his and patting her shoulder. "There, there, my dear, you're upset. Why don't you go to your room and stay there till this is all over?"

"Do not touch me! Do not touch me!" cried Judith, and dragged her hands away as Angus came in with a pewter mug on a tray.

"Leave the mistress alone!" he shouted, savagely offering the ale. "Drink and be damned to ye!" Jenkins took the mug, and Angus flung the tray clattering into a corner of the room and crouched like a wild beast. "Ou ay, hoo mony o' ye will there be round the hoose dressed i' the color o' bluid? The bluid o' the chieftains dead at Culloden stains yer damned body from neck to knee, but 'tis yours will be upon the skean o' Angus Maclaren!"

He drew his dirk and sprang. Jenkins had only just time to fling aside the mug and grip his wrists while Judith dragged the dirk away.

"Angus, Angus!" she panted.

Angus struggled feebly in Jenkins's grip. "Haud awa', ye sumph! I'll hae his pistol. It's nane too late to blow his harns oot."

The incensed Jenkins landed Angus with a crash on the floor. "You lousy rebel! Mr. Macdonald will have a rope round his throat yet for this." He wound his handkerchief round the bleeding scratch on the wrist that was all Angus had achieved. "You've 'ad my blood, though 'tis but a scratch; and I'll 'ave yours, you bleareyed old 'ighland riever."

Judith helped Angus, dazed and staggering, to his feet. "You should think shame, Angus, to behave so

241

crazily. Do you call this the way to make the gentleman kindly disposed toward us?"

"I thocht to mak' awa' wi' him," muttered Angus.

"He's more likely to make away with you after your deplorable behavior. . . . Pick up your tray, Angus, and take yourself off."

Angus, shaken and confused, staggered out, and Judith turned to Jenkins. The little scene had restored her self-control, but all sense of exhilaration had left her. She and Angus, by their joint exhibition of anxiety and rage, had surely made it abundantly clear now that the Laird of Glen Suilag was not far away. She was fighting a losing battle, but she must keep her colors flying. She opened her writing table drawer and locked the dirk away. "It shall stay there out of harm's way. . . . Captain Jenkins, what can I say?"

Jenkins was in good humor again. "Do not mention it, marm. By your promptitude you saved the life of your 'umble and admiring servant."

Angus returned. "Yer vittles is prepared," he growled at Jenkins.

"No, by gad. I prefer starvation. I've a wife and family at 'ome."

"Your meal was prepared by Janet, my cook," said Judith. "She loves anything in trousers, whether it be friend or foe. You can be easy, sir."

"The other body has had the start o' ye," said Angus. "He has had both the breasts o' the bird."

Jenkins was aroused to instant indignation. "Thomas? How dare the young puppy sit down to a meal before his superior officer! What I 'ave to put up with, marm, from young blackguards, you would 'ardly credit. I'm risen from the ranks meself, and these young aristocrats turn me profane. Too much blue blood in the veins to let 'em do any work, an' no red blood in the brain to make the damn thing active. . . . And think that

242

a reason for eating both breasts of a bird and leaving their superior the drumsticks."

He hurried from the room, Angus spitting after him. When the door shut Angus turned threateningly to Judith. "Gie me back that skean, mistress. I'll need it afore the nicht's oot."

"Oh, Angus," cried Judith, "don't you understand? If we treat them with courtesy they are more likely to be merciful if—if——" she broke off, then went on again. "That man is kind. He has promised not to burn the house. If he finds the Laird and we have been good to him he might—might——"

Angus interrupted savagely. "Na, na. The savin' o' the hoose is but a sop to comfort ye for the bluidy murder o' yer mon."

Judith sat down on the sofa thinking desperately, her hands holding her throbbing, aching head. So absorbed were she and Angus that they did not see Thomas strolling outside.

"Angus," said Judith, "one of us must go and warn the Laird."

"Na, na. Do ye no ken there is a cordon round the hoose? None can leave the hoose nor come to it."

"Angus, what if the Laird comes tonight? From the corrie one can hardly see the house, only a glimpse; he will not know they are here."

"Keep the middle window dark and he'll no come."

Suddenly Judith knew what they must do. "Angus, slip out of the window and across the larch wood. You must warn the Laird. You must! You can get away together. If they follow you, kill him. Kill him up there in the corrie."

She unlocked her writing table drawer and took out the dirk.

"Kill the Laird?" he muttered. "Are ye daft?"

"No. Anything to save him from the hanging at Carlisle. If you will not, I will. . . . But they would see my white dress."

He looked at her. Her eyes were wide and staring in her white face. . . . She meant it. . . . The brave wean! . . . Stretching out a shaky old hand he took the dirk from her. If she were to kill the Laird it would be a thing that would leave its mark upon her forever, and she had a long life yet to live; but for himself, he was old and need not endure the burden of memory for long.

"Ye are crazed," he said, "but I will e'en try it."

He stepped cautiously out of the middle window, turned round to give her his creaking smile, then turned back into the arms of Thomas.

"We do not allow your retainers to go walking in this heat, marm," said Thomas charmingly, as he twisted the dirk out of Angus's hand. "Was he going to cut you flowers with this instrument? Could I oblige?"

Judith shook her head speechlessly, and Thomas, plus the dirk, bowed gracefully and withdrew.

Angus came stumbling back. "What did I tell ye?" he asked sourly.

"What are we to do?" moaned Judith. "What are we to do?"

"Nothin'! Dinna fret. Wi'out a licht i' the window the Laird will no' come the nicht."

"But he might come tomorrow."

"Ay."

"And he cannot stay starving in the mountains forever."

"Na."

"Angus, can you not think of something to do?"

"Na," said Angus hopelessly.

Judith's hands went to her aching head again. "If only I could think! I feel I shall make some mistake— do something crazy before the night is over."

244

"I should no' wonder," said Angus gloomily. "All women are fules."

"Oh, Angus, Angus, what is going to happen? Will nothing stop it? Oh, my God, will nothing stop it?"

"Na," said Angus.

She dropped her head on her folded arms on the edge of the sofa. He stood by her, scratching his cheek and staring woodenly and hopelessly in front of him. . . . The long, hot day marched slowly on its way.

IV

It seemed to Judith that it would never be over and that the long, torturing hours of it would kill her. Early in the afternoon, for the sake of his own peace of mind, Jenkins locked Angus in his room; but Judith they left quite free. She made one attempt to get out and warn Ranald, creeping out this time by the kitchen; but instantly a Sassenach popped up beside her. She turned back and stumbled up the stairs to her room, where she sat in a heap on the floor, trying to think. But she could not think. Her head was splitting and felt hot and buzzy, and instead of thoughts silly little meaningless phrases kept saying themselves over and over in her mind. "A pint of cream and twelve eggs. A pint of cream and twelve eggs." And then—"Victory, after the worms have eaten them. Victory, after the worms have eaten them." And then again, "A pint of cream and twelve eggs." She wondered in sudden panic if she was going mad. Because she must not go mad. Tonight she might have to think clearly and cleverly, think to save Ranald's life.

She knelt upon the floor and tried to pray, her hands covering her face and her silk skirts billowing all round her, but the only words that would come were, "Please, God, give me sense," and then the word "sense" went on repeating itself in her brain like a tolling bell, and she could not say anything else. Sense. Sense. If she had sense she would be able to keep Ranald from coming to the house and be able in the end, perhaps, to get away with him to France. If she did not have sense he would be captured and hanged; and at the thought of the manner of his hanging her eyes dilated and she bit her lower lip to keep herself from screaming. . . . Sense. . . . If only they had not locked Angus up. He had not much sense, goodness knew; but his companionship would have kept her from going crazy.

From below her came the murmur of men's voices. Jenkins and Thomas were, she knew, in the parlor at their ease, Thomas on the sofa with his dirty boots on her chintz and Jenkins, with more consideration for her treasures, on a chair with his boots on the carpet. She had been in once and seen them like that. They were simply waiting. What for? She tried again to think. If only she could remember what exactly she and Angus had said in the parlor when Thomas was outside. Had they said anything about the light in the middle window? Her mind was such an aching blank that she could not remember clearly, but in any case she must be in the parlor when the light began to fail to see that no light was lit. Until then there seemed nothing that she could do, except sit on the floor and try not to think of what men who were as the devil for cruelty did to captured rebels.

She leaned her arms on the window sill and looked out at the hot, brooding garden and Ben Fhalaich shrouded in mist, trying to think instead of the beauty and tenderness of the earth that suffered these things. . . . Poor earth, that endured uncomplainingly the pollution and the shame of man's sin, committed with her green bosom below his feet and her trees arms about him and her air a caress on his cheek. Yet she had her revenge, for man's hideousness was a passing thing, and her beauty, though he sinned against it, was eternal.

And now it was almost dusk, a stifling dusk full of the menace of thunder. A sudden puff of hot wind blew over the garden, and the light of the world seemed to shudder and grow dim, like a candle flame caught by a draught, while behind Ben Fhalaich a great black cloud edged with gold was slowly mounting.

It was time that she went downstairs. She got up, staggering a little from weariness and the pain in her head, and as she did so she heard footsteps coming along the passage, the jaunty footsteps of Thomas. Her heart turned over. . . . What was he coming to tell her? . . . Had Ranald come another way and had they caught him? . . . The footsteps paused outside her door, and she tried to say, "Come in," but her voice would not come. Then something clicked and the steps went away again.

It took her a full two minutes to realize that she was locked in, for the key that morning had been as usual on the inside of her bedroom door and she had never noticed that it had been taken away; but when she did realize it the madness that she had been keeping at arm's length all day seemed to seize her. She ran across the room and hurled herself against the door, crying out. Then she ran to the window with some wild idea of jumping from it, but the window was very high with the stone terrace below it, and the creepers that Ranald had planted only a year ago had grown no farther than the lower window. Then she dragged the sheets off her bed to make a rope of them, but there were only two sheets and when she tied them to her bed, the only solid thing to which she could fasten them, they did not reach very far out of the window.

Sitting on the floor on top of the crumpled sheets, she fought to get back her self-control and remembered, as it came back to her, Ranald's skean-dhu that he had left behind him. It had belonged to a dead brother of his

247

and was probably blunt, but it might serve. She took it out of a drawer, testing the blade with her fingers. It *was* blunt, but it would do. She ran with it across the room and, dropping on her knees, began hacking at the wooden frame of the door so that she could get the lock and force it back. Her breath came in gulps, and the sweat that drenched her body soaked through and stained her silk dress. It seemed to her that the old wood of the door was hard as iron and her hands as strengthless as cobwebs. Every now and then she looked back over her shoulder to see how fast the dusk was coming on.

V

Thomas meanwhile went jauntily downstairs, tossing the key in the air and catching it again. The brilliant inspiration that had made him run upstairs that morning and pocket the key had been giving him intense satisfaction all day. His forethought had astonished Jenkins too—Jenkins, who always thought him a brainless idiot. . . . It was good to make the old fool sit up. . . . He reentered the parlor humming an air.

Jenkins was pacing up and down, his face empurpled by the heat and the distress of his mind. For Jenkins was set upon the capture of the Laird—that was his duty—but the tormenting of the Laird's wife, the very spit of his Jemima if a trifle more skinny, was not to his taste. He had refused to allow Thomas to lock her in until evening came. . . . The poor child's agony should last as short a time as possible.

"Done it?" he asked hoarsely.

"Done it," said Thomas, and rearranged himself on the sofa with the cushions in the small of his back.

"That murdering old 'ighland cattle lifter is safe under lock and key too. . . . You are sure that girl cannot get out? I don't want the poor child nosing round tonight."

Thomas fanned himself with his handkerchief. "Phew, it's hot! . . . I do not see what reason you have for being so certain the Laird will come to the house tonight."

"If 'e's not expected at the 'ouse why should the little lady and the cattle lifter be 'alf crazy with anxiety?"

"Are they?"

"Oh, use your eyes, Thomas, do!"

"Then we just wait and hope for the best?"

"That's it. Sit 'ere and sweat."

"By gad, it's hot!" continued Thomas. "Must be a storm coming. " Writhing about on the sofa in an access of heat, he suddenly kicked something under it. "Hullo! Hullo! Seems to keep her best china under the sofa."

"Now you be careful, Thomas," snapped Jenkins. "There's no need to go breaking up a woman's 'appy 'ome because you are going to 'ang 'er 'usband." Thomas dragged out the tray hidden by Judith and then forgotten, and Jenkins's tone turned to alert interest. " 'ullo? . . . Now look at that, Thomas. There you are. 'E was in the 'ouse before us."

"Well, I don't see how you make that out."

"Ah, you've no brain. Too much blue blood and education," triumphed Jenkins, getting his revenge on Thomas for the extraction of the key from Judith's bedroom door. "Look. That meal, Thomas, was eaten by a starving man. 'E's not cut the bird respectable with a knife, 'e's torn it with 'is 'ands. . . . There's the knife unused. . . . But starving though 'e was, 'e did not stop to finish 'is meal. . . . What do you make out from that?"

"He must have come in here, starving from the mountains, and they fed him. Then they heard we were coming, and he ran. . . . Mistress Macdonald pushed the tray under the sofa and forgot it."

"For an educated man, Thomas, that reasoning does you credit."

"What about your plan for catching him as he comes to the house? If he knows we are here he won't come."

"What a brain you have tonight, Thomas. You keep me marveling! But they are expecting him. That murdering 'eathen and Mistress Macdonald would not be all of a jig the way they are if they were not."

"They're afraid we'll catch him in the mountains."

"No, they wouldn't fear that. Do we look like catching an 'ighlander 'opping about in 'is blasted 'ighlands? You so overburdened with blue blood and me with weight, and both of us dressed in garments you can see a mile off?"

"What do you make of it then?"

Jenkins scratched his chin and gazed at the tray. " 'E must 'ave run away from a rumor, not a certainty. The little lady must 'ave arranged with 'im to give 'im some signal if the coast was clear, and now she's sick with fright he'll come, signal or no signal."

Thomas slapped his thigh in sudden excitement. "Got it! The light in the middle window!"

"What's that?"

"Mistress Macdonald and Angus were talking in here this morning, and I was outside keeping an eye on the men. I heard Angus say, 'Keep the middle window dark and he'll no' come.' "

"Yes?" demanded Jenkins excitedly. "What else did they say?"

"That's all I heard."

"You confounded young fool! Didn't you listen?"

Thomas was stung. "I did not join the army to practice eavesdropping," he said loftily.

"God bless my soul, then what did you join it for?"

"Fighting."

"Fighting? With a figure like yours? . . . Well, of all the young fools. . . . Well, you've 'eard enough for our purpose.... Get those candles from the writing table."

Thomas, a candle in each hand, paused. "I wonder if we are right about this? Surely the putting a light in a window would be a silly signal for her to make? I mean, someone else might put a light in the window accidentally."

"You don't know women, Thomas," said Jenkins profoundly. "It's just the sort of darned silly thing they do do. . . . A beacon set in the open window to light the warrior 'ome and attracting in all the moths. . . . The father's sword 'ung over the mantelpiece and likely to fall and 'it the children on the 'ead. . . . The 'usband's slippers put warming at the fire and setting the 'ouse alight. . . . They all do it, bless their 'earts."

They busied themselves with drawing the curtains across the side windows and well back from the middle window. They pulled the table forward and put the candles on it, lighting them with flint and tinder. Meanwhile the great black cloud that Judith had seen behind Ben Fhalaich had spread across the sky, and it was very dark. The first flash of lightning was followed by the first peal of thunder echoing across the glen.

"Phew! Startling, that was!" ejaculated Thomas.

"Make it cooler, let's 'ope," said Jenkins, and quite suddenly he stooped and blew out the candles. His nerve had gone, and his red perspiring face was drawn into lines of disgust and loathing.

Thomas wheeled round on him. "What in the world?"

"I don't like it," growled Jenkins.

"What? The storm?"

"No, you blasted fool. This decoying of a man to his death by putting a light in the window of 'is own 'ome. . . . It turns me sick."

Thomas advanced on him almost threateningly. "What? Squeamish? There's a war on isn't there? Did you think it was a picnic?"

251

"No, not likely, after Culloden. . . . 'Ere, what are you doing?" Thomas had seized the flint and tinder from him and struck them together. The flame leaped out again in the darkening room, and he relit the four candles. The two men stood on each side of the table, glaring at each other, while outside a storm of thunder rain came pelting down.

"Ever see a man 'anged, drawn, and quartered, Thomas?"

"No."

"They cut 'em down before they are a quarter dead and start the quartering on a live man's body. . . . Nasty to see. . . . That is what they'll do to the Laird of Glen Suilag when you and I 'and 'im over to authority."

"What's that got to do with us? It's only our business—" He broke off, for the sound of footsteps on the stairs was audible through the pattering rain.

"Who's that on the stairs?" ejaculated Jenkins. "Didn't you shut that girl in? . . . Lock the door, you fool!"

Thomas made a dive for the door, but he was too late and Judith was upon them. The scene seemed to burn itself into her brain—the four candles blazing by the middle window, the scarlet coats of the men, the lightning flickering across the sky—flame, it was all flame, and Ranald would be burned in it unless she put it out. She tried to run across the room to blow out those terrible candles, but Thomas caught her and held her, her face pressed against his coat. "Noise! Noise!" a voice in her mind kept saying. "Make a noise." She tried to scream out to warn Ranald, but she could not; no sound would come. She felt paralyzed and stifling in darkness. From far away she heard Jenkins saying, "Now, now, my dear, be easy now."

With a sudden twist she got her head free and fastened her sharp little teeth into Thomas's hand. She bit him hard, and he yelled like a child and loosened his grip. "Noise!" tolled that voice in her mind, "noise!" She dragged Thomas's pistol from his belt, unconsciously pointing it out of the middle window, and fired. There was a blinding flash of flame in her eyes, and the room seemed full of smoke. It seemed to her then that there was flame everywhere, in the room and in the sky and in her own brain. . . . The whole world was on fire.

Through it all Thomas's voice came to her. "Gad! That's done it! That's warned him! He'll have doubled back up the corrie when he heard that! Come on, Jenkins, we'll get him yet."

He rushed out of the room, and she heard him shouting for his men. But Jenkins did not immediately follow him. With a gesture of real delight he drew the curtains across the middle window and bowed to Judith.

"I congratulate you, marm," he said.

Then he too ran out and she was alone, swaying backwards and forwards, muttering a sort of mad paean of praise. "You'll not catch him now! He is safe. Safe up there in the mountains with the rain and the clouds to hide him and the heather for his bed. I'll go there too. O God, O God, let us die in the hilltops where men never come and only the whaups are crying and the water weeping. Water is sweeter than blood, and rain than tears."

Gradually the madness ebbed out of her, and she was conscious again of herself and of where she was and of what she had done. She was Judith, standing alone in this curtained, empty room with four candles burning on the table. She was Judith, and she had saved Ranald. . . . She had made no mistake. . . . She stood perfectly still and upright in her triumph, the lovely folds of her dress billowing out around her. . . . She had made no mistake. . . . How quiet it was after the turmoil. The storm had lessened, and there was no sound now but the pattering of the thunder rain on the stones outside and footsteps that came across the terrace, halting and dragging. . . . Footsteps? . . . She flung up her head sharply, listening. And the curtains were moving as though someone were pulling at them, trying to get in. O God, what would she see through that middle window?

In a moment she knew. The curtains were dragged aside and he stood there, leaning against the window frame, gasping, the lightning flickering behind him. One hand was pressed to his side, and a red stain was creeping though his fingers over his tattered shirt. His face looked white as death, and she knew what she had done.

"Ranald," she said, "I've shot you."

He let go of the window frame and lurched toward her, pitching over onto the floor. Now that the very worst had happened she was shocked into complete sanity and was conscious of nothing at all in the whole world but the man at her feet and what he might yet want of her. She knelt down by him, her love making her creep as close to him as possible, yet her reverence for the dying keeping her from touching him.

"You've saved me from them," he whispered; "but you—what will you do?"

"I shall just wait," said Judith.

"For what? . . . Love and life over and done for you."

She felt his grief for her and bent over him, smiling at him though he was nearly gone from her, her voice very clear and slow that it might reach him, "Do you hear what I say? . . . I shall remember what you said. . . . Life is never over. Love is never done."

CHAPTER V

I

THE Laird's body was laid in Judith's four-poster in the big west bedroom, and all night long, while the unleashed wind raged across the mountains from the sea and the rain drowned the world, Angus watched by it. This Judith relinquished to him. She had been alone with Ranald when he died, Angus shut out; so this final duty should belong to Angus.

He would not let her stay in the parlor, where her husband's blood stained the floor, and the candles, burned down to their sockets, still stood by the middle window; so she went to the little south bedroom over the porch. Janet, her servant, crooning over her softly, undressed her, brushing her hair and putting on her night-shift and making her lie down in the little four-poster that had been Ranald's before his father died. Judith submitted like a good little child, even drinking the milk that Janet brought her and kissing her good night very sweetly when her ministrations were over. . . . Janet went down the passage sobbing. That Mistress Judith, always so fiery and independent, should be so sweetly reasonable in her grief made her afraid, for Janet was old and wise and knew that this apparent sudden change of character betoken a shock that would be terrible in its aftereffects.

But the aftereffects had not come yet. Judith lay in the dark room with her eyes on the whirling, reverberating darkness outside the uncurtained windows. Every now and then lighting shone out, illuminating the tossing branches of the larch trees and Ben Caorach pallid against the streaming sky; and whenever that happened

Judith smiled, for Ben Caorach had seen the moment that had been the symbol of all that was eternal in their love; and while Ben Caorach still stood, she thought, her faith too would stand. "Life is never over, love is never done," she had said to Ranald, repeating his creed rather than her own to comfort him; but now she felt that what she had said was true. Love and life went on and on, and however painful they were to the perishable body that was gripped and torn by them, yet they must be good, or they could not so endure.

So Judith lay in the queer exaltation of great grief, and not even the terrible sound of Angus wailing for the dead, coming to her fitfully through the sound of the storm, could disturb her peace. She was in that state of exhaustion which gives a curious sense of lightness to the mind. The usual interaction between mind and body seemed to have been suspended by weariness; her body was just an exhausted thing that seemed to have very little connection with the rest of her while her mind floated above it, thinking clearly and peacefully.

Even when morning came, lovely and cool, with limpid, dancing air and sunlight sparkling on wet trees and grass, her calm was still with her. She got up and washed and dressed herself, fastening all the buttoms with a slow, studied absorption and brushing her hair with meticulous care.

Then she went to the west room, flinging the windows wide to the sun and the fresh wind from the sea. Angus had fallen asleep in his chair by the bed, his head hanging on his chest and his mouth sagging open. He looked pitiably old and gray and broken, almost horrible; and she shuddered a little. It was a relief to turn from him to the young god on the bed. For Ranald's body, in the combined dignity of youth and death, had a beauty that was godlike. It was the moment of the body's last triumph, coming between the disfigurement of illness or injury and the corruption of death, conquering the one and yielding to the other with the trumpets of beauty still sounding.

"You will never be old, Ranald," said Judith. "Thank God, you will never be old." Standing between the figure on the bed and the painted picture on the wall, Judith felt him vividly with her; but he was a divided Ranald, spirit and body two separate things. Yet what did it matter? Though the visible man was soon to be taken away, the invisible would remain; and her faith was surely strong enough to exult in what was left her. . . . So with her head held high she went downstairs to do all the many things that had to be done.

II

Her exaltation lasted until the funeral. They buried the Laird on a day of storm, and Judith, outraging the custom of the time, followed her husband's body to the grave. All round her stood Ranald's people, and beside their grief her still composure looked utterly heartless. But until the day of her death she never forgot the smallest detail of the scene; it haunted her always. The gray clouds tearing across the sky, the lowering purple of the heather spreading like a pall over the hills, the skirling of the pipes minging with the lamenting of bareheaded, bearded men. The rain drove in her face and tore at her cloak, and there at her feet was a deep hole in the ground. . . . It was then that she realized what had happened. . . . Ranald was dead, and she had killed him. . . . Ranald, who used to walk over the hills and ride Mactavish up and down the glen road, who used to love to dance with her when evening came and the violins were wailing in the great hall at her home; Ranald, who could shoot and ride and fight and dance and argue with the best, would do none of these things again because she had killed him. They were putting him down in a deep hole in the ground away from all the things he loved, and it was her fault.

She made no sign at all; but when it was all over and the crofters had gone, and Angus touched her on the arm to take her away, she would not move. "Mistress Judith, Mistress Judith!" he pleaded. "Mistress Judith, ye mun coom hame." But she would not move, and Angus was forced to leave her and go and fetch Janet. Looking back as he stumbled away, he saw her standing there very upright, her slender figure buffeted by the wind. As he went he shook his head and muttered to himself, for he did not like the look of it.

Yet when he and Janet came back together they met Judith walking quietly home, as composed as ever. She went into the parlor and sat by the peat fire and let Janet take off her wet shoes and stockings and rub her cold feet. She was very good all day, eating what she was told to eat and doing the piece of sewing that Janet put into her hands, but yet Janet and Angus were very unhappy about her. When darkness had come and the lights were lighted and the curtains drawn, Angus lingered at the door, afraid to leave her. . . . He had noticed that she had sewn up the petticoat she was making the whole way round, so that it was impossible to get into it anywhere. . . . He was deadly afraid for her. She was strong, both in body and mind, nerves and character; but she had surely borne more than a girl of nineteen could bear without injury.

"You must go to bed now, Angus," she said, smiling at him. "You are very tired."

"Na, na," muttered Angus and then, suddenly and fiercely, "Mistress, ye mun no' sleep i' that west room the nicht."

"Why not?" asked Judith haughtily. "It is my room. I have told Janet to put it ready for me again."

"Ye mun no' do it," said Angus. "I will no' hae ye do it."

258

Judith threw up her head, her cheeks scarlet. "Angus, am I the mistress of this house or are you?"

It was a flash of her old spirit, and Angus was so relieved by the sight of it that he gave in and left her.

And then it began. She had not known that misery could be like this. It overwhelmed her so utterly that everything went down before it. She had no faith left and no hope. She did not believe now in anything at all but the terrible fact of death. Ranald had once been, and now he was not any more; there was nothing left now of all his charm and strength and beauty, his high hopes and splendid promise; it was all destroyed, and by her. . . . She had done it. . . . Her sewing dropped out of her fingers, and for hours she sat there in her chair facing the window. Her despair was so great that she had no sense of the passing of time nor of the dimming of the light as the fire died and the candles guttered down. But she heard, and with increasing vividness, the rain pattering on the terrace outside, and mingled with the rain was the sound of footsteps halting and dragging. Her eyes on the middle window and her hands gripping the arms of her chair, she watched the curtains sway and part and Ranald come through them. . . . It happened all over again. . . . But this time, though she struggled hard to get up and go to him, she could not, for she seemed bound fast in her chair, and she had to sit and watch him die uncomforted. And then he was not there any more; there was nothing there, not even a bloodstain on the floor; she knew there was not because she knelt down on the floor to look. With the little sanity she had left she knew that she must not stay in this room, so she got to her feet and went upstairs to bed.

She undressed and climbed into the four-poster, lying flat on her back with her arms outstretched. But she could not go to sleep because she was so dreadfully cold. "You must go to sleep, Judith," she told herself. "You must go to sleep, or you will be ill," and she wrig-

259

gled her toes backward and forward to try and get a little warmth into them. But it was no good; she was cold as ice, as cold as Ranald was lying out there in the rain. "Mo chridhe," she said, "I did not mean to do it." But there was no answer. There was no sound but the moaning of the wind outside and the creaking of the old boards in the passage outside her room.

Lying there she began to think of all the Macdonalds who had died in this bed and whose bodies had lain here in the dignity of death, as Ranald's had done. It seemed to her that it was their voices that she heard crying in the wind and their footsteps that went up and down the passage outside her door. . . . They must be very angry with her. . . . This alien girl who had murdered her own husband and yet dared to call herself by their name. . . . But she was too miserable to be frightened. She did not know that misery could be like this. . . . When Janet came to her in the morning she was still lying flat on her back with her arms outstretched and she had not been to sleep.

And so it went on for several days and nights. She did her work as usual in the day, and Janet and Angus hoped that it was going to be all right and that she would win through. They did not know that every evening when dusk came she sat in her chair and watched Ranald coming in through the middle window, and they did not know that the power to distinguish what was real from what was not real was leaving her. They did not know, either, what were the things that she thought about when she lay sleepless and shivering in her big bed upstairs.

III

The breaking point came on a lovely, warm, moonlight night. She sat in her chair and looked at Ranald lying on the floor, and it seemed to her that she was being perfectly sensible and thinking very clearly and well. She was almost proud of herself because her thoughts seemed so wise and right. It seemed to her that Ranald must be coming to her every night like this because he wanted to take her away to be where he was. He was angry with her. She had destroyed his life and his work, and he did not think it right that she should live on in the sunshine while he lay buried deep down in the earth. She did not think it was right either. She was a murderer, and murderers were always put to death. She ought to be killed, but there did not seem to be anybody to do it. She would have to do it herself. She *would* do it. It would be a reparation.

Once she had made up her mind she felt quite happy. She thought that if she took her own life, coming to him of her own will and act, perhaps then he would be kind to her and forgive her and not torment her any more. Sitting there thinking it all over, with what she thought as such sense and calm, she decided that she would make reparation at the tarn of Ben Fhalaich. Ranald had once said laughingly, when he was telling her about the tarn, that savage Macdonald forebears disposed of their enemies there. Well, she was a Macdonald enemy, for she had killed a Macdonald; so it was right that she too should be disposed of there. And she had another reason for wanting to go to the tarn. Ranald had spent the last night of his life there, and if she too spent her last night there they would be close together. He would be waiting for her, perhaps, in the little cave; and they would lie there together, two poor ghosts who loved each other.

"I am coming, Ranald," she said, and she ran almost eagerly across the room and out through the middle window, across the lawn and through the larch wood and round the loch. The moon was so bright as she climbed Ben Fhalaich that she could see each leaf and fern and heather bell like a pattern of lace upon the mountainside, yet she did not notice that it was lovely, for since Ranald's death the beauty of the world had been as completely blotted out for her as though she had been blind.

The climb exhausted her worn-out body horribly, and when she got to the top she was shaking all over, her dress drenched with the dew and her body with sweat. As she dragged herself to the tarn's edge she looked like a wounded bird. The tarn! She was sobbing with thankfulness when she reached it. Its black, fathomless water looked cool and kind to her hot, aching eyes. Only a little while longer and it would be over. For just a little while she would have to suffer, as she had seen Ranald suffer, gasping for breath, the life of a strong body resisting the grip of death to the point of agony, and then it would be all over and they could be together, and she would be forgiven because of what she had done. She crept round the tarn toward the cave of Ben Fhalaich, stumbling blindly over the stones, for she wanted to be as near to the cave as possible when she died. It seemed to her clouded mind that Ranald was in the cave waiting for her and that when she was dead he would come out and take her.

She was there now, as close as she could get, at the place where the stream from the cave crept across the stones and lost itself in the tarn. Darling little stream! She loved it so much. It had come from where Ranald was. It should take her with it into the tarn, and when she was dead it should carry her spirit back to Ranald in the cave. . . . Stepping delicately, as delicately as the stream itself, she went with it into the tarn.

But though she did not know it she had chosen the one place where the ground beneath the water sloped gently. At the further end of the tarn she would have gone in instantly out of her depth, but here she found herself standing in ice-cold water up to her knees only.

The shock of the water on her heated body brought her to a standstill, paralyzed by its grip. She stood there swaying, the bitter cold of the water an agony and the shock of it a shock to her mind as well as her body. It jerked her mind out of the mist of misery that had engulfed and clouded it, and for a moment she was herself again. . . . What did she think she was doing, it asked her? . . . "What am I doing?" she whispered. "Ranald, what am I doing?"

And it was then, in that glimmer of normal consciousness, that she first heard someone sobbing quite close to her, someone sobbing in the cave. She thought it was Ranald, and she cried out to him, "Ranald! Ranald!" Then she realized that it was not a man sobbing; it was a little child. What little child? Her mind had fallen back again into the mist, and she forgot she was childless and she thought it was her own son. She had brooded so much this last year on the child she had not got that he had become very real to her. She was quite certain it was he who was crying now, and like a flash she was out of the water and inside the cave, the sobbing bundle clutched tightly against her.

Duncan was a small child for his eight years, almost microscopic, and though but eleven years younger than Judith herself, he fitted into place in her arms as though to the manner born, his face buried in her neck and his body curved round hers. Judith was now word perfect in her Gaelic, so that its softness leaped very naturally to her lips to comfort the child. "Why is it that you cry, then, child of my heart? Is it yourself that is left all lonely in the hills? Laugh, then, mo chridhe, and let your mother comfort you."

She carried him to the entrance to the cave, so that the moonlight fell upon him, and looked down at his face. And then she began to laugh and cry together, for this was no child of hers! His freckled face was filthy dirty, with white streaks across it where tears had

263

ploughed their way through the grime; the travesty of a kilt that he wore was torn out of all recognition, and if he had ever been washed by his mother it was so long ago that he had forgotten it. He was a crofter's child, not one that she knew, not one of Ranald's people. Perhaps he was from Achnabar, where the Laird was dead and the Laird's son was dead and all their people scattered. In any case he was a child, and his sorrow seemed to fill the world. She sat down at the entrance to the cave, crooning over him. "Hush, then, little son! What ails you? Is it yourself will be telling me what ails you?"

He gazed at her wide-eyed, choking back his sobs. Who was this lovely lady? For lovely he thought her, in spite of her wet draggled skirts and wild hair and the smears of dirt that had been transferred from his person to hers. For one wild moment he thought she was one of the green people, and that she had come to carry him away to Tirna nOg where he would be lost forever to the world of men; but then he realized that she could not be because her face was warm against his and her tears were wet, and the flesh of the fairies was cold and they never cried. So he plucked up courage and asked her who she was. "Is it yourself that comes from Glen Suilag, lady?" he asked her. She nodded, and his eyes grew rounder and rounder. "Is it yourself that is the lady of the Laird?" She nodded again, her lips trembling. "Is he dead?" he asked. "Yes," she said, and at that Duncan did not cry any more but tried to wriggle out of her arms.

"What is it that ails you?" she asked him again. "Tell me, child of my heart."

So he told her, and she listened, her mind unclouded and understanding quite clearly what he said. So he had made a mistake too. They had both of them made mistakes. Somehow that comforted her, and she was able to comfort him. It would have happened just the same, she

264

told him, if the Sassenachs had not found him beyond Ben Caorach; in the end they would have found Glen Suilag. So he must not be unhappy any more, he must be happy because he pulled the heather for the Laird's bed and gave him his bit of oatcake to eat, for the Laird was very hungry and he must have liked that bit of oatcake.

"Dhé, but he *did* like it," said Duncan; "all gone it was before I had the time to turn myself about." And at the thought of Ranald, the living, human Ranald, wolfing up Duncan's oatcake as he had wolfed up his meal in the parlor, Judith broke down and cried and cried and Duncan cried too, for company, and the tears of the the two of them washed Judith's mind clear of any vestige of madness.

When they had cried their eyes dry they found that dawn was gray in the sky. Judith was astonished that the night had passed so soon. For how many hours had she sat in the parlor at Glen Suilag reliving her tragedy? How long had it taken her, crazy and exhausted, to climb up Ben Fhalaich? What had she been doing? What had she been thinking? "God forgive me," she whispered, and clutched the warm human boy who had been her salvation tightly against her. A bird cried out over her head and looking out she saw that the dawn had just touched the mountaintops with saffron and amethyst.

"You must go home now," she said to Duncan. "You must go home to your mother, little son." But he clung to her and did not seem to want to leave her.

Had he a father, she asked him? No, he said, his father had marched with the Laird of Achnabar to fight for Prionssa Ban, and he had not come home again. Had he brothers or sisters? Yes, he had eight brothers and sisters and hard put to it was his mother to be filling their bellies with food.

"Then say to your mother," said Judith, "that Mis-

265

tress Macdonald of Glen Suilag loves you and will be thanking her for the loan of you. If it is your mother's will that you shall live at Glen Suilag with me, then 'tis I who will be filling your belly and teaching you to be a good child. Say this to your mother, and if it is her will that you should come to me, then come to Glen Suilag tonight. Have you understood, little child?"

He had, and the prospect seemed to please. He kissed her and ran off into the mists, jumping from boulder to boulder beside the tarn and leaping up the mountain like a hare.

Judith watched him go and then dragged herself to the stretch of bracken that overlooked Glen Suilag. Here she watched the sunrise of a perfect day. Peak after mountain-peak was lit by the sun till they stood all round her like flaming torches ablaze with all the colors in the world, while down below in the glen, where lay Ranald's body and all her dead hopes, there was still darkness. To Judith it seemed that those flaming peaks were candles standing round a bier, beautiful flames lit in a desperate effort to ward off darkness. . . . Beautiful. . . . She realized suddenly that she knew they were beautiful. The beauty of the world was once more apparent to her. The bier was still there at the heart of her life, and would be until she died; but grouped around it were other lovely things, and now she could see them. Sitting there she watched the glen come back to life. The darkness stirred and lightened, and there was here a gleam of silver water, there a tossing green plume or a gleam of purple heather, and everywhere trails of soft peat smoke from the crofts. So gradually and silently that the moment of its final passing could not be recognized, the veil of night was lifted and Glen Suilag lay flaunting its incomparable beauty at her feet. Tirna nOg Ranald had called it once, the land of heart's desire. It was still there. It was Ranald's adored hidden country

266

that he had vowed to make quite perfect. . . . And she had killed him so that he would not.

Looking at it, Judith knew what she must do. Her reparation must be not to destroy her own life, but to take up his and live it for him. She could do what he had meant to do. She would build Utopia in Glen Suilag.

That she could not do it in any visible way she knew quite well. She was alone, and financially she was ruined, but by endless striving she could keep a hold on an ideal so that it did not die. This was a moment of illumination for her and she saw quite clearly how it is that great things are brought to birth in the world. An idea is conceived in the mind of a man of vision, an idea perhaps so greatly fantastic that in the eyes of the world its translation into actual fact seems a task impossible of accomplishment; but because to him his idea is the chief thing in life, he must attempt the impossible and fight to realize it, the world jeering a little as he fights and fails and dies. Yet the idea is not dead; for in it, like the light in a lantern, is enshrined the spirit of the man; and because of the very law of the world, that ordains that like shall turn to like, that spirit attracts to it other spirits of the same nature, so that as the years go by the light of the ideal burns brighter and brighter until it bursts into a great flame that lights the whole world.

So it should be, Judith vowed, with Ranald's ideal of perfection in Glen Suilag. He had not realized it, but his spirit was in it and by adding her spirit to his she would keep the lantern of it burning. She would fight until she died to do this, and others coming after her, lit by her light, would do the same. . . . She wondered for the thousandth time whether there was any truth in what Ranald had said about the return of spirits to this world. Would two of those others who came after be Ranald and herself again? It did not seem possible, and yet she had noticed again and again that life was always a rounded thing that ebbed and flowed and swung full circle back again. Dawn was followed by dawn and sunset by sunset; the seasons revolved continually, and the sky over her head seemed to curve round her in the likeness of a circle. Progress was not a thing that arched straight forward; it swung along in circling eddies, each circle advancing a little further forward; and might it not, in each sweep back, gather up again into its life the spirits that had given it being? . . . Perhaps.

Judith got up with a long, sobbing breath. She was a visionary no longer; she was an exhausted, heartbroken girl who had no illusions at all about the life that lay before her. Struggle and failure and loneliness were in front of her, and very often, she felt sure, her belief would fail her utterly. Yet she had something to cling to now, for she had something to do. In the days when belief was strong in her the doing of it would be a joy, and in the days when belief failed it would be a blessed habit that kept her sane. And when all was said and done, she told herself, work and belief and fighting, quite regardless of the thing worked and fought for and believed in, could in themselves make life worth while.

IV

But she blocked up the middle window. She would make it, she told herself, utterly impossible for anything at all to pass through that window. When she sat in the parlor and saw Ranald coming to her through the parted curtains she would know that what she saw was not reality but a picture projected by her own imagination. . . . Months afterward she was ashamed of what she had done; it had been a morbid way of fighting a morbid grief, but at the time it helped her, and she never unblocked the window again. . . . One day, she thought, when the tide had turned and the march of life had

268

come round again full circle, some other girl would unblock it, and the old parlor would be flooded with sunlight as it had been on the day when Ranald brought her home.

But for the present there was no sunlight in Glen Suilag. Conditions were terrible in the Highlands, for the victors had chosen for their revenge, as Ranald had known they would, the destruction of everything for which their enemies had cared. They broke the power of the chiefs and persecuted the priests; they destroyed religion and education and all the old customs. . . . The Highlanders might not wear the kilt or play the pipes or dance the reels.

Ranald's fortune was lost in the general shipwreck, and Judith lived in a house whose beauty gradually faded into pitiful shabbiness and went out every day to work among a people sullen and diseased with starvation and distress. The bitter shadow of defeat lay over the Highlands, and the calling of the whaups and the patter of the rain came always as a crying of despair.

In groups, in battalions, and one by one Judith's relations came to Glen Suilag and argued with her. Of what use, they asked her, to stay here? She would go mad with loneliness, they told her, shut up here all by herself. And what possible help did she think she could be to her crofters? How could one woman alone fight this ghastly postwar poverty? She was young, they told her, and still beautiful. She must forget all this and come away and start life over again. Outside her terrible mountains there was still love and laughter and dancing and all that made life good. But to all of them Judith returned the same answer. She could not leave Glen Suilag. Her life, she said, was bound up in it in a way that she could not explain. When they tried to make her explain she only shook her head, and they were obliged to give it up and go away, frantically commending her to the care of friendly neighbors.

But these same friendly neighbors, when they came to see Judith, were treated very badly by her. . . . She did not want them. . . . They took up time that should have been given to her work, that utterly hopeless work of building Utopia in Glen Suilag, and they distracted her mind and encouraged the weakness of self-pity in her. So she turned them out with the utmost rudeness, and they departed huffed. She was "queer," they said; one of those hopeless people one could do nothing for.

As the years went on it may be that she regretted her self-chosen isolation, for she was desperately lonely.

While Angus lived she had someone with her who loved and understood her, but Angus did not live for very much longer. With the Laird's death the mainspring of his life had been broken, and it seemed to Judith only a little while until she stood by his grave, which she had bidden them dig by Ranald's, and heard her people lamenting for him.

Duncan, though he loved her, was never a son to her. She was too young to be his mother, and he was, too, a creature of the wilds who was driven mad by the civilized life she tried to make him lead. She had to let him be what he wanted to be—her servant and not her child —and in the end he married and left her and she did not see him often.

As time went by her life was one long self-stripping. To help her crofters she sold nearly all that she had of value: her jewels and her dresses and much of her furniture and even her lovely portrait. But Ranald's portrait she would not sell, nor the furniture in her bedroom and in the parlor, nor her white satin dress with the yellow roses; for these were her friends and part of her life and she could not part from them.

But it was not only her possessions that she gave. Her ceaseless toil robbed her of health and strength and beauty, so that she was very soon an old woman, worn out and ugly. . . . And at the end of it all there was nothing to show for it. Poverty and sin and suffering were as rampant in the glen as ever, and Glen Suilag, the house itself, was scarcely more than a tumble-down ruin. Mistress Macdonald was mad, people said, and sometimes, when despair had her by the throat, she was inclined to agree with them; but at other times she knew that by her ceaseless fight she had kept something alive in the glen—a vision, an idea, Ranald's idea that had his spirit in it—and by her outpouring of herself she had fed it and strengthened it so greatly that it had in it now the stuff of eternity. When she felt this she was very happy, regretting not one shred of her lost health and beauty; but she could not always feel this, and at these times it was very hard to go on.

V

The hardest time of all for her was when she was too old to work any longer. She was one of those vigorous people to whom work is in itself a joy, and in addition hers had been to her husband and child and religion and sacred trust, the whole purpose of her existence. Without it she was desolate.

She had to spend most of her life sitting in her bedroom now, for all her years of tramping about the glen in wild weather had given her rheumatics, and she could not get up and down the stairs. Her heart was weak, too, from the strain she had put upon it, and she often felt very ill. And she was not a good patient. She was of the type that rebels furiously against weakness and pain, fighting it to the last ditch, and her two servants found her very difficult to deal with. They neither loved nor understood her, and they let her see it. . . . And perhaps she was not very lovable to those who did not understand. The strength of her character, unsoftened by the love of children, had turned to hardness, and her continued absorption in one idea had made her narrow-minded and unable to enter into the concerns of others. And she was proud—appallingly, fiercely proud, bitterly resenting her own weakness and her dependence upon others. She was not attractive to look at, either. Her body, that had never known physical love or a child at the breast, had become withered and hard and dry, and her face was raddled and lined from toil and exposure to wild weather. . . . Not a nice old lady, people said; and they did not come to see her if they could help it.

So she sat by herself in her chair by the fire, her gnarled hands resting on its arms, and lived her life over again in her thoughts, so as to keep her mind off the pain and death that still lay in front of her. For though she would not for worlds have owned it to anyone she found old age and death very frightening. The gradual failure of her powers was hard to endure, and the fear that she might at the end lose her courage was terrible to her.

When she felt very old and very bad-tempered she would look up at the portrait of her young husband and think how absurd it was that they should be united, that radiant young man with his bottle-green coat and his gay assurance and his ugly, unlovable old woman in the shabby, patched old clothes. And then sometimes she would cry a little, for she wanted him now as she had never wanted him before. It was not the young man that she wanted—he seemed very far removed from her now, more like her grandson than her husband—but the man that he would have been if he had lived. She would not be such a horrid old lady now, she told herself, if he had been with her always. She had once been soft and sweet and lovable, and his love would have kept her so. If they could have grown old together, old age would have lost half its terror, for they would have understood and helped each other and made little jokes about their difficulties and ailments. . . . For only the old, she thought, can understand the old. The young endeavor to be helpful but only succeed, poor things, in being nothing but a nuisance, always fussing and bothering and behaving as though they know best when the fact of the matter is that they know simply nothing at all. . . . Yes, she wanted Ranald the old man, her husband, the father of her children. She did not for a moment doubt that if he had lived his love for her would have lived too. Their feeling for each other would not have passed with the passing of youth and beauty. There was a poem that he had read to her when they were very young, and she often read it to herself now, holding the book very close to her dim eyes and saying the words slowly to herself.

Let me not to the marriage of true minds
Admit impediments. Love is not love
Which alters when it alteration finds,
Or bends with the remover to remove:
Oh, no! it is an ever-fixéd mark,
That looks on tempests and is never shaken;
It is the star to every wandering bark,
Whose worth's unknown, although his height be taken.
Love's not Time's fool, though rosy lips and cheeks
Within his bending sickle's compass come;
Love alters not with his brief hours and weeks,
But bears it out even to the edge of doom.
If this be error and upon me proved,
I never writ, nor no man ever loved.

Yes, she thought, that was love, a thing that went on and on. If it didn't go on and on it wasn't love. Love was not an emotion but the very fact of eternity, God Himself, of whose essence all that endured partook.

But as the day of her death drew near she began to live more and more in the past, and sometimes, in spite of her aches and pains, she almost forgot that she was an old woman and thought that she was a young girl again. The young man in the picture, who had seemed so remote from her, was remote no longer; he was very vividly present with her, and the scene of the past in which she lived most acutely was not the day of his death, but the day when he brought her home to Glen Suilag as a bride.

It seemed to her one evening that she was sitting opposite him again at the little dinner table, dressed in her white silk dress with the yellow roses, with her brown hair tied back with a yellow ribbon. The glory of a Highland sunset stained the world outside the windows, and he was telling her again of the fantasies that he believed in and she was laughing at him, loving him for them but not believing a word of it. He was talking about their love. "Today is its flowering time," he said, "but it has roots and it will have a fruit." She asked him, "Do you mean that we have loved before on this earth, and that after we are dead we will come back and love again?" And he answered her, "But we shall not be dead. We shall not come back as ghosts, child of my heart; we shall come back as living, immortal creatures." She heard the very tones of his voice and laughed at his earnestness. He laughed too, and their laughter echoed in her dreams all night.

But next morning, when she woke up, though in her bodily health she felt much worse, yet her mind was clearer than it had been for weeks. She knew quite well that she was an old woman and that what she had thought had happened last night had not happened at all. The man in the picture was aloof again, separated from her by a long stretch of bitter years. She felt very miserable and not at all well, and she would have liked to stay in bed, only that would have been a confession of weakness, so she struggled up and sat in her chair as usual.

But though she knew that last night had been a fantasy she could not get it out of her head and she still heard Ranald's voice saying, "It will have a fruit." She began to wonder, as she had wondered at intervals all her life long, if Ranald was right and if such a thing could really happen. She was a religious woman. She believed in God and in the immortality of all that was worth while in life, including the spirit of a man at its highest and best; but how the spirit of man lived on she did not pretend to know; she did not see how anyone could know. Perhaps it lived on only in what it had created; perhaps it was absorbed into the great flood of spirit that flowed through the world like blood through the veins of a man; perhaps it had some individual life of its own, coming or going according to the purposes of God; perhaps it did all these things. . . . Who could tell?

All day long she turned the pages of her Bible trying to find something that would give her some leading. "The souls of the righteous are in the hands of God." "Then shall the dust return to the earth as it was, and the spirit shall return unto God who gave it." "The resurrection from the dead." These three trumpet blasts sounded in her room, as they had sounded down the ages; but they told her nothing definite, they only reiterated the fact of life without telling her the where and the how. And she wanted to know. She wanted Ranald's fantastic idea to be true. She wanted, in spite of the suffering of human life, to live it again. She wanted to be young and sweet and soft once more, giving Ranald all that she had never given him and being to him all that she had never been. She wanted them to live out their lives together to the very end. She wanted, through long years of struggle, to help him try and translate his ideas into action, even though at the end of it all they failed again. . . . For she was old enough to realize that failure is one of the most unimportant things in life.

And so, as the spring dusk crept over the garden, Judith Macdonald began to pray. Very humbly she asked her God that she and Ranald might come back to earth again, living out their lives as it must surely have been the will of God that they should do. . . . For Judith was not so blasphemous as to lay the disasters of her life at the door of her Creator. The blame for the horror of war and the cruelty of man she put where she should have put it, upon man himself. . . . Yet she felt that her prayer was rather presumptuous, and she asked pardon for it if it was so, for who was she that she should dare to lay her hand upon the future? Yet she dared. When dark fell, and her maid came in to light her candles, she was still praying this same prayer.

The curtains were drawn now, and her maid had gone. Two lighted candles stood on the mantelpiece and two on the table by her elbow. The corners of the room were full of shadows, and the wind was blowing. The house, as always on windy nights, was full of strange creakings and mutterings. . . . Judith thought that she heard footsteps coming along the passage, and she turned her head to one side, listening painfully, for she was a little deaf. . . . They were the light, dancing footsteps of someone who was very young, and they paused for a moment outside her door and then came into her room. Peering into the shadows she saw a girl's face, a small, pointed little face with lips smiling at her, lips delicate yet determined, dark eyes with gold lights in them and dark hair lying in the nape of the neck in little curls. With a joyous upleaping of the heart Judith leaned forward, gazing intently at the vital little face; yet even while she gazed it had gone and she found herself staring at shifting shadows only. . . . Fancy, she told herself, surely only fancy, and leaned back in her chair with a sigh. . . . Yet if it was fancy it was one that curved her mouth into a smile and lit lights in her eyes, a radiant, lovely fancy that wrapped her round in a peace she had not known for months.

For a long while she sat there, exulting in what she had seen; yet even now the habit of conflict was so strong in her that she could not accept it without question. That girl! She had looked so young, so inexperienced, such a child. If she was the Judith of the future she was a Judith born into the world without the knowledge that had come to the Judith of the present through long years of life. Somehow Judith had thought that if she came back to earth again she would come back with the lovely body of a young girl but with the mature mind of a woman. She saw now that that would be absurd—such a creature would be a monstrosity. If she came back she would come back with a young mind and heart, and a character strong with the strength of the past but undisciplined by the suffering of the present. Experience and wisdom would have to be gained all over again. . . . Yet surely she would remember. . . . Surely, surely she would remember. . . . It could not be that her love and her suffering would have left no trace on her spirit.

The wind rose and the rain pattered against her window, and she began to be terribly afraid for that other Judith. She would be a creature born into the world with that terrible gift of free will a weapon in her hands that she could use as she liked to make or mar her. She would have it in her power to go where she liked and do what she would. Would her choice bring her where Ranald was? Would it bring her back to Glen Suilag? And, if she came, would she be a creature fitted for the perfect union of love for which this present Judith ached and longed? There could be no true union without true individuality, the old Judith knew that well; but would the young Judith know that? Would she know that to find and make herself was the first duty of life? The old Judith began to pray that some miracle might

277

happen to show these things to the young Judith; that some experience might come to her that would force her to see with clear eyes and choose courageously. . . . Surely it would be so. . . . It must be. . . . It must.

They brought her some supper and she ate it. The candles fluttered down, and she was so tired that she could not think any more, so she got up and put herself to bed, moving with more pain and difficulty than usual. She was glad when the struggle of her toilet was over and she was safely between the sheets, with the flowered curtains of her bed drawn all around her. But yet she felt a little apprehensive. She wondered what the night had in store for her, and she was afraid. Her last memory, as she fell into a doze, was of herself as a young girl coming into this room and seeing this bed for the first time, and wondering with a pang of fear if she would have to die in it.

When they came to wake her in the morning she was dead. They wondered if she had cried out for help in the night, and no one had heard her above the sound of the wind and the rain. It was rather terrible, they thought, that she should have died alone like that; but yet it was typical of her. Her pride was so great that perhaps she was glad, when she finally surrendered to death, that no one saw her do it.

They buried her in the glen beside her husband and Angus, and, as no one loved her, no one mourned for her. . . . Only the sea gulls, as they sailed down the wind, cried and lamented.

EPILOGUE

The Finding

Yet for the great bitterness of this grief.
We three, you and he and I,
May pass into the hearts of like true comrades
    hereafter,
In whom we may weep anew and yet comfort them,
As they too pass out, out, out into the night.
So guide them and guard them Heaven and fare them
    well.   —SAMUEL BUTLER

EPILOGUE

I

THE sun was blazing into her room when Judy woke up the morning after her birthday party. Her first feeling was one of surprise that the curtains of her bed were not drawn all round her as Judith had always drawn them, but were pulled well back as Judy always pulled them. Her second feeling was one of horrified astonishment at the sight of her own gaudy silk striped pajamas. . . . What frightful garments! . . . And what was that corpulent black ball snoring at the foot of her bed? . . . A dog. . . . Why, of course, Sarah! . . . Then she sat up and pushed the hair back from her face, drawing a great breath of bewilderment and astonishment and palpitating joy. . . . So that was it!

Further thought was interrupted by the entrance of her mother and Jean with a tray of breakfast.

"How are you, darling?" demanded her mother.

"Very well, thank you," said Judy cheerfully.

"What sort of night did you have, darling?" asked Jean tenderly.

What sort of night? Judy smiled rather a peculiar smile and seemed to be meditating. "I had dreams," she said at last.

"Stomach," said Lady Cameron decidedly. "I thought so. Put your tongue out, darling."

Judy's tongue shot out with the suddenness of an erupting jack-in-the-box, but there was nothing the matter with it; it was a blameless rose-pink all over.

"Well, I don't know, I'm sure," said Lady Cameron, and felt her daughter's pulse and forehead. The pulse was beating quietly like a good little clock and the forehead was cool. "There doesn't seem to be a thing the matter with you. Whatever made you faint like that?"

"There's a lot of mystery in life," said Judy solemnly, but her eyes were shining.

"Could you eat any breakfast, darling?" asked Jean. "We've only brought you tea and toast. . . . That's all we thought you'd feel equal to."

Tea and toast! Judy glared at it. She was starving. She could have eaten an entire ox. "Thank you," she snapped.

"Well, try and eat the toast," said Lady Cameron, "and then lie down again and keep quiet. I shall keep you in bed till lunch, of course."

Judy smiled sweetly.

"Do you hear me, Judy?" said her mother sharply. "You are not to get up."

Judy smiled yet more sweetly.

"Do you hear me, Judy?"

"Yes, darling, I always hear you."

They draped a dressing jacket round her, piled pillows behind her back, and left her toying feebly with the toast and tea. As soon as they had gone she wolfed it up in two minutes and leaped out of bed. Indoors seemed to be stifling her; she wanted to get out of doors where she would be able to think properly. She washed and dressed and crept downstairs, followed by Sarah. From the dining room came the chinking of china and the delicious smell of sausage and coffee. And they'd given her tea and toast!

She let herself out of the front door and went to the loch the long way round, so that they should not see her from the window. It was gloriously cool and fresh after the storm, with feathery white clouds floating across a bright blue sky and every sprig of heather and blade of grass jeweled with drops of rain.

As she climbed up Ben Fhalaich, her thoughts busier just now over the everyday joys of love that were com-

282

ing to her rather than over the great fact of it, she was in a mood to notice its little intimate beauties rather than its grandeur. She knew all the names of the plants now, for Ian had taught them to her, and she knew at what levels she would find them all. Down by the loch was the lovely yellow mimulus, the meadowsweet and ragwort, while higher up were scabious and harebells. Higher up still the real mountain plants began, the ones that she loved particularly. There were the pale green starfish leaves of the butterwort, that in early summer had flowers like violets, the red buds and starry yellow flowers of the bog asphodel, and the pink and orange sphagnum moss. Best of all there were the cotton grass, the mystic canna-bawn, and the lovely, fragile grass of Parnassus. And everywhere, the whole way up, were the heather and bog myrtle.

She scrambled up until she came to a jutting bit of rock where she could sit down and see the glen at her feet. It was incomparably beautiful this morning, more beautiful than she had ever seen it. The whole scene had the brilliant clearness of the rain-washed background of the picture in her room. The blue loch and the green larch trees and the gray house with the flower-filled garden, the crofts with peat smoke curling up into the quiet air, the heather-covered hills behind ringing it round and protecting it. Was there in all the world a spot of earth that could compare with this valley that was her home? . . . Tirna nOg, the land of heart's de-sire. . . . For a moment her throat felt lumpy and there were tears in her eyes. Then she blinked them away and began to think, her chin cupped in her hands, her thoughts going back over last night, twelve short hours that seemed to have lasted for a century.

All that had happened was absolutely clear to her; she saw it all in a series of pictures. The wearing of Ju-dith's dress had opened a door into the past that had sent it flooding into her memory. First there had been the terrible picture of Ian coming in through the middle window. Then blackness. Then a curious picture in which she seemed to be standing in her bedroom watching her mother and Jean putting her to bed. That had been very odd. It had seemed as though she were right outside her own body. Could she have been? Had she been for a little while jerked right out of material things so that she lived only on that plane of life where they had no existence? After that she had lain flat in her bed and had what, she supposed, people would call a series of extraordinarily vivid dreams about a woman who had lived at Glen Suilag nearly two hundred years ago. But she knew they were not dreams. That woman was herself, and she had not been dreaming, but remembering. She smiled as she thought how bewildered and frightened she had been by her half-remembered memories and Ian's idea of possession. It all seemed so simple now and not at all alarming.

She wondered if Ian last night had had the same experience. She felt sure that he had, but if so why didn't he come to her? From where she sat she could see the road to the village, and the little inn where he was staying; but no kilted figure came out through the door hurrying to the arms of the beloved.

At first she felt annoyed with him but then she laughed, for his nonappearance was so typical of him. Like all worthwhile people he was a mass of contradictions. He was a romanticist to the very core of his being, perhaps one of the worst of the species that had yet been let loose upon the earth, but his romance, like gold in the rock, was not always very easy to get at. It did not issue very easily in pretty speeches and actions. Smiling to herself, Judy pictured his probable behavior. He would wake up and think out patiently and thoroughly what had happened to him, and he would be glad about it with the same deep gladness that was flooding her through and through. Then he would get up and eat a large breakfast of porridge and eggs and bacon, he would go to the surgery and attend to his patients, he would do any jobs of work that needed very urgently to be done, and then, but not before, he would come to her. Perhaps when he came he would say wonderful things to her and be the man that he had been on the night he brought her home. But on second thought she thought that he would not be, for he was a little different now. That man had never known opposition and hard work and failure and ridicule; but this man had, and the easy expression of enthusiasm was not so easy to him. But in any case what did she care what he did say or didn't say, or did or didn't do? The fact of his love was all that mattered to her, and of that she was as certain as she was certain of the rock on which she sat.

For a little while longer she stayed there, knowing the meaning of the word joy, and then, tilting her chin and setting her mouth firmly, she went down the mountain to grapple with her family.

II

Breakfast over, Lady Cameron went to the kitchen to harass Elspeth, and the others strolled desultorily into the drawing room. The storm had kept them all awake, and they sank languidly into chairs, dividing the *Times* into three and erecting its pages between them and a fatiguing world.

"Sir James," said Jean, "would you like to change with me? Manlike, you've kept the most interesting half for yourself."

"On the contrary, my dear, with the unselfishness of my sex I gave you the middle and kept the advertisements."

"But that's what I want. The autumn fashions are just out."

Charles raised a rather yellow face from his portion of the *Times* and held it out to her. "I've finished with the blooming weddings if anybody wants them."

"Thank you. Anybody interesting married?"

"Lots of blasted fools. Never seem to learn not to."

Sir James looked up from the disarmament problem. "Weddings seem a sore subject with you this morning, Charles."

"You may say so. Judy's and mine due in a month, and billing and cooing distinctly in the diminuendo."

"I'd noticed that. Why?"

"I'm all for billing and cooing myself, but Judy doesn't seem to have time for it these days. She's too busy scratching about in the dust of the past."

"Shall I go?" asked Jean tactfully.

"No. I'm only grousing."

Sir James waved a soothing hand. "Yes, Charles, I'd noticed it. I'm sorry. I don't think Judy is quite herself these days."

"Glad it's not escaped the legal eye."

"Take her away from here," said Jean suddenly. "This place isn't healthy for the imaginative; they breathe in nonsense along with the mist. . . . Look at Ian."

"I've done nothing else for the last month," said Charles bitterly, "and I don't see what there is in him for Judy to make a fool of herself over."

Jean flushed. "Are you suggesting——"

Charles heaved himself to his feet, as near losing his temper as it was possible for him to be. "Yes, I am. I'm suggesting that your brother has played the dirty on me."

"How?"

"Charles!" said Sir James warningly.

"Now let me get it off my chest. Jean won't mind, she's got too much sense."

"No, go on," said Jean, and smiled at him. She enter-

286

tained the liveliest feelings of friendship for him. In fact, for friendship, her feelings were very lively indeed.

"Ian's in love with our Judy," growled Charles. "He'd like to make her the Lairdess, or whatever they call it, of this horrible hole."

"Yes, I think he would," said Sir James. "But he can't help that, Charles."

"I'm not saying he can. I've every sympathy with the fellow, blast him; keen on our Judy myself. But he's not done the decent by me and Judy."

"What should he have done?" asked Jean.

"What any sane man would have done. Either murdered me or taken himself off to the Balkans. But has he adopted either of these decent courses? No. He's stayed here and insinuated himself into Judy's life by pouring sentimental Jacobite treacle all over himself and Judy till they're so stuck together that you can't tell t'other from which."

"You do Ian an injustice," said Jean hotly. "He's not underhand."

"Then what the devil is he?"

"Bewildered. He's in love for the first time and doesn't know what to do about it. He's just drifting."

"That's about it," said Sir James. "So is Judy. Better have it out with Judy, Charles."

"Is that your honor's advice?"

"Yes. Drifting's dangerous."

"I'll do what you say," said Charles. "Take the lid off the dustbin and know the worst."

The entrance of Lady Cameron cut them short, and he fled to the larch wood. He didn't feel like Lady Cameron this morning. He didn't feel like women at all. What with one thing and another he was beginning to think that there was a good deal to be said for a bachelor existence. Lonely, of course, but dashed peaceful.

But at the end of the larch wood, by the loch, he collided with Judy coming down from Ben Fhalaich.

"Oh," she said, "I want to talk to you, Charles."

Her chin was tilted in the way he knew. . . . No escape. . . . Sighing he lowered himself to a fallen log and lit a cigarette. Judy sat opposite him, her eyes tender and troubled, and he looked away from her, for she was too sweet to be looked at by a man who had lost her. . . . Dashed pretty little thing, she was. Obstinate as the devil, but adorable. Pluck and grit she had; a mate in a thousand. She'd wear well. . . . But he'd lost her. He felt her now to be as illusive as the smoke rings from his cigarette that were curling away over the sparkling loch toward the dark, brooding mountain. That dashed mountain! He loathed it. With its rather arrogant air of possession and its look of rooted strength it reminded him of that fellow Ian Macdonald.

Judy's voice, gentle but determined, cut into his thoughts. "Charles, I've got a lot to explain to you. You'll have to use your brains."

"Haven't any," muttered Charles.

"Use your heart, then. You've got one of the best I've ever come across."

"Judy, that sounds like old times."

For the life of him he couldn't help looking at her for a moment. She was leaning toward him, her strong little face softened with the rare tenderness that made it perfectly irresistible.

"You thought I'd changed toward you, didn't you? But I haven't. Ever since my eighth birthday, when I fell down and hurt myself, and you took the bull's-eye out of your own mouth and put it into mine to comfort me, I've thought you a perfect duck."

"Blushing, that's what I am."

"But, Charles dear, I don't want to be Mrs. Perfect Duck."

Charles dropped his cigarette, grinding it under his heel, and a hard note came into his voice. "Now we're getting there."

"Please, Charles, if you could manage not to take this to heart I'd be awfully glad."

"Dashed fond of you," he muttered.

"I am of you."

He began to get a little worked up. "Then hang it all, Judy, why chuck me over? We've been engaged for several centuries—you started filling up your bottom drawer with dusters and petticoats and that when you were sixteen—and we were going to be married next month. Why, the wedding presents have even started arriving. . . . Quite a little posse of alarm clocks this morning. . . . Why, dash it all, Judy, you can't do a thing like that."

"It's difficult, but I can because I've got to. . . . Now comes the time for you to use your brains, Charles."

He lit another cigarette. "Well, fire away."

"Ever since I came here, Charles, I've been having the most extraordinary experiences, and last night I had the most extraordinary of all."

"Well?"

"I can't tell you about them; I couldn't find the words, and if I did you'd think me mad; but I can tell you what they have taught me."

"Well?"

"Don't you think, Charles, that there comes a time in one's life when one suddenly discovers one's individuality?"

"Yes. I did that the first time I had toothache."

"I did it when I came to Glen Suilag. In London I was only conscious of being a girl among other girls, just one of a crowd, with a body that would grow old and die like other bodies; but when I came here to this lovely solitude, where one cannot be one of a crowd because there are no crowds, I became conscious that I was Judith. I became obsessed by myself. . . . Judith. . . . Judith. . . . Judith. . . . A real individual who will never die."

"What?" he ejaculated.

289

"There's worse to come, my poor Charles. . . . Listen. . . . If one is an individual and eternal person then one is important and there must be a place for one somewhere in the order of things. . . . Don't you think so? . . . First you find yourself, and then you find where to put yourself. Individuals are no use alone. Somewhere for all of us there is a place or a person or a piece of work to which we must link ourselves."

"Yes?"

Her eyes slipped from Ben Fhalaich to the loch, and up to the cloud-flecked sky over her head, and she held out her arms for a moment in an unconscious gesture, forgetful of him. "I have found them all three in Glen Suilag."

He stamped out his second cigarette. "A lot of high-falutin nonsense," he said angrily. "Why not say straight out that you are bored with me and intrigued by that fellow Macdonald? What's wrong with the truth?"

"Nothing," said Judy. "But what you say is not the truth. I'm not bored with you any more than I'm bored with father and mother. You three are still to me what you've always been, but what I feel for Ian is bigger than anything I've ever felt before. It's not just a question of love. It's a question of life. There is a certain kind of love that is not only an incident in life but life itself, because it links you up with every kind of life that endures. In loving Ian I don't only love a man, I love the work that he does and the world in which he lives and everything that he stands for. . . . I am one with them all. . . . I always have been, and I always will be."

There was a long silence. "Is that all?" asked Charles at last.

"Yes, that's all. . . . Oh, Charles, you must simply hate me, but do you understand a little? I can't bear it if you don't understand."

"Well, I've got the gist of it."

290

He got up and walked a little away from her, not looking at her. The movement cut her to the heart.

"Oh, Charles, must you go?"

"Well, I thought that *was* the gist of it."

"Yes," said Judy slowly, "I suppose it is."

He forced himself to turn round and smile at her. "Well, good luck to you, Judy. God bless you and all that."

"Charles, do you mind terribly?"

"Well, I don't know. . . . I dare say I shall be able to peck a bit at lunch. I'm just going up the corrie. So long."

"Charles, do say you understand a little?"

"Oh, lord, how women do go on!"

"But do you?"

"Yes, old girl. I didn't grasp a lot of your gassing, but I gather that you've found your job." He smiled at her. "It's a good moment when one finds one's job. I remember the day when I decided on the army—felt no end bucked."

"Charles, you *are* a dear."

"Aren't I? . . . Sweet. . . . Well, old girl, my job's trailing round the world singing *Tipperary* and hitched by the braces to the good old Union Jack; and yours seems to be keeping an eye on that lunatic Macdonald and this moldy little glen, and your job and mine don't fit, so —well—I'll bury the little affair up in the corrie —no flowers by request."

She watched his trim figure going briskly round the loch, and she felt bad about it. . . . Of course he'd soon be mended up. . . . He was constitutionally incapable, with his good-nature and friendliness, and his inability to refuse anybody anything they wanted, of holding out against any nice, determined girl who decided, nicely and with determination, to marry him. . . . She gave Jean six months to cope with the situation. . . . And they'd be very happy. He'd be so good to Jean, and spoil her so much, that her purring satisfaction would envelop him as well as herself, and they'd both get very sleek and fat and lazy. . . . But still, she felt bad about it.

III

She made her way through the larch wood to the garden feeling very tired. Not that she meant to give in to it. It was her intention to explode the final bomb before lunch.

She found her parents in the drawing room arguing about Sir James's new pajamas, which had arrived pink and green when ordered lilac and gray.

"I don't know what Hope's are thinking of," said Lady Cameron. "They know your age perfectly well."

"I think I rather like them," said Sir James gently.

"Don't be ridiculous, James! . . . Judy, what are you doing here? I said you were not to get up."

"Yes, darling."

"You have deliberately disobeyed me."

"Yes, darling. . . . As a matter of fact I've been for quite a long walk. It's lovely after the storm. The bog myrtle smells like incense, and there are fairies playing in the corrie."

"It's no good discussing the beauties of nature to distract my attention. . . . I said you were not to get up."

"Yes, darling. I heard you."

Sir James cleared his throat. "You ought not to have disobeyed your mother, Judy."

"No, I oughtn't. But I did."

"Take these detestable pajamas out of my sight, James. . . . Well, Judy, what is it?"

"I've just jilted Charles."

There was a dreadful pause.

"I think you're probably right," said Sir James.

Judy gave him a quick, grateful glance. With him there was never any need to argue or explain. They always understood each other perfectly without wasting time or strength or words. She braced her shoulders and turned back to receive her mother's broadside. . . . Lady Cameron was on the whole a patient and enduring parent, but there are times when even a worm will turn. . . . Although she had feared this she was furious.

"Judy, what in the world are you thinking of? The wedding day is fixed, and what on earth are we to do about the wedding presents? . . . Good heavens, I wrote to Buzzard's about the wedding cake only this morning."

"Oh, mother, mother, what does all that matter!"

"Matter? Of course it matters! It's monstrous, Judy. Just think of the trouble you're causing everybody. And what will grandfather and the aunts say? They've always thought you a terrible minx, and now it will take me hours to explain you to them. And poor, poor Charles!"

"He's taken it very well. He'll be all right. I'm going to marry Ian Macdonald."

"Then you are quite crazy, Judy," said Lady Cameron. "A man like that! He's everything I dislike."

"But it's not you that's marrying him, mother."

"Let her alone," said Sir James. "She's outgrown Charles."

"Don't be ridiculous, James! It's this place has turned the child crazy."

"The place has not turned her crazy, but it has made her outgrow Charles."

"Father," said Judy, "how understanding of you. . . . Do you like Ian?"

"Yes, I like him. But I don't think you will find life as soft and easy with him as it would have been with Charles."

293

Judy threw up her head. "I don't want life to be soft and easy."

Her father smiled at her. "Then Glen Suilag has made you grow even faster than I thought."

He gathered up his pajamas and left them to it—his unvarying course in domestic argument—and the battle raged for half an hour before Lady Cameron was vanquished.

"You don't know what it will be like, Judy," she stormed for the twentieth time. "It will be no life for a young girl. Think of the winters here, the cold and the darkness and the storms. And this dreadful old house—no comforts, no amusements, no anything—and the loneliness of it all."

"I know all about that," said Judy.

"But you don't know," snapped her mother, "and you won't listen when I tell you. . . . And then the man himself. An idealist living the life of a savage and expecting his wretched wife to do the same. . . . I know that type, Judy. He'll love you, but he'll have no mercy on you."

"What do you mean by mercy?" asked Judy. "Central heating?"

"You know quite well what I mean, Judy. He'll make you work as hard as he does himself. He'll have exaggerated ideas about the duties of a wife. He'll even use your money trying to put this wretched place on its feet again."

"But of course," said Judy.

Lady Cameron almost moaned. Her father, Judy's grandfather, had made a fortune out of a new kind of stocking suspender, and much of it would come to Judy when he died. The thought of the proceeds of that sacred suspender being wasted by Ian on his wretched crofters was almost more than she could stand.

"He's a fortune hunter," she declared with bitterness.

Judy blew up like a mine. "You dare say that!" she

stormed. "Ian has never even heard of that loathsome suspender!"

Lady Cameron, a just woman, withdrew the accusation. "I beg your pardon, Judy. No, he's not a fortune hunter. . . . Not enough common sense for that."

"You don't understand a man like Ian."

"Perhaps not, dear. . . . But no honorable man would have asked you to marry him while you were still engaged to Charles."

"He didn't."

"But, my dear Judy, you said—"

"I never said he had asked me to marry him. . . . He hasn't. . . . What I said was that I was going to marry him."

Lady Cameron gave it up. "Go and lie down," she said. "I may not understand the modern girl, but at least I will be obeyed by her when I am her mother. You're looking tired out. I'll send lunch up to you. Ridiculous, the way you pile things one on top of the other. Breaking off an engagement on top of a thunderstorm and a fainting fit. You'll be having one of your headaches now."

"And you give in, darling, about my marrying Ian?" said Judy sweetly.

"I suppose so. I'm not consulted nor, apparently, is Ian, but you've got your father on your side as usual."

Judy departed flushed with victory. Sir James, hearing silence in the drawing room, came tentatively back again to find his wife collapsed on the sofa.

"I shall have to take a good long rest to get over this holiday, James," she said. "I shall go to Bournemouth."

IV

Up in her room Judy finished the delicate invalid lunch brought to her by Elspeth and then stole downstairs, waylaying Angus in the hall.

"Angus, I'm starving. Bring me some of that cold roast beef."

"Ay," said Angus, "where to?"

"The drawing room," said Judy.

When he brought it to her she was sitting in front of the harpsichord, singing and playing very softly so that they should not hear her in the dining room.

Today there is sunlight caressing the dew,
Today clouds go chasing all over the blue,
Today echo answers the cry of the dove,
Today there is laughter and singing and love.

And now I have tasted the fullness of bliss,
And now I have given my heart with a kiss,
And now I hold heaven close clasped to my breast,
And now my whole being is hushed and at rest.

"Do ye want yer roast beef or do ye no' want yer roast beef?" he asked disagreeably.

"I want it," she said. "I'm starving. Pull up that little table, please, Angus."

While she ate it he stood and watched her, his youthful, bright blue eyes fixed on her. She looked up at him between mouthfuls. She did so wonder if he, too, had been remembering.

"Do you know, Angus," she said, "that you have the eyes of someone who is very young? Why is it? Do you think it is because your love goes on and on and never grows old?"

He smiled at her suddenly, his disagreeable expression breaking up into mirth and tenderness. "Maybe!" he said. Then his habitual gloom descended upon him again. "How mony more months will ye wait afore ye settle down wi' the Laird? I'm ower muckle tired o' waitin' for ye to hae a bit o' sense."

"It has been a long wait, hasn't it, Angus?"

"Ou, ay."

By the way that he was looking at her she knew that he, too, had remembered.

"Oh, so you understand? . . . Angus, where have you been all this time?"

But Angus seemed to have no idea. He growled a little, and then, cocking his head to one side, listening, he winked at her. "'Tis the Laird comin' doon the drive," he said, and left her.

Judy turned to the harpsichord and began singing again very softly and rather flat. This was a great moment for her, and her heart was pounding so that it was impossible to keep in tune.

My life is now given for weal or for woe,
My life is your own now wherever we go,
My life is your vassal, your child and your slave,
My life your possession through death and the grave.

God shield us from partings, hobgoblins, and tears,
God save us from demons and dangers and fears,
God keep us together the length of the day,
God grant we keep laughing the whole of the way.

The door opened and shut, and Ian was standing in front of her, by the window, his hands deep in his pockets. He made no comment on the song she was singing, and he looked so much as usual that for a dreadful moment she wondered if his sleep last night had been dreamless.

"Is the family putting on weight in the dining room?" he asked.

"Yes. Cold beef and treacle pudding."

"Good. . . . I hoped I'd see you alone. . . . I couldn't get here before; there were things to do. Are you all right?"

"A bit dazed. How are you?"

"Dazed too."

She looked up at him anxiously. Had he remembered? "How long is life?" she asked him softly.

Instantly his face lit up and his head went back. He looked happy and self-assured, like the man in the picture in her room, and he answered her in the tone of one repeating words learned by heart long ago.

"A man living a life is like a man writing a book. He may break off after a few chapters, but he comes back to his work again and again until the book is finished."

"And will you and I come back again and again until we have built paradise in our glen? Glen Suilag will grow mighty tired of us."

"Not it. We are as much a part of it as the bog myrtle and the heather. It does not tire of its children."

"We needn't go on," she said; "we both remember."

"Naturally. We are the same people. We thought we were possessed by the dead, but we weren't. We *are* the dead."

"No, no, the living. There are no dead."

"Can you tell me what happened to you last night?"

"Yes. I lived again a bit of my life as I lived it nearly two hundred years ago."

"That's exactly what I did."

"How did it begin with you?"

"It began when I was back at the inn. Quite suddenly —I remember I stopped stock still in my room with the shock of it—it seemed as though I was out of time. At

298

one moment I felt enclosed in time, like a picture in a frame, and the next moment the frame had suddenly fallen away and at night, while I slept, I remembered everything."

"So did I." She got up and came to him, looking up and speaking with an effort. "You knew it was I who shot you?"

"Yes. To warn me."

"That's why the middle window made me feel mad with grief. . . . But I shan't feel like that any more now that I understand. . . . And we'll unblock the window." She slipped her arms round his neck, feeling like that once more, and for the last time. "I didn't mean to do it, Ian, I didn't mean to do it!"

"Silly donkey! That's all past. . . . Think of the future. . . . Our flowering time was short, Judy, but the dead flower left a fruit."

He laughed and in the grip of his arms as he put them round her she felt all the power and the strength of life and love, past and present and to come. They were good and glorious, these two, and they were one, and held by them she believed in them and laughed out of her sense of lovely security. . . . Not even though she could see, out of the corner of her eye, the road that wound up Ben Caorach, linking their hidden country to a world of darkness whose power to overwhelm individual creations of loveliness did not decrease as the centuries went by—not even so was her faith shaken. . . . That world of darkness was not as powerful as it thought itself, she had discovered.

"We'll do it yet, Ian," she cried triumphantly. "We'll do it yet."

"Yes," he said and then, bending his head to say a pretty thing almost in the manner of the old Ranald, "Judith, you are the sun and moon and stars above the glen, the candle and the warm flame at its heart."

Angus, who was listening shamelessly and with satisfaction outside the door, withdrew at this point to polish up the silver for the first time in weeks.

use this handy coupon to order directly from the publisher

Bestselling novels of history, drama and adventure by
TAYLOR CALDWELL

Please send me:

_____THE BALANCE WHEEL V2278 — $1.25
_____THE EAGLES GATHER V2245 — $1.25
_____LET LOVE COME LAST V2317 — $1.25
_____TIME NO LONGER V2842 — $1.25
_____THE TURNBULLS N2222 — 95¢
_____THE WIDE HOUSE V2200 — $1.25
_____MELISSA V2407 — $1.25
_____THE EARTH IS THE LORD'S
V2370 — $1.25
_____DYNASTY OF DEATH A2242 — $1.50
_____THE DEVIL'S ADVOCATE V2573 — $1.25
_____THERE WAS A TIME, Taylor Caldwell.
story of life's pain and the glory of love. V2915
— $1.25
_____LET LOVE COME LAST
Saga of a great man destroyed by his family.
V2885 — $1.25